A TANGLED WEB

William C. Johnson

Published by Central Park South Publishing 2024
www.centralparksouthpublishing.com

Typesetting and e-book formatting services by Victor Marcos

ISBN:
978-1-956452-67-9 (pbk)
978-1-956452-68-6 (hbk)
978-1-956452-69-3 (ebk)

*Oh, what a tangled web we weave
When first we practice to deceive.*
—Sir Walter Scott

CHAPTER 1

There have been many romances in the world…some more complicated than others…but few top this one.

Ensign Kevin Boyce was just enjoying a beer at the Supply Corps School Officer's Club in Athens, Georgia, when he first saw Greta.

She wandered in with another Georgia University coed, and they both drew the attention of every lascivious eye in the place as they sashayed across the floor, directly in front of the bar, and then wiggled their way into a booth toward the back of the room.

Kevin thought the petite blonde was pretty, "cute as a button," as his mother would say, the type she always wanted him to marry. But Kevin had his eye on the brunette, who was full-bodied, statuesque, and absolutely gorgeous. Maybe not his mother's type but, at this stage of Kevin's life, he was more driven more by his libido than his mother's opinion.

Given the rustling in the room right after the two girls passed by the bar, Kevin knew that, if he was to have any chance, he needed to act quickly. So, he jumped up and began to saunter, as quickly as a guy can saunter, over to the booth where the girls were now comfortably seated. He arrived before anybody else, but given his lack of experience, stammered a bit at first, not sure what to say to the girls.

Fortunately for him, the brunette wasn't nearly as inexperienced, or shy.

"Hello, good-looking," she cooed, batting her eyes and smiling broadly. "What can we do for you?"

She had a vague European accent, which, although a bit intimidating, made her even more attractive to Kevin.

What can she do for me? He thought, his mind mulling over the options.

Finally, he blurted out, "I was wondering if I might do something for you?"

"Well, for starters, you can sit right down here," she answered as she scooted over to her side of the booth and patted the seat beside her. "And tell us who you are and where you're from."

"I'm Kevin Boyce," he answered, "from the glorious state of Kansas."

"Well, Mr. Kevin Boyce, from the glorious state of Kansas, I'm Greta Schmidt, from West Germany, and this is my friend Betsy Casey, from Georgia.

"We're pleased to make your acquaintance," Betsy added with a southern drawl. Kevin acknowledged her words with a nod, before turning his attention back to Greta.

"West Germany, huh," he acknowledged, "I thought I detected an accent."

"Damn. I was hoping I was fully Americanized by now."

"I'm glad you're not. Where are you from in West Germany?"

"A town called Uberlingen, on the north shore of Lake Konstanz."

Kevin couldn't take his eyes off Greta. She was that striking, with a distinctively Nordic look. She had high, prominent cheekbones on a rectangular face framed by lustrous, brown hair flowing naturally to her broad shoulders. Best of all, her soft, brown eyes sparkled with curiosity and wit, hinting at the kind of self-confidence that could only be forged through an abundance of successful life experiences.

"Is it nice, Uberlingen?" he asked.

"Absolutely. It's a resort town, with hills, lots of spas and magnificent views of the lake. Kind of like places in Kansas, I assume?"

Kevin laughed at Greta's sarcasm.

"Hardly. But my hometown, Wichita, was a nice place to grow up. No hills. No spa. No lake. Just lots of flat land. Which describes Kansas as a whole. It's very flat, which I like."

Unlike you, Miss Schmidt, he mused. *Which I like even more.*

A smile crept across Greta's face, as if she knew what he was thinking.

"So, it's 'flat.' That's the first word that comes to your mind when you think of Kansas?"

"Not just that," he answered with a blush, "There are wheat fields, oil derricks, silos and very friendly people."

"Like you?"

"Of course. Listen, I'm a wonderful guy. Wait 'til you get to know me."

"That what I'm trying to do," Greta answered coquettishly. "But it isn't easy."

"Touché. Would you like a beer?" he asked.

She arched one eyebrow. "I said I was German, didn't I?"

So, that's how their relationship began, innocently enough, with lots of harmless banter and a few beers. But, mostly because of Greta, it didn't stay that way very long. The third time they met at the Officer's Club, she invited herself back to Kevin's room and was the aggressor in a bout of lovemaking unlike anything Kevin had experienced so far in his young life. She was insatiable, and although her lips professed her passion pretty well, her hungry body did it even more emphatically.

After that, the two got together almost every night, whether it was in the BOQ or Greta's dorm room, occasionally to make love but often just to talk. They seemed to have different opinions on almost everything, from philosophy to religion to world affairs, but they never allowed those differences to affect their feelings, or their sex.

So, as the months passed, their relationship deepened into something pretty special, which presented Kevin with a dilemma when he got orders to report to a ship in San Diego. Should he leave Greta behind and risk losing her? Or invite her to join him there, which would be a significant escalation to their budding romance.

One complicating factor was that he knew that his ship, the *U.S.S. Buck*, was scheduled to go to the Far East, and probably Vietnam, shortly after he reported, which would leave Greta stranded in a strange town, for close to a year, which wouldn't have been so bad if they were married but would be intolerable for a single girl like Greta.

So, not being ready for marriage, Kevin did what he considered to be the chivalrous thing and broke up with her.

However, as it turned out, Greta had no intention of letting him do that.

****

Kevin's heart was pumping and his legs quivering as he approached the ship that was to be his home for the next few years. Although one of the smallest warships in the Navy, the *Buck* was impressive enough to intimidate the newly appointed supply officer who grew up in Kansas, several thousands of miles away from the nearest ocean. Sure, he had seen ships from afar during his training to be a naval officer, but this was the first time he had seen one up close, and Ensign Boyce was in awe.

Before boarding, Kevin paused for a minute at the gangplank and surveyed the ship from stem to stern, taking in all the sights, smells, and sounds, thinking how foreign and inhospitable it looked. Like a wild animal ready to pounce.

Welcome home, sailor boy, he thought facetiously, after seeing there wasn't anything particularly welcoming about the *Buck*. The forward deck bristled with dual gun mounts; their barrels pointed skyward. Above them was the bridge, its leering windows daring any intruder to try something, just so the officers could blow them away. And aft of the bridge was a towering four-legged mast, cluttered with electronic devices, ominously scanning the skies for perceived danger. Then, behind the mast was what looked like a helicopter deck, and, finally, another dual gun mount protecting the ship's rear.

All in all, to Kevin's eye, the *Buck* was a very formidable fighting machine, but hardly someplace you could comfortably call home. Still, he was eager to embrace his new life as a sailor, and this ship seemed to be as good a place to do it as any. Certainly, it was better than the tangled underbrush of Vietnam that U.S. soldiers might soon be encountering.

Kevin had picked his arrival time carefully to insure the smallest possible audience. *Most of the sailors will be ashore,* he thought, giving him the opportunity to find his quarters, unpack his duffel bag, and take a quick tour of the ship alone.

To get my sea legs, so to speak, he thought.

After mustering up what little courage Kevin had left, he walked briskly up the gangplank, his head high, his chest out, trying to appear more confident than he felt. Complicating things, though, the walkway swayed a bit under his feet, making each step more of an adventure than he would have liked.

Then, once on board, Kevin found himself assaulted by a plethora of unfamiliar sights and sounds. He heard metal scraping against metal, most likely from a work crew preparing a deck for painting, and the hissing of steam from the vents scattered haphazardly around the ship. Even the ropes tethering the ship to the pier creaked loudly, as if the *Buck* was straining against them, eager to get underway. The smells were intense as well, with diesel and cooking odors contaminating the normally fresh sea air.

Only one sailor was visible, and his back was turned, eyes gazing out to sea. But, when Kevin cleared his throat, the guy jerked around, a startled expression on his face.

I'll be damned, Kevin said to himself. *This guy is in charge of the ship and seems more scared of me, a lowly Ensign, than I am of him. Go figure.*

"Permission to come aboard?" Kevin asked, snapping off a crisp, well-rehearsed salute.

"Permission granted, sir," the petty officer answered with a salute of his own.

When Kevin reached the main deck, the sailor continued, "I assume you're Mr. Boyce. Please leave your bag here, sir, and report immediately to the captain in his in-port cabin."

A lump rose in Kevin's throat, forcing him to swallow again before asking, "The captain wants to see me now?"

"Yes, sir," the sailor answered. "Captain Riley said to send you to his cabin the minute you come on board."

"I didn't think he'd be here now. Do you know why he wants to see me?"

"No sir. You'll have to ask him that. I just know he's been waiting around on the ship for you to arrive. Must be something important.

Damn, Kevin cursed under his breath. He had hoped that his experience would be more like Ensign Pulver in the movie "Mister Roberts," and that he could avoid the captain for days by hiding out in the supply office or in his cabin.

Sensing Kevin's hesitation, the petty officer pointed toward the bow and said, "His in-port cabin is just off the wardroom. Through that hatch and down the ladder."

But Kevin was stalling, not because he needed directions, but because he was afraid of what the captain might have in store for him. *Come on, Kevin, how bad can it be?* he comforted himself, *I haven't had time to screw anything up. Not yet at least. He probably just wants to welcome me to his wardroom. Nice touch.*

Emboldened by this wishful thinking, Kevin dropped his duffle bag, walked over to the nearest hatch, scooted down the ladder and within seconds was outside the captain's door, steeling himself for the inevitable.

He knocked three times, and stood at attention, ready to salute his commanding officer. But there was no time for that.

Suddenly, the metal door burst open and a surprisingly large man, his rugged face obviously weathered by the sea, brushed past Kevin as if the young ensign wasn't even there.

"I don't want to know you, or your name, because you're not staying," the captain snarled over his shoulder as he passed. Then, he leapt up the ladder to the main deck and, in a surprisingly few lengthy steps, departed the ship, a perplexed Ensign Boyce trailing along in his wake.

Kevin thought to himself. *What the hell does he mean, I'm not staying? I haven't even reported in yet. Can he do that?* Then, he remembered that the captain of a ship is about as close to royalty as an American ever gets. He has full authority to do whatever he wants.

They were twenty-five yards down the pier before the ship's bell rang twice and the words, "*Buck* departing," crackled out over the ship's loudspeaker. Kevin knew it was Navy custom to "ring" the captain on and off his own ship, but this was the first time he had heard it in person. It was impressive but a little eerie at the same time. *Could this be the first, and last, time I hear that sound? Could my Navy career be over before it even begins?*

The Admiral's office door was wide open when they arrived, so Commander Riley barged in and announced, in a voice loud enough to be heard all over the base, "Look at what they sent me, Admiral McClinton. Look at him. A baby-faced officer barely old enough to shave, let alone handle the duties of a supply officer. This is ridiculous. I'm not taking him, sir."

Admiral Hubert McClinton, though small in stature, and balding, was even more respected and seasoned than the *Buck*'s captain, and tough as nails as well. He had earned Commander Riley's respect, admiration, and friendship over the years, but that didn't seem to matter much at that moment. The captain wanted Kevin off his ship and would go to any lengths to make it happen, even if it meant treating his old friend disrespectfully.

Admiral McClinton looked up from his paperwork, and smiled sweetly, a little too sweetly, not the least bit intimidated by the bluster of the larger officer hovering over his desk menacingly. After gazing emotionlessly at Commander Riley for a few seconds, the Admiral then turned his attention to Ensign Boyce, who was standing at attention in the back of the room.

Commander Riley is right, the Admiral thought, *this guy does look young. In fact, he could probably be my grandson. Kind of nice-looking, though, in a hayseed sort of way.*

Kevin was nice looking. He had a Greek nose, and a cherubic face framed by close-cropped blonde hair, and a strong jawline. His steely blue, unwavering eyes seemed confident beyond his apparent years, even in this uncomfortable circumstance. And, his long, lean body was taut, like an athlete ready to leap into action if needed, which, hopefully, would not need to be the case.

"Look, Wayne. I have Mr. Boyce's record right here," the Admiral finally said, pulling out a file from the pile on his desk. "He graduated from the University of Kansas, with honors, finished high in both OCS and his class at Supply Corps School, and seems perfectly qualified to be a supply officer on the *Buck,* or any other ship in my fleet, for that matter."

"Then, put him on some other ship, sir. I don't want him on mine."

"It's not your call, Commander. It's mine and let me be clear. This young man is going to be your supply officer, End of story."

"It's my call whether he stays as my supply officer though, right Admiral?"

"Just give him a fair chance, Wayne," the older man replied, softening his tone a little, then turned toward Kevin, "And I'm rooting for you, Mr. Boyce, so my old friend here will have to eat his words. And, believe me, if you do well, I'll make sure he does."

"Aye, aye, sir," Kevin replied, a little twinkle in his eye.

But Commander Riley wasn't quite done yet.

"Root for him all you want, but my last two supply officers came to me right from that crappy school in Athens, no real Navy experience, and both failed miserably. I sent a letter to you, you might remember, and also to the guy in charge of Supply Corps School, saying I would never take another wet-behind-the-ears officer to essentially manage, and screw up, everything on my ship. So, I'm not taking him, sir. There's just too much at risk here. We may be at war soon."

The Admiral looked up with flinty eyes, now hardened by Mr. Riley's tone. "War or no war, you're taking him, Mr. Riley. You got that. And that's an order."

When Commander Riley didn't move right away, he went on, "For God's sake, Wayne, get the hell out of my office before I lose my temper. And take your supply officer, Mr. Boyce, is it, with you."

On the walk back, a red-faced Commander Riley said nothing but, even from a few feet away, Kevin could feel the heat of his boiling anger. Once back on board, and with the announcement "*Buck* arriving" still echoing off the metal walls of the ship, the captain looked back over his shoulder, and snarled, "This isn't over, sailor. The first time you screw up, you're gone. So, don't unpack, and I still don't want to know your name."

Then the captain slammed the steel hatch, leaving Kevin alone to ponder what he had gotten himself into, and even why he joined the Navy in the first place.

****

The next day, things improved a little bit for Kevin.

As luck would have it, one of the officers stationed on the ship was a lieutenant j.g. named Ron Cowell that Kevin knew when he attended the University of Kansas. Ron was now serving as the communications officer of the *Buck* and was happy to help his fellow alum get settled in as a member of the wardroom, even if it might not last long. The first advice he gave his old schoolmate was not to worry too much about Captain Riley. "His bark is much worse than his bite. And he's probably already forgotten the whole episode."

"Thanks for the encouragement," Kevin answered. "But I'm pretty sure the captain isn't that forgetful and I'm guessing my days on the *Buck* are numbered."

"Well, numbered or not, you might as well enjoy them. Let me introduce you to a few of your shipmates."

So, Ron escorted Kevin up to the wardroom where several of the other officers were having a cup of coffee.

"This is our new supply officer, gentlemen. Mr. Kevin Boyce," he announced. "If you want to be well-clothed, fed, and paid, you might be nice to him."

The nearest officer stepped up, hand extended, and introduced himself. It was Lt. Mike Horning, a big bear of a man who was in charge of operations. Played football at Michigan and was obviously blessed with all the physical tools needed to keep the deckhands in line.

"We call him Tiny. Who knows why?"

Next, Kevin was introduced to Lt. Mike West, appropriately nicknamed Gramps. He was the grizzled old Chief Engineer of the Buck, who had enlisted in the Navy twenty years before, and had made it through OCS after failing the chief petty officer's exam twice.

He liked to tell his men he wasn't smart enough to be a chief, so they made him an officer. Needless to say, his men loved him for it and Mike had earned the right through the years to sport a scraggly beard, which was in sharp contrast to the other, clean-shaven, young-looking officers in the wardroom.

Next, Kevin met Lt. J.G. Buddy Penn, the officer in charge of weapons, who despite being the top warrior on board, was the friendliest of the lot.

"Welcome aboard, Pork Chop," Buddy said, offering his hand, a big smile creasing his face.

Kevin recognized immediately the derogatory but affectionate term supply officers were called in the real navy and appreciated it. It meant he was accepted as one of the guys.

Then, Ron informed Kevin that the most important officer Kevin needed to meet wasn't onboard yet. "Your roommate will be Joe Thrasher, an ensign who recently graduated from Annapolis, but he's going to DASH (Drone Anti-Submarine Helicopter) school right now to learn how to operate our choppers. You know about them, right?"

"Not really. Except obviously they are small, and unmanned, and dangerous to subs."

"We'll have to see about the 'dangerous to subs' part. Our job is to test that. We have two on board, both just big enough to carry two torpedos. We're the first ship in the Navy to have them and the captain is eager to get them into the air. All we need are the requisite replacement parts, which have been on order for months now. For some reason, the guy you replaced couldn't get them here, and eventually the captain ran out of patience, which he's prone to do."

"I've already seen that," Kevin said, now knowing what he needed to do first to succeed here. *Get those damned parts on board, Mr. Supply Officer,* he told himself.

****

For days, Kevin successfully avoided the captain. He holed up in his small office, looking over the records, checking receipts and transfers, verifying stock levels, and doing all the necessary things prior to officially taking the reins as the *Buck*'s supply officer. Helping Kevin was First Class Petty Officer Tom Hertz who, although he had worked closely with Kevin's tarnished predecessor, seemed very competent. Still, Kevin needed to oversee Hertz's work closely, especially in the beginning, to make sure he could be trusted.

"This doesn't make sense," Kevin said to the doughy-faced petty officer at one time. "I checked our open purchase orders, and the helicopter replacement parts were ordered six months ago, with a scheduled delivery one month after that, and they still aren't on board. What's up with that?"

"Yes, I know," a chagrined Hertz responded. "We've had the helicopters here for months now but can't operate them without those parts. So, we've been waiting, which is something the captain isn't very good at."

Kevin replied, "I don't blame him. What can we do to get them on board now?

"They keep telling us the manufacturer is behind. But I don't believe them. Why would they have released the helicopters to us if the parts aren't even manufactured yet? Doesn't make sense."

"No, it doesn't. We need to do something."

"We could send another message I guess." Hertz replied, "maybe a little stronger."

Kevin rolled his eyes. Sending messages hadn't gotten them anywhere to this point. Something more direct was required.

"I think I'll call the officer in charge of the warehouse," he said, "and see what I can do on a more personal level."

"Do you know him?" Hertz asked.

"I will shortly," a determined Kevin answered.

So, Kevin dialed up the warehouse himself, asked for the Supply Officer in charge, a Lt. Tom Murphy. He was connected immediately.

"What can I do for you, Ensign Boyce?" an impatient-sounding Mr. Murphy asked.

"Please call me Kevin. Can I call you Tom?"

"Of course. But I'm pretty busy right now, Kevin. Why the call?"

"You aren't related to Brian Murphy, are you? He was in my class at Supply Corps School."

"Lots of Murphy's in the world," Tom answered, his tone cold, "And no, I don't know anybody named Brian Murphy. Could be a distant relative, though. I have a slew of cousins scattered about."

"You from the Midwest?

"Yes. Can't you tell by my accent? My family originally settled in Iowa, up near the Illinois border. And I grew up in Cedar Rapids."

"You a Hawkeye?"

"No, a Cyclone," Tom said, "Iowa State in Ames."

"Know it well. I'm a Jayhawk. Went to Ames several times for basketball games," Kevin said, trying to build some kind of rapport.

"Makes sense that you went there for basketball," a now-relaxed Tom jabbed, "I can't imagine somebody from K.U. traveling that far to see their football team play."

"Careful, Tom, we actually beat you guys once when I was in school."

"Once? You're probably still celebrating. But enough about your woeful football team, Kevin. What can I do for you?"

So, Kevin explained his dilemma, that helicopter replacement parts, probably warehoused in one of the buildings under Tom's control, had been on order for an inordinately long time. And could he please check into it?

"Sure thing," Tom replied, "and if you want bet on the next Iowa State/KU football game, let me know."

"I may have been educated in Kansas but I'm not that stupid," Kevin replied.

A few days later, Robert Wade, the fresh-faced young supply clerk, stuck his head into the office and said, "Sir, guess what? Those helicopter parts you two were discussing the other day, well, they just arrived this morning. We're checking them in now. How lucky was that?"

How lucky indeed, Kevin told himself. *Sometimes, Mr. Wade, you have to give luck a chance to work.*

That night, as Kevin was getting ready for bed, there was a soft rap on his door, and when he opened it, there stood the Captain, in full uniform, standing tall and at attention, saluting Kevin.

What the hell? the supply officer thought as he snapped to attention himself and hesitantly saluted back. He surely painted quite the picture, barefooted, and in his skivvies.

The captain smothered a smile, then said, "I salute you, Mr. Boyce, because, although I don't know how you did it, you got our replacement parts. And we get to fly our DASH helicopters tomorrow. I invite you to come up on the bridge with me and catch the show."

Kevin noticed the captain used his name for the first time.

"Thanks. I will, but I didn't do much. The parts just happened to –" he started to humbly explain.

However, the Captain would have none of it. "Happened on your watch, sailor and, in the Navy, that's all that matters. Thanks for doing your job."

He turned to leave, then, tossed one last comment over his shoulder, "Oh, and Mr. Boyce, you can unpack now. Welcome aboard."

And, just like that, Kevin was accepted into the wardroom of the *U.S.S.Buck*, not only by his fellow officers but by his Captain as well. And his Navy career had been officially launched.

CHAPTER 2

Several months into his new job, Kevin was enjoying a cup of coffee in the wardroom when the Captain made one of his rare appearances there.

"Kevin, I just learned that the Secretary of the Navy might visit our ship next week, and the Admiral says he wants to do a dress rehearsal tomorrow. Tour the spaces. Inspect the crew. The whole nine yards. And he wants everybody in dress whites."

"Why dress whites?"

"It's bullshit, but he wants to impress the top dog. Something about a funding bill that needs the Secretary's support."

The next day, Kevin was particularly busy. He had only a few minutes to put on his starched white uniform and make sure everything was in order before heading topside for the inspection. Shoes shined? Check. Belt buckle polished? Buttons lined up? Everything seemed in order when he grabbed his lid and took his place in front of his division just seconds before the inspecting party appeared.

The Admiral was first to arrive, followed by the *Buck*'s Captain and Executive Officer. Everybody seemed in a particularly good mood, even jovial, as the Admiral stepped forward to address the Supply Division with a friendly smile on his face.

"Ensign Boyce, nice to see you again," he said, "Are you and your men ready for inspection?"

"Yes, sir, we are." Kevin said after saluting.

Then, the Admiral's expression became deadly serious. He arched his eyebrow and asked again. "Are you sure you and your men are ready, Mr. Boyce?"

"Yes, sir, I am."

Kevin heard titters behind him, but he didn't turn around to see who was laughing until the Admiral stepped past him and addressed the first man in line, who happened to be Hertz.

"Sailor, do you see anything inappropriate about how your division is dressed?"

The supply clerk smiled and answered, "Yes, sir. I do."

Kevin was astonished that Hertz would respond that way. But he remained silent as the Admiral stepped to the next man in line and repeated the question.

"Yes, sir," that sailor said as well, "I see something very wrong."

More laughter. Kevin was chagrined until he noticed that everybody was looking at him, not in shock or pity, but with broad grins on their faces, as if they were watching a comedy show.

"Mr. Boyce, will you remove your lid please," the now-surprisingly cheerful Admiral McClinton asked.

When he complied, Kevin got the joke. In his haste to get to the inspection, he forgot to change the khaki cover on his hat to white. So, he had been standing in front of all of his men, and the inspection party, resplendent in his pressed dress whites, brass freshly polished, with the wrong-colored hat on his head. One tan lid in a sea of white.

Everybody got a big laugh out of it and, fortunately, the Admiral seemed amused as well.

"Don't worry, Mr. Boyce," Captain Riley whispered to him. "Nobody expected much out of you anyway." Then he laughed along with everybody else, a sight Kevin had never seen before. A serious Mr. Riley was a force to be reckoned with. But a smiling one? Absolutely scary.

As the inspection team moved on toward the forward deck to meet with the Operations Division, Admiral McClinton held back a little and, with a broad grin on his face, comforted Kevin, by saying, "No problem this time, Ensign Boyce, but should the Secretary of the Navy visit your ship in the next few days, I would appreciate it if you could wear the right-colored lid, okay?"

Then, he turned serious again and whispered, "I should be done with all of this nonsense shortly, and I have something important to discuss with you in private. So, please wait for me in the wardroom."

About thirty minutes later, the Admiral entered the wardroom to find a nervous Ensign Boyce waiting. He wasted no time with pleasantries.

"Young man," the Admiral began, "I've been reviewing your file again and I must say I'm impressed. Company Commander at Officer Candidate School, second in your class at Supply Corps School, crypto officer with the highest security clearance. Quite a record for somebody so new to the Navy. And I'm here to offer you an easy way to polish your resume even more."

Kevin cocked his head slightly, like a cocker spaniel might do, but said nothing. He was waiting for the other shoe to drop.

"Occasionally, when the *Buck* is in port, I'd like you to sneak onto another ship and test their security."

Kevin felt the blood drain from his face. *Sneak aboard? Test their security? I think not.*

"Lieutenant Commander Brad Smith from Naval Intelligence will be in touch soon to explain the details. Listen. I really appreciate you doing this for me, Kevin. Oh, and one other thing. Nobody, not family members or shipmates, not even your Captain, can know that you're doing this. Word gets around fast in the Navy."

Kevin started to object but Admiral McClinton gave him no time for that. He abruptly turned and left. Obviously, what had seemed like a request was really an order, which, as Kevin was beginning to realize, was often the case in the Navy.

Then, about a week after the ship returned from a training exercise, an unfamiliar officer knocked on the supply office door and stuck his head in, a big smile on his face. He addressed Kevin in a deep, sonorous voice, "Ensign Boyce, may I speak with you in your cabin, please?"

"Of course, sir," Kevin answered. "But what's this about?"

The senior officer's expression didn't change. "In your cabin, please," he said.

When they were alone, door closed, the officer extended his hand to introduce himself. He was a friendly-faced guy, with ice-blue eyes and a big smile on his face, accentuated by deep dimples. He had close-cropped brown hair and, in marked contrast to the amiable expression on his face, he stood quite erect as he addressed Kevin, like he was at attention or something.

"I'm Lt. Cdr. Brad Smith, with Naval Intelligence out of the San Diego office, and I want to discuss more fully the assignment Admiral McClinton talked to you about."

"He really didn't say much about it," Kevin explained. "But, based on what he did say, I think you're talking to the wrong guy."

"I don't think so, especially after meeting you. We need someone who looks young, and naïve, and harmless. Check, check, and check. Who thinks fast on his feet. Check. Who's new enough to the Navy that few know him. Check. So, despite your misgivings, Kevin, you're our guy and, if you don't want to do it, after promising the Admiral, well, you'll have to tell him yourself."

Realizing the futility of fighting the inevitable, Kevin shrugged his shoulders. "Okay. What do you want me to do?"

"About once a year, every ship in the Navy gets a surprise inspection. One of the things we check is their security, and what we want from you is simple. Just sneak onto the ship a day before the inspection and plant fake bombs…so the inspectors can find them the next day."

"So I just slip onto the target ship undetected," Kevin repeated back for dramatic effect, "Hide fake bombs. Sneak back off the ship. And go on about my business."

"That's it."

"One question, sir. How the hell am I supposed to do that?"

"You'll come up with something. One thing others have found effective is to just join a loading party going onto the target ship, sneak away for a few minutes and plant the 'bombs' in the most secure spaces you can find, in gun mounts, torpedo tubes, the engine room. Then, join another group of sailors leaving the ship. You let us know where the bombs are stashed, and we take it from there."

"Will I have a fake ID?"

"Of course not. That'd be like cheating. But, as part of the loading party, you won't be checked anyway. I can assure you of that."

"But what happens if I get caught?"

Brad Smith paused for a second, seemingly pondering the possibilities, then answered honestly, "I wouldn't let that happen if I were you."

****

Occasionally, Kevin received a letter from Greta. Despite his attempt to break up back in Athens, she acted as if the relationship was ongoing. Still, he didn't feel that way and he craved the kind of female companionship not available through letters.

So, Kevin got in touch with an old college flame who now lived in San Diego. Her name was Sally Thomas, and, after exchanging pleasantries, she agreed to meet him in the bar of a downtown hotel, the *U.S. Grant,* which was only a couple of miles from the naval base where the *Buck* was docked.

Although Kevin had ended the romantic relationship at the time, and had no interest in restarting it now, he still was excited to see Sally again, as a friend. He remembered her to be a pretty, highly personable sorority girl with blonde curly hair, dimples, and a ready smile that drew everybody in immediately. Kevin couldn't wait to see how much of that Kansas farm girl freshness Sally had retained over the several years they'd been apart.

The *Grant was* a relatively small hotel, elegant by San Diego standards, with a tiny bar that served anybody sitting in the lobby. As Kevin adjusted his eyes to the unexpected darkness, he spotted the still-adorable Sally sitting in an overstuffed sofa in the corner. She already had a white wine in front of her.

Her pixyish hair looked the same, as did her face. And yet, somehow, she seemed different. Kevin didn't know what it was, maybe her confident manner, or just the smartly tailored blue jacket and skirt she was wearing instead of the ever-present blue jeans she wore in college. Of course, seeing him in his dress uniform, she probably had the same thought.

"Sally, you've grown up," he began.

"So have you, Mr. Navy Officer."

Kevin laughed. "My good friends call me Pork Chop now."

Sally got an incredulous look on her face. "My goodness. Why?"

"In the Navy, all supply officers are called Pork Chop. I don't know why. Maybe because we're in charge of feeding the crew."

"Well, Mr. Pork Chop, you sure look handsome in your uniform. And are those medals on your chest?"

Kevin looked down. "Mostly for good behavior."

"That would be a big change. Come. Sit beside me. I ordered you your favorite drink, a Purple Passion. You remember. Vodka and grape juice," she replied. "Just like we used to drink back home, at our barn parties."

He laughed, then sat down onto a tufted couch, which had a diminutive table in front of it and a large California landscape painting behind.

Kevin said nothing for a minute, his mind taking him back to those idyllic college days when putting vodka and grape juice into a personalized jug and drinking it behind hay bales was as risqué as things could get. And how being with Sally now made him feel strangely, but warmly, nostalgic.

"I don't remember that drink," he replied after settling in and forcing himself back to the present.

Sally laughed. "Or anything else about those barn parties either, I suspect."

"Wow. What a blast from the past. Barn parties. We always had a good time and I remember kissing you there."

She furrowed her brow, her face somber. "I don't think so. I was a very serious student"

"And a hell of a kisser."

They both laughed heartily, just like the old days. Openly, and without embarrassment.

Then, Kevin turned to the waiter, who was politely waiting for the silliness to end, and said, "I'll have a Blackjack, neat. No grape juice, please."

It was amazing that, here, in such a posh setting, it still seemed like they were back at the Wagon Wheel, their favorite beer joint in Lawrence, or on the grass under the Campanile, just babbling to each other about inconsequential things that seemed huge at the time.

As usual, Sally carried the conversation. "You remember my roommate, Mabel?" she said. "Well, she's on husband number two, and having an affair with husband number one. And Kelly, the kind of spacey one we used to double-date with? She's now a translator at the United Nations."

Kevin did a double take. "Get out of here. I didn't think she spoke one language very well."

"You mean English?"

"You got it."

And they both laughed again.

"Sandra Nixon is studying to be a doctor," Sally goes on, "I think she's in residency."

"She's too good-looking to be a doctor," Kevin replied.

Sally acted mock offended. "You wouldn't say that if she were a guy."

"Frankly, you're right," he agreed, "Because I'm not into guys."

"Well, I'm glad to hear that," Sally responded. "Any girlfriends at the moment?"

"None to speak of," Kevin answered quickly, not really considering Greta a girlfriend any longer, "I'm leaving for the Far East soon, and it wouldn't be convenient anyway."

"Vietnam?" She asked.

"I don't know for sure, but I hope so."

"That makes you different than any other guy I've met," she said, "Most would rather run off to Canada."

"I guess so. I understand that's the mindset of those behind us in school, but not my buddies," Kevin answered, "All of our fathers and uncles joined the military. It was just assumed we would, too. And everybody did."

"You're right, as I think about it. That sure changed in a hurry, didn't it? But, with what you know now about Vietnam, why would you want to go?"

"It's what we've all trained for and, honestly, despite everything that's happened, I'm still patriotic. At this stage of my life, I feel it's my duty to defend my country."

"And those of us who can't do that, love you for it."

Then, Sally gave Kevin a chaste kiss on the cheek, leaving him wanting more. But, wisely, he didn't follow up on the impulse and they ended the 'date' as good friends rather than the lovers they once had been.

****

After his meeting with Lt. Cdr. Smith, Kevin was naturally worried about his new undercover assignment. But he didn't have time to think much about it.

Instead, his mind was on the looming deployment to Westpac, and what now seemed like their most likely destination, Vietnam. Like most of the crew, Kevin had mixed feelings about going to Vietnam. On one hand, it was what the ship's crew had been training for, and they were eager to test their capabilities. On the other hand, being in a combat zone, any combat zone, was risky.

Granted, America wasn't officially at war in Vietnam yet, and those few U.S. military people helping the Vietnamese were called "advisors." But that was just semantics, or political posturing. Everybody knew that America was committed to defend the South Vietnamese if necessary, and it was only a matter of time before that commitment would lead to "boots on the ground," as the military liked to say.

So, Kevin was preparing as if the U.S. was already at war, and the *Buck* would be a combatant sooner rather than later. He was scrambling to get the appropriate provisions, stores, money, and ammunition on board for an extended tour of duty, and the ship was engaged in training exercises that would test their real war capabilities ahead of any actual event.

They were practicing "plane guarding" the carrier, for example, in a position just aft of it where they could pick up the pilots of planes that went into the ocean. And they were battering the shoreline of San Clemente Island with heavy artillery in case they were called on to support a major invasion. Also, they were testing capabilities that went right to the heart of what the *Buck* was designed to be, an anti-aircraft, anti-submarine fighting machine.

Among the most promising of those capabilities were the two experimental drone helicopters, which theoretically could greatly extend the range of the *Buck* torpedos. But their effectiveness still had to be proven, and the first attempt to use the drones didn't go well at all.

Using sonar, the technicians in CIC (Combat Information Center) were able to track the target submarine and, with radar overlays, they maneuvered the drone to a position above it. But, when they dropped the 'homing' torpedoes, one misfired and the other just headed out to sea, never to be found again. The captain was livid, and he let everybody know it, in a voice loud enough to carry all the way to Hawaii.

Ensign Joe Thrasher, Kevin's new roommate, was most directly in the firing line of Commander Riley's wrath but handled the abuse with aplomb. He went methodically about his business for the second launch, which, fortunately, went much better.

The shore bombardment of San Clemente Island went well too, but it was an eye-opener, or more appropriately, "ear-opener" for Kevin. He had gone to crypto school before reporting to the *Buck* and, therefore, was the only officer on board qualified to code and decode highly confidential messages. So, during General Quarters, when the *Buck* was in a combat situation, Kevin's duty station was in the crypto shack, a very small cabin high up in the superstructure of the ship. It was a hot, poorly ventilated, tiny metal room, just off the radio cabin, where he would wait for any encrypted messages that would come in. Few did, especially during exercises, so Kevin just sat there, uncomfortably on a hard-back stool, twiddling his thumbs, sometimes for hours on end.

Except when the ship was doing shore bombardment exercises. Then, all hell would break loose, as the massive guns exploded without warning, sending the cabin, and Kevin, sideways a foot or two. To him, it seemed like he was on the receiving end of the shell rather than the sending end.

Eventually, the training exercises were concluded, the ship was back in port, and Kevin's hearing had returned to normal when he heard a knock on his cabin door. It was the Officer of the Deck (OD) telling him that there was a "knock-out woman" on the pier who wanted to see him.

He couldn't imagine who it could be, but it was Greta, of course.

What's she doing here? And how the hell did she got through security? Kevin asked himself, before realizing that a girl with her looks could charm her way by any young security guard as easily as a knife can slide through soft butter.

"You should have told me you were coming," a smiling Kevin suggested.

"I like to surprise you, sailor boy," an obviously excited Greta said while hugging him as if she didn't want to lose him again.

Kevin felt an unexpected tingle shoot through his body and a stirring in his loins as he held Greta close. He pulled back to look at her. She was even more attractive than he remembered, with her high cheekbones and her loving brown eyes gazing deeply into his in a highly seductive way.

Greta reached out for Kevin again, and gave him another hug, this time holding on for several long minutes, her face down and her silky hair caressing his face. She smelled fresh and dewy, without the hint of perfume. Kevin squeezed her back, letting her know in every way he could how thrilled he was that she was there.

My life just got more complicated, he thought, *but I'll figure it out. I have to if I want to keep this delightful creature in my life. And why wouldn't I? Why wouldn't any guy?*

Greta tilted her head upward, and Kevin found her lips, his mind still sorting through what he would have to do to balance all his job responsibilities with entertaining her appropriately. Then, her tongue found his and all bets were off. After the long, passionate embrace ended, and Kevin had control of his tongue again, he blurted out, "I'm not sure you're aware that the *Buck* is leaving for Hawaii in a few days."

"I'm aware, and that's fine. I'm only here a few days anyway," she responded, "so it will work out perfectly.

Obviously, she doesn't know how busy a supply officer can be before his ship leaves.

"I won't be in the way," Greta said coquettishly, striking a provocative pose that undercut her message perfectly. "And, if you're not available, I'll just find something else to do with my time," she purred, fluttering her eyelashes at him provocatively.

"I need to work during the day, but my nights are yours," he promised.

"When do your nights start?"

Kevin looked up at the sky briefly, as if pondering his answer. "When the sun is over the yardarm," he finally replied cryptically.

"And what the hell does that mean?"

"It's an old Navy saying that originated when the British gave their sailors shots of rum during the day as a reward for their hard work. The first shot came around 11 a.m., which coincidentally was when the sun peeked over the cross mast called the yardarm."

"So, your nights begin at 11 a.m.?"

"More like, by custom, they begin whenever a sailor is ready for his first drink."

Then, Kevin looked up at the sky, glanced down at his watch and said, "And, for us, I think the sun is over the yardarm right now."

To which she answered, "I love this yardarm thing," and they headed for the nearest bar, which was a few miles away, in downtown San Diego.

So, driven by purpose and passion, Kevin got up at 5 a.m. each morning, worked until the 'sun was over the yardarm,' then mustered up enough additional energy to rekindle his romance with Greta in the evening. And rekindle they did, with days sunning and playing volleyball at Mission Beach, followed by nights that would start at a different restaurant in La Jolla or Del Mar, but always ended up in Greta's hotel room overlooking San Diego's picturesque bay.

Once there, Greta was full service. She would wiggle her way out of whatever clothes she was wearing, then, dance provocatively in front of Kevin as if she was on stage. He didn't have to do much himself, just lie back on the bed, fingers intertwined behind his head, and enjoy the show as best he could, until it culminated with Greta straddling him and bouncing up and down, her boobs going every which way, until he was totally spent.

Then on the final night, after a romantic dinner at the Marine Room, and a stroll on the moonlit beach outside the restaurant, Greta changed the script a little bit, with a strip tease dance reminiscent of the one Marilyn Monroe gave President Kennedy on his forty-fifth birthday, except that, unlike Marilyn slinking off the stage fully clothed, Greta ended her act totally nude, beside the bed, breathily singing her version of "Sailor Boy."

Kevin, and his member, gave her a standing ovation.

And the next day the *Buck* deployed, with an apologetic and exhausted supply officer on board. For days, he thanked his staff profusely for covering up for him the last few days in port, as he attended to "other, more urgent, matters," as he worded it.

Having seen Greta, they seemed to understand.

CHAPTER 3

The *U.S.S. Buck* was only a few days away from docking in Honolulu when the first small signs of a storm appeared. Up until then, the only excitement on board had been when the *Buck's* sonar picked up the ping of a Soviet sub. But, with a freshening wind and an ominous choppiness to the sea, any experienced seaman could guess what would soon be in store for the ship.

Of course, Kevin was anything but experienced, so he missed all the signs. He noticed his desk moving a little more than usual as he put the finishing touches on the ledgers that reflected what he had accomplished the last few weeks in port. But he wasn't all that concerned until he thought about the drone helicopters tethered on the aft deck. Kevin had made them secure enough to handle normal weather, but not the pitching and yawing of the ship he was feeling right at that moment.

So, he decided to go topside and check on them. Big mistake.

Once outside, Kevin stepped onto a slippery deck that was sloped precariously away from him. That should have been a warning sign, but Kevin missed it entirely. Instead of ducking back into the relative safety of the cabin, he turned aft toward the ladder leading to the helicopter deck just as the ship began a slow roll back the other way. With his back to the bow, Kevin didn't see the massive wave crashing over it.

Suddenly, he was under water, and everything was green and salty, and disorienting. He felt himself lifted up and carried by the wave toward the gunwales, his last protection before being washed over the side.

Is this it for me? He thought as he thrashed around trying to find something, anything, to latch onto. Suddenly, he felt something coarse and hard run up his arm, and instinctively grabbed what turned out to be the aptly named "lifeline," a rope that encircled the ship, above the gunwales, as a last line of defense before washing overboard. Kevin held on for dear life and, when the wave finally passed over him, and the ship began to right itself, he found himself hanging partly over the outside of the ship, both hands still gripped tightly onto the lifeline.

Then, before the ship could roll precariously in the other direction, he scrambled up and back onto the deck, then, slid toward the door he had exited. Fortunately, he was able to unlatch it quickly, and fall back inside.

With water sloshing around his feet, Kevin was able to secure the latches from the inside, then, fall against the door, his chest heaving with exertion and fright. His heart was beating so loudly he could hear nothing else, not even the noise of the storm. But he was safe, and that was all that mattered.

A few minutes later, First Class Petty Officer Hertz came out of the supply office, followed closely by storekeeper Wade, and they were both shocked to find

Kevin, soaked, and shivering, and scared, looking up at them from a puddled hallway. They picked their boss up and helped him back to his cabin.

"What the hell were you thinking, sir?" an obviously concerned Hertz asked, "You're lucky to be alive."

"I wasn't thinking," Kevin answered in a weak, quivering voice.

"Not a good thing aboard ship, sir," Hertz clarified. "The sea stands ready to gobble up non-thinkers."

Just then, a voice crackled over the loudspeaker. "Attention, all personnel. Normally we don't have to say this during a typhoon. But would everybody please stay inside the ship and off the decks. This includes pork chops, by the way. As you were."

Kevin understood the dig, as did everybody else onboard but, knowing he deserved it, he just buried his head into his pillow and tried to sleep. Unfortunately, the soothing roll of the ship that lulled him to sleep most nights was now something very different: a carnival ride of jerking and straining that felt like it was testing every screw and bolt holding the ship together.

Then, to add to his discomfort, the loudspeaker burst into life again. "Attention all crew members. If you're not on duty, please go to the main inside passageway and secure yourself. Looks like we are going to take a direct hit from this storm. Repeat. Please go to the main inside passageway. Everybody who isn't needed at their duty station, secure yourself in the main passageway. That is all."

Kevin dressed quickly and, instead of following the 'suggestion,' headed up to the bridge, which was his usual duty station during operations. But, when he got there, the captain spotted him immediately, made a grimace, and shouted over the roar of the storm, "What the hell are you doing here, Boyce? Get below deck immediately!"

"Remember, Captain, I'm the designated Safety Officer, and this is my duty station."

"The only safety you need to worry about right now is your own, from both the storm and me, if you don't get your ass out of here. We're going to need you when things calm down."

Kevin did as he'd been told, but not before the ship slid down the backside of one massive wave, giving him a front-row seat on a wall of water higher than the ship's superstructure tumbling over the ship's prow, and washing over the roof of the bridge.

He thought to himself, *What an awesome and frightening sight. If I survive this storm, I'll remember what I just saw forever, unfortunately.*

Finally, the wave tumbled noisily, but harmlessly, over the roof and onto the deserted decks below. Then, just as suddenly, as the water had exploded onto the bridge, it subsided enough for Kevin to grab a railing, and scramble down the ladder to the relative safety of the passageway below. Once he reached the main passageway, in the bowels of the ship, he saw another disconcerting sight. Almost the entire crew was there, feet propped against one bulkhead and butt against the other, with faces as green as the seawater that had just washed over the ship.

It took everything Kevin had to slide down next to an unfamiliar sailor, position himself uncomfortably between the two bulkheads and stay as rigid as possible as the ship fought him, like a bucking bronco trying to throw its rider to the ground.

The only thing the crew could see was the attitude indicator on the far bulkhead, a crude instrument designed to measure the tilt of a ship as it pitched and rolled. There was awed silence as everybody watched the needle go into the danger zone to the right, setting off a "capsize" alarm. Then, back to the left with the same alarm clanging in a way that just added to the terror everybody was feeling.

"Must be broken," one crew member finally muttered, "As far as I can tell, we haven't capsized yet,"

"No. Not yet," another replied. "But stay tuned."

Nobody laughed. Everybody felt too helpless, frightened, and seasick to appreciate the humor in the situation. Especially seasick. Many crew members had already thrown up, their vomit sloshing around on the floor of the deck below their feet. The stench was unbearable.

If there's a hell, Kevin thought, *this is it.*

After what seemed like hours of constant and violent motion, the ship finally began to right itself, and calm down a bit. The crew was visibly relieved. One by one, they picked themselves up, circumvented the pools of vomit in the passageway, and returned to their bunks or duty stations.

Surprisingly, within a few hours, the sky was blue, the sea like glass, and there was no visible evidence of the cruel storm that had tried to flip the ship and kill everybody on board. It's as if the sea had been beaten into submission and was offering up its apologies in the form of perfect weather.

With their safety assured, the mood of the crew was pensive one minute and giddy the next. They had survived an ordeal that would test the heartiest of crews, and most onboard couldn't decide whether to celebrate or just give thanks to whatever deity they believed had answered their prayers.

When the cleanup work was done, most of the crew wandered topside and gathered near a gun mount, or an air conditioning duct, to share their stories. The more they talked, the higher were the waves, the stronger the winds, and the louder the noise. But, exaggerated or not, all agreed that they had never seen anything like it.

"And here's to our pork chop," one crew member toasted with his mug of coffee, "Who says he didn't get sick once through the whole storm."

"If you believe that, I've got a bridge to sell you," another countered.

"OK. But don't try to sell me a boat. I'm really not in the market for one of them right now."

****

Unfortunately, the storm put the *Buck* a day or two behind schedule, necessitating an underway replenishment to restock stores, commonly known as an "UNREP."

Normally, the ship would be taking on fuel and/or supplies from a tanker or a "reefer" that was equipped specifically to do the job but, because none were in the area, a nearby cruiser, the *Canberra,* agreed to pass along enough emergency rations to get the *Buck* safely to their next port of call, which was Honolulu, Hawaii.

The sea had turned choppy again and that, plus the size disparity between the two ships, made the operation particularly tricky. The two ships had to synchronize their speed and direction so that they were side-by-side, only a few dozen yards apart from each other. Then, high lines and hoses had to be attached between the two ships so supplies could be passed from the larger ship to the smaller one, all while hurtling across the waves together, at a relatively high speed.

In this kind of operation, the critical thing was to maintain a consistent distance between the two ships, which required an OD (Officer of the Deck) and helmsman that were both quick-thinking and totally in tune with each other. Obviously, the OD was very important since he made all of the decisions during the operation, but the helmsman was equally important because he had to turn the helm (wheel of the ship) quickly in whatever direction the OD ordered, just to keep the ship going straight on course.

Normally, Captain Riley would be the OD but, this time, Executive Officer Elmer Bess was allowed to do it as part of his training. Kevin was to be in his normal place on the bridge as the Safety Office, whose sole responsibility was to monitor the activities and report on them later. Not very exciting, perhaps, but it would give Kevin a front-row seat at one of the most complicated and intricate maneuvers a naval ship is required to do.

Everything was going smoothly until the helmsman was ordered to turn toward starboard and he made a split-second move toward port. He was able to correct his mistake instantly, but the damage was done. The centrifugal force between the two ships had sucked them together and, although they only tapped each other, the metal projections sticking out from the larger cruiser punctured the skin of the *Buck*.

Of course, any time the skin of a ship is compromised at sea, it's not good, but this time it didn't seem that serious until Mr. Bess gave the command, "All back full," which caused the *Buck* to slow dramatically, while the larger ship kept moving forward at the agreed-upon speed. There was a loud, ripping sound as the metal projections of the cruiser tore holes in the forward port section of the *Buck*, allowing seawater to invade some of its spaces.

The captain immediately relieved the Executive Officer as OD, and yelled, "All ahead full," thereby synchronizing the two ships better as they separated, avoiding any further ripping of the *Buck's* port side. However, the damage had been done, and seawater was gushing into the bow of the ship.

The *Buck's* "damage control" team rushed to the bow of the ship and shored up the penetrated compartments as best they could by closing and locking a number of watertight doors. Then, they set up pumps and hoses to drain the water out of compartments that were still secure.

The *Buck* tipped precariously toward the bow as the Captain slowed the ship down in order to limit the amount of water pouring into its damaged hull. Eventually, the ship stopped taking on any more water and, although a photo of the event from above would look like the *Buck* was about to sink bow first, the ship had actually stabilized.

Kevin tried to move toward the ladder leading off the bridge but had to get down on all fours in order to avoid falling. As he crawled, he saw a sign lying on the deck that was normally hanging on the bulkhead at the back of the bridge: ***A collision at sea can ruin your whole day.***

No shit, he commented to himself.

Several days later, the *U.S.S. Buck* limped into Pearl Harbor, under tow, and was tied up at the Naval Shipyard to undergo repairs to the ruptured exterior skin of the ship. Even more importantly, while that was going on, the Navy planned to launch an investigation into what had caused the collision, with Kevin as a key witness.

Obviously, the careers of Lt. Commander Bess and the helmsman, were at stake, because the Navy doesn't look kindly on a collision at sea, no matter what the extenuating circumstances.

CHAPTER 4

Normally, any arrival into dry dock is a somber affair. No bands. No visitors. No banners. And *Buck's* arrival was no different except that there, under a crane and straddling the hoses and wires that snaked across the pier to the ship, was the unmistakably shapely image of the indefatigable Greta.

She was quite a sight, dressed in a blue sundress, the top of which was amply filled, and seemingly held up by only two tiny spaghetti straps. She was trying, with limited success, to keep her dress from billowing up a la Marilyn Monroe, and yet, she was still able to muster a theatrical wave toward the *Buck*.

As usual, the captain was the first one off, dressed outrageously in surfer shorts and a loud Hawaiian shirt. He did it to please the small crowd who, because he was arguably the best ship handler in the Navy, had gathered to see him "park" the ship.

Close behind him, however, was Kevin who, after receiving permission to depart the ship, braced himself as Greta rushed over, embraced him, and elicited a cacophony of catcalls from the crew.

Then, the two lovers leaned back, waved to the sailors, and Kevin further entertained them by giving Greta another, more passionate kiss, bending her over backwards while she kicked her shapely right leg up behind her, and let her left arm dangle as if she were a rag doll.

"Greta, what the hell are you doing here in Honolulu?" He whispered when they finally disengaged enough to talk.

"It's a long story," she answered.

"Well, let's find a drink somewhere, and you can fill me in."

"I hoped you'd say that. I have a taxi waiting just outside the gate," she responded.

Kevin hesitated. As the supply officer, there was so much he needed to do now that the *Buck* was finally in port. Requisitions to deliver. Supplies to get on board. But, looking into Greta's pleading eyes he realized the decision wasn't really his to make.

Whatever Greta wants, Greta gets, he sang silently. *At least for the next few days.*

So, the taxi took the two young lovers to the Barefoot Beach Bar, at the Hale Koa hotel on Waikiki Beach, a resort owned by the U.S. government and operated for the use of military personnel only. It turned out to be the perfect setting for them to ease into the Honolulu beach scene, enjoy a couple of surprisingly inexpensive drinks, and for Kevin to hear Greta's long story about why she decided to surprise him. Except, when they finally settled into beach chairs outside the bar area, Mai Tai's in hand, with a pink and yellow sunset spreading across the sky before them, the story wasn't really that long.

Greta explained, "A college friend of mine is from Honolulu, and when she told me she was going to visit her parents, I asked to tag along. That's all there was to it. Kind of spur of the moment."

"Pretty ballsy of you."

"What is this 'ballsy?'"

"You wouldn't understand," Kevin answered diplomatically, "But one thing is becoming clear. Absolutely nothing keeps you from getting what you want, does it, Greta?"

She smiled coyly, then fluttered her eyelashes as she answered, "You got that right, sailor boy, and tonight, guess what I want?"

They embraced and snuggled up to each other, without saying anything more for quite a while, delightfully soaking up the silence, finishing their second drinks and enjoying the last brilliant gasp of pastel colors that were slowly fading into royal blue before darkness fell.

"Do you have a hotel room, perchance?" Kevin asked.

"Why, dear sir, I have something even better. I'm sharing a suite with my friend, and she's staying at her parent's house tonight. So, I have it all to myself."

"Near here?"

"Within walking distance, in fact. Why do you ask?"

"No reason, I guess. Just that that it's getting a little chilly here and maybe it would be warmer there. What do you think?"

"I can pretty much guarantee it will be warmer there," Greta said, snuggling closer to Kevin, her ample breasts pressed against his chest, and her hand exploring the inside of his leg as a preview of coming attractions."

"Well, I don't really have anything else scheduled," Kevin replied, moving her hand away for the moment. He had to save himself for later. Then, the two lovers disentangled and, with a passion-fueled zip to their step, walked briskly to the end of the beach, then the quarter mile or so to Greta's hotel, where they bounded up the stairs two at a time to Greta's suite, giggling all the way.

Their race to nirvana was temporarily suspended while Greta fumbled with the lock, and then, she threw the door wide open so both could enter the suite together in a mad dash to the bedroom. Along the way they tossed items of clothing everywhere, in the living room, in the hallway, until they reached the bed and, both completely naked, slipped under the silky sheets.

Once appropriately positioned, the two young lovers kissed and groped and thrusted their way to a simultaneous coital climax that took both of them a little bit by surprise.

"Next time we may want to be a tad more patient," Greta breathlessly suggested as she lay back into the pillow, her right hand across her face.

"Me and my little friend would agree with that," Kevin joked.

Then, Greta threw back the sheets, readjusted her body a little, and sat up in bed, her full and perfect breasts exposed, now flushed and pinkish. As was her face, probably from passion and whisker burns.

Still fully exposed, Greta began to pepper Kevin with questions.

"So, tell me about life on the *Buck*?" she asked.

"Not much to tell really, other than me almost drowning and the *Buck* colliding with another ship."

"You almost drowned?" Greta sat up straighter, covering her breasts a little in the process. All of a sudden, she was much more interested in what Kevin might say than what he might do. Her eyes widened and her mouth was agape.

"I was pretty stupid," Kevin began to explain. "I went out on deck during a typhoon. Almost got washed overboard. The lifeline saved me."

"I'm not sure what a lifeline is," Greta confessed, "but I'm glad it was there. What about the collision? That sounds even more serious."

"You have no idea."

Then, Kevin gave her a vivid account, including the fact that he was on the bridge as safety officer at the time. She asked a number of questions about UNREP's, the type of ship they collided with, the amount of damage. All of which Kevin answered generally and carefully, so as not to disclose what he perceived to be confidential information. Although, when he thought about it, the fact that two ships collided at sea probably fell into the category of something the Navy brass would rather keep to themselves.

But, what the hell. She is my girlfriend and lover, he assured himself. And *anyone in authority would understand why I had to tell her about one of the biggest events in my life, at least so far. Besides, she won't tell anybody else. I'm sure of that. Who would she tell?*

"Some safety officer you are," a now-grinning Greta quipped.

"Just to be clear," Kevin said with an upraised hand, "There was nothing I could do to prevent the collision. My job was just to sit there and observe."

"Glad you're not in charge of my safety," Greta responded with a wink. "That's all I'm going to say. I like people who do more than just observe."

Taking that as an invitation, Kevin dove under the covers as Greta tried to wiggle away. He found what he was after quickly and she stopped wiggling just long enough to let him pleasure her once again. Afterwards, the now fully sated couple collapsed back onto the bed, their bodies covered in perspiration, their faces beet-red, and their hair matted back against their foreheads.

"I must look awful," Greta queried.

"You could never look awful," Kevin murmured, then rolled over, his back to Greta, with the intent to go to sleep. But she wasn't done with her inquiries just yet. She immediately hit him with additional questions like "How long to fix ship?" and "What will happen to those who caused the collision?"

"Well, barrister," he answered formally as he turned back over, "Let me consult my notes."

Remembering the Navy warning about loose lips sinking ships, Kevin verbally danced around her barrage of questions for a few minutes more, providing just enough information to seem responsive while still staying away from anything that he felt might get him in trouble. The closest he came to disclosing something he shouldn't was when Greta asked about the helicopters she had observed on the aft deck of the *Buck*. He told her they were used very rarely, mostly when hunting submarines.

"Wow. What an advantage," she posited, "That should greatly increase the range of your torpedos, right?"

It was Kevin's turn to arch his eyebrow, not expecting such an educated question. "I suppose so, if they worked, which most of the time they don't."

"Why not?"

"I'm curious Greta. Why do you care about these things?" To which she answered with a wink, "I'm interested in everything you do, sweetheart. You're a very important navy officer after all, and I love your war stories."

Kevin was flattered, but still cautious. Eventually, the conversation turned to the pending war in Vietnam.

"When will the U.S. get fully involved?" she asked, "And what does it mean for the *Buck*, and for you?"

But Kevin couldn't tell her much because, ironically, he didn't know much. In fact, at the time, any ordinary U.S. citizen knew more about the war than the military people that were supposed to be fighting it. Soldiers and sailors were only told things on a "need to know," basis, and, frankly, other than what was going on at their base or on their ship, there wasn't much they really needed to know.

A running gag on the *Buck* was for somebody to circulate front page war articles from the *San Diego Union*, under a metal cover marked "Top Secret."

"I could ask you the same thing," Kevin replied, "When do you think the U.S. will be involved?"

"I don't know, but I don't think the U.S. should be involved at all," Greta answered sitting up even straighter against the bed's backboard. "It's a civil war there, nothing more, involving only the Vietnamese people. Let them sort it out themselves."

"I know it seems that way from where you sit, but we have to stop the march of communism somewhere. Might as well be there."

Greta scrunched up her face, as if she had been assaulted. Then, abruptly, she smiled sweetly and said, "That's a subject for another time. Right now, I want to know everything about how you expect the war to impact you."

Fortunately, most of Greta's questions were benign enough that Kevin could tell her something interesting without disclosing much. As an example, he told her that, as far as he knew, they were on their way to Subic Bay in the Philippines, not to Vietnam, and then on to a photo shoot in the South China Sea. Beyond that, he really didn't know much.

"A photo shoot?" Greta asked, arching one eyebrow.

"Some bullshit PR stunt. Probably to please a Senator or some such."

"Just your ship?" she asked.

Realizing he'd probably said a little too much already, Kevin redirected the conversation as best he could to a safer subject. "Who knows? I only know what we're doing. Which is to go to the Philippines next, which I hear is not that great for officers."

"Why? Sounds wonderful, and exotic."

"Maybe too exotic. I hear the town just outside the base is the worst sin city in the Far East. A sailor's paradise. But, for officers, the only safe place to drink is the O Club on the base."

"Why's that?" Greta asked.

"Because officers in town are a prime target for the petty thieves lurking in every alley there," Kevin explained. "At least, that's what we've been told. The Shore Patrol can't really guarantee our safety anywhere but on the main drag. Better not to take a chance."

Greta may have wondered why the strongest military in the world couldn't protect their own in what was essentially a "Navy town," but she didn't pursue the subject any further. Her interest lay elsewhere.

"I wonder what South Vietnam is like. I hear Saigon is beautiful."

"If I go, are you going to meet me there?" he asked facetiously.

"I'll check flight schedules," she answered with a wink.

CHAPTER 5

The *U.S.S. Buck* left the shipyard a week after entering it, good as new, but instead of heading out to sea as Kevin thought was the plan, the ship crept up the harbor a few hundred yards and tied up at the Pearl Harbor Naval Station.

Soon thereafter, he learned the delay was to accommodate a Court Martial hearing that would determine culpability for the ship's collision with the *Canberra*. And Kevin was ordered to be there, as the star witness. As the Safety Officer during the operation, Kevin was in a perfect position to see events unfold, and the court wanted to hear his account.

He testified that the initial contact was caused by "helmsman error," which was never in question, but also that the damage to the ship was exacerbated by the XO's command to back down full. Once the speed of the two ships got out of synch, Kevin said, the small initial punctures of the *Buck's* outer skin grew into large holes that allowed thousands of gallons of seawater to pour into several port side compartments.

"In my opinion," he further testified, "the quick thinking of the captain to assume the conn and back down the engines probably saved the ship."

After Kevin finished answering questions, the Captain, Executive Officer, and helmsman all testified and essentially corroborated what he had said. So Kevin suffered no repercussions. No reprimand. No letter to his file. No nothing. But the helmsman was censured, as was the XO, probably ending his chances of commanding his own ship someday.

When he returned to the *Buck*, Kevin found a large package on his desk containing everything he needed to carry out the undercover assignment the Admiral had asked him to do a few weeks earlier.

There was a sailor's uniform in the package, but also an envelope marked **Top Secret,** which contained two pages of instructions, the floor plan of the *U.S.S. Leary* with target spaces marked, and three cardboard rectangles marked "Bomb" in big, bold, red letters.

The typhoon had been frightening for Kevin. As was the collision at sea. But, for Kevin, pretending to be a sailor, sneaking onto an unsuspecting sister ship, and planting bombs without getting caught could be the scariest thing yet.

He asked himself, *what if somebody on the Leary figures out what I'm doing?* Then, dismissed the thought entirely. Getting caught was not an option.

To make matters worse, the assignment was more complicated than he'd been told it would be. His target ship, the *U.S.S. Leary,* wasn't tied up next to the *Buck* as he had been led to believe. Instead, it was located several hundred yards away, and could only be reached by passing a number of military personnel, and probably some security people, along the way.

So, on his very first undercover assignment, Kevin needed to improvise.

His first trick would be getting off his own ship without being recognized. His second would be getting past any security along the way. And the third would be getting onto the *Leary* itself undetected. Not to mention getting off it in one piece.

Kevin decided he would wear his officer's uniform to exit the *Buck,* carry his sailor's uniform in a duffle bag, then find somewhere close to the *Leary* to switch uniforms. Awkward but doable. Then, he would just join a loading party as the Naval Intelligence officer had suggested, and once on board, sneak away to plant the bombs.

I just might pull this off, Kevin told himself, feeling a little more confident than before.

But it didn't last long. As he neared the *Leary,* he heard a gruff voice yell at him from behind. "Sir, you're in a restricted area."

Kevin turned around to see a burly sailor, shore patrol band wrapped around his sizable bicep, standing with his hands on his hips, and a combative look on his jowly face.

"That pier is for crew members only," the patrolman continued after an uncomfortable second or two looking Kevin over. "Are you assigned to one of the ships tied up here . . . sir?"

"Actually, I'm from the *Buck,* which is several piers down. I'm here to visit my brother, who's an officer on the *Leary,*" he lied.

"What's in the bag?"

Uh, oh. The fake bombs may be hard to explain. Not to mention the sailor's suit.

"Change of clothes," Kevin answered, looking earnestly into the guard's eyes. "My brother and I are taking a little R&R in your fine city."

His act seemed pretty convincing, at least to Kevin, until a bead of sweat trickled down his nose and dropped to the ground. Fortunately, it wasn't noticed by the shore patrolman.

"OK," the guard finally said, averting Kevin's steadfast gaze. "Enjoy Honolulu with your brother, sir."

After the patrolman walked away, Kevin looked around for some out-of-the-way place where he could change his clothes but saw nothing. No barracks or dorm. Eventually, he saw a large Quonset hut with a small "Submarine Force, U. S. Pacific Fleet" sign over the door.

Not perfect, he thought, *but there must be a restroom in there someplace. If confronted, I'll just plead innocence... and a bursting bladder... and hope for the best.*

Luckily, just to his right as he entered was a restroom. Ahead of him stretched a long hallway lined with doors, at the end of which sat one very bored, very young woman behind a small reception desk. She was chewing gum and reading a magazine, oblivious to Kevin's entrance.

Thank God for the indifference of youth, he told himself as he ducked into the restroom, changed quickly, left the bag containing his officer uniform in an empty locker, and emerged a minute or two later dressed like a sailor recruit, all without the girl even looking up from her magazine.

After peeking out the front door to make sure the shore patrolman wasn't still lurking about, Kevin exited and made a beeline for the *Leary,* Fortunately, just as he hoped, Kevin saw a line of sailors walking single file onto the ship, each carrying a case of vegetables or fruits.

So, Kevin grabbed one of the cases and joined the line. Once on board, Kevin followed two sailors into the food storage area, stashed his case there, and ducked through a hatch into the areas of the ship where he needed to hide the bombs.

He went first to a storeroom in the rear of the ship, then to an enlisted men's sleeping compartment, and finally to the engine room, where despite his clean uniform, he was able to convince a sailor he actually worked there. Then, he scurried topside, joined a group of seamen leaving on liberty, and made it back to the submarine headquarters building undetected.

Once back in his officer's uniform, and out of any real danger, Kevin seemed to float back to the *Buck,* his heart pumping, adrenaline coursing through his veins, and his confidence soaring. "*I may be a pretty good supply officer,* he told himself as he crossed the gangplank, *but I'm a helluva spy. I just can't wait for my next undercover assignment.*

Be careful what you wish for, Mr. Boyce.

Kevin was right about one thing, though. His first undercover operation was a success. A few days later he even got a cursory note from Lt. Commander Smith simply stating, "Inspection went well. Commendation letter entered into your file. We'll be in touch."

Kevin wished he could share his joy with Greta. But, telling her about an undercover operation to plant fake bombs on a Navy ship would certainly violate his pledge to protect confidential information.

So, he had to gloat alone, which was not nearly as much fun.

The day before the *Buck* left Honolulu, Kevin and Greta decided to go to the beach, ostensibly to try surfing. But they discarded that idea when they couldn't get their boards out far enough in the surf to catch a wave. So, they commandeered two lounge chairs that were close enough to enjoy the show being put on by real surfers.

But, as Kevin should have realized beforehand, Greta quickly became the show.

She was dressed in a lime-green two-piece bathing suit, with a halter top barely able to do the job it was designed to do. She had been to the beach every day and had a slightly golden tan that was in stark contrast to the darker skin of the bathing beauties who visited the beach area more often.

Which was just one of the reasons she stood out. Greta's breasts were impressive, of course, and her legs long and shapely, like a model's, and, although she wore a big, floppy white hat and sunglasses, she couldn't hide her best feature, which was her striking face. Few noticed the pale-skinned, blonde-headed guy lying beside her. Although Kevin had been lifting weights on the ship, and his normally lean body had a little more definition than normal, he was still just a guy, and obviously, Greta wasn't just a girl.

Despite the attention she was getting; Greta focused her full attention on Kevin. And, as was often the case, she wanted to talk politics again, and why America was in Vietnam. Kevin offered up his time-worn defense that communism was spreading throughout the Far East and needed to be stopped.

"Why?" Greta asked, "Why does it need to be stopped? If the Vietnamese want to be a Communist country, why should America interfere with that?"

"Because rather than have communism thrust upon them, South Vietnam should be free to choose their own way of governing." he countered, "We're supporting the people in their effort to be free."

"I'm not sure the people feel that way, or just the puppet government you inserted in Saigon, but no matter. If they want to fight to govern themselves, that's their business," Greta said, sitting up straighter and covering herself by throwing a Terry cloth robe across her shoulders. She was readying herself for verbal combat. But she changed tactics.

"I guess I'm just worried about you going there," she admitted. "The place is a powder keg, about to blow, and I don't want you coming back with limbs missing, or worse."

"That won't happen, my dear. I'll be on a ship far from any real danger."

She turned her back to him, then looked over her shoulder, her eyes a little moist. "It's just that I love you, Kevin, and I don't want to lose you over something as stupid as helping the South Vietnamese decide what government they're going to have."

It's ironic, Kevin told himself, *that the first time Greta tells me she loves me is after an argument, with her back turned away from me.*

But Kevin knew she was right about one thing. After the Philippines and after the photo shoot, he was indeed headed to Vietnam. And based on messages he had read in the last few days, they would be an active participant in the war, "plane guarding" behind the carrier, searching enemy junks, and softening up the beaches for a landing. And Greta was right about another thing, too. Although far from the real action, Kevin could still end up in harm's way, for a long time, and the romance that had deepened considerably in Hawaii might suffer.

****

The next day, the *Buck* got underway for the Philippines.

Other than tracking the occasional Russian sub or trawler, there wasn't much for the crew to do, and so, it was a particularly freeing time for Kevin. He had time to catch up on his work, of course, but also to read books, and just think about things.

I understand the angst everybody's feeling back home, because I'm not sure we should be in Vietnam either, he acknowledged to himself, *but that's not my decision. I'm trained to keep my head down, obey orders, and just do what I do best, which is make sure the crew is fed, paid, and happy.*

But, given that the ship was headed to war, the "happy" part will depend on events outside his control. So, Kevin vowed to enjoy himself as much as possible before then, by taking advantage of the balmy weather to catch up on his tan, lift weights a bit, and indulge in his favorite leisure time activity, which was to wander up to the bridge to watch the real Navy at work.

Captain Riley was especially fun to watch. He was a caricature of the kind of sea captain you read about in books. Chiseled features, leathery face, steel-hard eyes, and a very demanding personality.

Kevin's roommate, Joe Thrasher, was enjoyable to watch as well. Everybody knew he was a superstar in the making. He graduated third in his class from the Naval Academy, had major responsibilities as both the Combat Information Officer (CIO) and the DASH officer, and was slated to make admiral someday. Kevin was on a very different career path, hoping eventually to be an ad man, or a cartoonist, not as lofty an ambition, to be sure.

But the two had become fast friends because they shared similar traits. They were both college athletes. They were both ambitious, tempered a bit by an impish sense of humor. They were loyal to a fault. And, above all, they were patriotic.

So, when Kevin watched Joe on the bridge as Officer of the Deck, it was almost like watching himself and, often, when the watch was over, the two would go down to the wardroom and do a post-game analysis, just as they might have in college after a ballgame.

Talking to Joe was as close as Kevin would ever get to "driving" the ship himself, and he loved their brainstorming sessions. The two officers were busily recapping Joe's performance in their cabin one night when the XO, Commander Bess, poked his head in the door and asked if he could talk to Kevin alone.

"Sure," Joe answered, thinking some logistical matter needed to be handled. But what the XO wanted to discuss was much more serious than that.

"I just want to get something off my chest, Kevin," the diminutive officer blurted out after Joe left. "I feel like you didn't support me at the Court Martial hearing in Hawaii, and I really didn't appreciate it."

"What do you mean, Elmer?" Kevin responded, genuinely confused. "I just told what happened. It was helmsman error. The collision wasn't your fault, which the panel concluded as well."

"I'm talking about after the collision," Elmer spat out, his face now contorted and red as a beet. Obviously, whatever he was about to say had been eating at him for awhile. "You were on the bridge with me," he began carefully, "You saw how crazy everything was. Tell me. Did you think the skin of the ship had been punctured the first time the two ships tapped each other?"

"No sir, I didn't," Kevin answered truthfully.

"Well, neither did I, for a very good reason. The damage wasn't visible from the bridge. Obviously, I would never have given the order to back down if I had seen the Canberra had penetrated our hull."

"But, sir, shouldn't you have known that was possible?" Kevin ventured the thought carefully after a brief pause. "Or, at least, waited until you had a clearer picture of the situation?"

"Come on, Kevin, you were there. You saw the chaos, and confusion. You know how difficult it was to get actionable information."

"I wasn't the OD in charge, sir. I was just observing," Kevin carefully countered, "With all due respect, sir, it was your job to assess things and make decisions, not mine."

"I just think you could have expressed a view more sympathetic to me when you were testifying," Elmer argued.

"That wasn't my job at the hearing, Elmer," Kevin countered, his brow furrowed but his voice even keeled.

"I know. Just the facts." The XO interrupted, "Protect your own ass."

"I wasn't protecting my ass. I was just answering the questions I was asked, truthfully and honestly."

"Like the Boy Scout you are," Elmer uttered.

"I wasn't in the room, Elmer, when you testified," Kevin stated, ignoring the barbed remark, "Did you tell them that you couldn't see the damage from the bridge?"

"No. Wasn't my place to," he answered, his eyes now watering a little, and his lip quivering. The anger had passed, and Elmer was coming to grips with what he had done. It was an uncomfortable moment for Kevin.

"Wasn't my place to, either" Kevin asserted as he tried to make contact with Elmer's now averted eyes. After a second or two, the XO looked up, tears now gone, but with a more contrite look on his still damp face.

"I keep asking myself the same question," Elmer went on, "Did I panic? Was the moment too big for me? Maybe the Captain would have reacted the same way. Who knows?"

Of course, Kevin knew the answer to that question. The captain certainly would not have done what Elmer did because, as soon as he heard the order, he reacted instinctively and appropriately, reversing it.

"The point is, Elmer, you're a fine Navy Officer. A great one, in fact. And the Court Martial panel gave you your job back. They didn't take away a stripe or two, which they might have done, you know."

"But they blamed me for the damage to our ship. It'll go on my record. I doubt I'll ever get command of my own ship now."

"If anybody can overcome this, it'll be you. You just need to 'soldier on,' and finish out your career on a high note. Very few Navy officers get their own ship anyway."

Elmer pulled his shoulders back, his eyes now totally dry, and looked into Kevin's eyes with a pleading look that Kevin understood perfectly.

"Our talk is just between us," Kevin assured him, "My word."

"Thank you again," Elmer responded, with a smile, "Now, get back to work, Mr. Pork Chop. And that's an order."

Kevin grinned back, visibly relieved.

"Aye, aye, sir," he answered.

*****

Kevin had mixed emotions about the *Buck*'s next port of call, which was Subic Bay in the Philippines.

He was glad to have a layover before heading to Vietnam but wished it could be somewhere more interesting. From what he had heard, the base was like a zoo, with too many ships and, literally, swarms of sailors just milling about.

And the adjoining town, Olongapo, was rumored to be a real hell hole.

So, Kevin was surprised by the gorgeous scenery the *Buck* glided by on its way into port. The place looked like a tropical paradise, with lush greenery, palm trees, and even an occasional sandy beach popping up here and there, like you might find in any of the more popular island paradises in the Asia Pacific.

There were no people around, which surprised him, and the pungent smell of flowers and the sounds of exotic animals and birds were the only things greeting the crew as the ship rounded the final bend into the harbor.

Then, everything changed abruptly, from hushed calm to frenetic military activity, first with the skyline of towering, gray superstructures of dozens of Navy ships, all armed and ready for combat. Then, barely visible behind them was the base, bustling with cranes, vehicles, and sailors, all moving purposefully in no particular direction.

There was a war-infused energy and anxiety in the air that was palpable.

The *Buck* tied up next to three other destroyers who were lashed together and extending out from one shared pier. The ships had created their own small community within the confines of the base, with gangplanks, lines, electrical wires, and hoses leading from one ship to another. There were crowds of sailors moving across the ships both ways, unimpeded, but the vast majority were headed ashore on liberty, knowing it was their last chance to drink and party before heading into harm's way.

The *Buck* slid comfortably into the outermost position and, when all the lines were secured, and the gangplank in place, the OD made the liberty call over the loudspeaker, releasing droves of *Buck* sailors to scurry off the ship, with the skipper leading the parade as usual.

A few sailors were forced to stay on board, though, to help bring on supplies and, with help of his right-hand man, Tom Hertz, Kevin supervised that activity.

When the work was completed, Kevin went to his cabin to take a shower and was putting on his liberty clothes, when he noticed an envelope on his desk marked "CONFIDENTIAL" in large, red, block letters. He knew immediately what it was.

Inside were cardboard "bombs" he was to plant on a nearby ship, a memo, and a card from the same Lt. Cdr. Brad Smith he had met in San Diego. Evidently, the guy was the commander of all Naval Intelligence Activities operating out of San Diego, and that included *Subic Bay*. So, he was here.

The memo read, "The *U.S.S. Davis* is tied up next to you. Please plant these bombs per your prior instructions and come see me at Naval Intelligence headquarters on base when your assignment is over."

Differently than the last time, Kevin was looking forward to going undercover again. At least it beat the drudgery of office work, and he still remembered the adrenaline rush he got after his last operation, and his thinking at the time that he might have found his true calling.

Fortunately, by the time Kevin got topside in his sailor suit, another ship had tied up outside the *Buck*, so it seemed easy to join a group of sailors crossing the *Buck* to the *Davis*, do his dirty work, and sneak back onboard the *Buck* among sailors leaving for liberty.

Kevin was surprised how calm he felt. He now knew from experience that the IDs of sailors passing from one ship to another were never checked. The real trick was getting off and back on the *Buck* without being recognized, which would require a little cloak-and-dagger work, but given that most of the crew was off on liberty, it was certainly doable.

So, in his sailor suit, Kevin slipped out a hatch on the port side of the *Buck*, away from the OD, merged into the mob of sailors on their way to the *Davis,* and was on board the target ship within minutes of leaving his cabin. Like the *Buck,* the *Davis* was a Sumner-class destroyer, so Kevin knew his way around. He went down the starboard side of the ship and ducked into the passageway where the supply office was located. He was in familiar territory.

"Kevin, is that you?" a voice called out from inside the office.

Uh, oh. Who the hell could that be?

Kevin chose to ignore the greeting. He walked by the door quickly, and ducked through the hatch to the crew's quarters, where he could hide in the head if necessary.

But he wasn't quick enough. A hand grabbed his arm, spun him around, and Kevin was staring into the face of Mitch Cable, an old friend from Supply Corps School. What bad luck.

"Kevin, what are you doing here?" Mitch asked. "And why the hell are you dressed up like a sailor?"

Kevin averted his eyes and stared at his shoes, the way he did when his father caught him doing something wrong. Then he looked up sheepishly.

"I was playing a trick on a fellow officer, and I guess I ended up on the wrong ship. Too many beers, I'm afraid." Then, he gave his friend a crooked grin.

Mitch was unconvinced and asked, "Really? What's in the bag?"

Kevin looked at the bag like it was the first time he saw it, and answered, "Nothing of importance. Well, good to see you, Mitch, I better be going, or I'll be late for my prank. We should grab a drink while we're both in port."

Mitch sensed there was something amiss. His old friend was confused and out of sorts, which was uncharacteristic of Kevin. Maybe it was the beers.

"Why don't I help you back to your ship?" Mitch said. "Where is it located?"

"We're tied up right next to you."

"OK, buddy, let's go topside, and yes, I'd love to get together later. You can tell me all about this trick you were trying to play. But, for now, we need to get you back to your ship and tucked away safely in your bunk."

Mitch escorted Kevin up to the main deck of the *Davis*, placed him gingerly onto the first step of the metal gangplank between the two ships, and tried to support him from behind as Kevin "staggered" his way back toward the *Buck*.

Another acting job, Kevin thought. *It's surprising how often I have to play some kind of role in real life. Whether it's dancing around the truth with Greta or impersonating a sailor.*

Kevin was grateful that he had some limited acting experience back in the day. Before joining the Navy, he had agreed to play the lead in a community play, and he was putting that experience to good use now. Even the OD on the *Buck* was fooled by the stumbling and staggering Kevin did as he tried to cross from one ship to the other. The guy grabbed Kevin's left arm and guided him safely on board.

Mitch hollered across, "He's all yours now, and good riddance. Mr. Boyce has had a few too many and needs to be escorted to his stateroom."

Upon second glance, the OD saw that, indeed, it was his Supply Officer masquerading as a seaman. He got a bewildered look on his face and started to ask something, but a suddenly straightened up and sober Kevin spoke first, in a stern voice, "Listen, I can explain everything, but I'm not going to. Is that understood, sailor?"

The OD shook his head vigorously up and down, and replied, "Yes, sir."

Then, without saying another word, Kevin brushed by him and hurried down to his stateroom where he changed back into his officer uniform, and then, within minutes, returned to the main deck to ask the same sailor for permission to disembark, confusing the poor guy even more.

Then, after a brisk walk across the base to the Naval Intelligence headquarters, Kevin found himself standing at attention in front of the same Lt. Commander Brad Smith he had met in San Diego several months before. Only, this time the guy didn't seem so affable.

"So, Mr. Boyce. How did your operation on the *Davis* go?" Brad asked, leaning back in his chair and intertwining his fingers behind his head, still without a smile.

Kevin didn't beat around the bush. "Bad luck, sir. While trying to hide the "bombs," I ran into an old friend from Supply Corps School and, even in my sailor suit, he recognized me."

"And did what?"

"Escorted me off the ship."

"He didn't report you to the captain. Or turn you over to the master-at-arms?

"No, sir. I think he did me a favor…for old time's sake."

Finally, Brad smiled, and gestured for Kevin to sit in the straight-back chair in front of his desk. He commented," Sounds like you got lucky, Mr.Boyce. As did we. I'll just cancel the inspection of the *Davis* scheduled for tomorrow, and we can all go on about our lives."

"I can go on liberty, then, sir?"

"Absolutely. But before you go, I want to talk to you about your girlfriend, Greta Schmidt," the intelligence officer said with a smirk, obviously enjoying the moment. "If you don't mind."

Chapter 6

Kevin wondered how this guy knew Greta and why he would bring her up now. He leaned forward a bit in his chair, eager to hear more.

Mr. Smith pulled a thick tan file folder from a drawer and placed it on the desk in front of the perplexed supply officer without opening it. Kevin could see an unfamiliar woman's name written on the tab, which made him more confused, and anxious. Then, from another drawer, the intelligence officer pulled out a small notebook which he placed in front of himself, also unopened. All very dramatic.

Kevin decided to let the intelligence officer carry on his little show without interruption. He just waited quietly, acting bored, while inside his heart was beating frantically. After a few seconds looking down at the folder and notebook before him, Mr, Smith raised his steely-blue eyes, peered directly into the young officer's eyes, and began to speak. His brow was furrowed, and the smile gone. He was all business and, to Kevin's eye, way too theatrical, like an amateur actor might play the role.

"When the Navy approached you to plant 'bombs, it was for the reasons the admiral told you. You were young and unassuming, somebody we thought could board ships unnoticed, wander around easily, and, above all, handle the pressures of undercover work."

"The admiral said something about being athletic, too."

Mr. Smith didn't appreciate the sarcasm.

"OK, but that's beside the point, isn't it?"

"What is the point then, sir? I'm waiting."

"I'll get right to the point then. We have reason to believe Greta's a Soviet spy."

"You've got to be kidding," Kevin responded, shaking his head. "What in the world gave you that idea?"

"I'm not at liberty to say. And it isn't confirmed yet, which is why I wanted to talk to you before doing anything. We think you can help us sort things out."

"I don't need to sort anything out. Greta is no more a spy than I am."

"We need to sort that out as well," Brad countered.

"You think I might be a spy?" Kevin blurted out while rising partway out of his chair. "That's utterly ridiculous, Mr. Smith."

"She may have turned you. She certainly has the skill and charms to do that."

"So, you're saying she went to Athens, Georgia, of all places, attended the University of Georgia, found me there, a lowly supply officer, hung out with me, and turned me into a Russian asset?"

The intelligence officer nodded knowingly, "It's a long shot, I admit, except we know she was never enrolled at the University of Georgia, she's five years older than most graduate students, and has followed you to both San Diego and Honolulu."

"Maybe she's in love with me."

Brad rolled his eyes and continued, "Plus, we believe she grew up in East Germany."

Kevin shook his head in disbelief, then looked Brad square in the eyes and asserted, "I know for a fact thar she was raised in West Germany."

"For a fact?"

"Well, she told me that, and described her hometown perfectly. I believe her."

Brad looked away for a moment, then, sat up in his chair, folded his hands on his desk, looked Kevin directly in his blue eyes, and countered, "I know that's what she told you. And, honestly, Greta Schmidt might have grown up there, if there actually is such a woman. But we believe the woman you are dating is actually Lena Mueller, whose file is there in front of you. She was schooled in East Berlin, and, while there, became a die-hard Communist. If we're right, the Russians brought her to Moscow for training when she was nineteen years old, and "Greta Schmidt" is just her current cover. She's had many others through the years."

Kevin opened the folder and saw the picture of a teenage girl that, to his eye, looked nothing like Greta. "This isn't her," he argued, "the teeth and hair color are totally different. The shape of her body isn't the same, either."

"Nonetheless, we believe it is her. Lena has matured a lot through the years and gone through what we call a Soviet makeover. Hair, boobs, lips. All changed. So, it's no surprise to me that you don't recognize her now."

"Greta isn't this Lena woman, I'm sure of that, and I know she's not a spy."

But, as defiant as he appeared, Kevin's head was spinning. *Could this guy be telling the truth? Could Greta be a commie? From East Germany? And five years older than*

I thought? Hard to believe. If she's a spy, why isn't she in Washington D.C. seducing some senator's aide? Or in New York, hanging out with U.N. representatives, or translators? Why is she sipping Mai Tai's in Hawaii, with a newly minted supply officer from Kansas, who isn't even in a position to know much about anything. Just doesn't make sense.

"Listen, Mr. Boyce, I understand your skepticism," a now-subdued Brad agreed, "and, frankly, we have no real solid proof that your Greta is actually Lena. And no proof at all that she may have turned you. What we do know is that Lena is now in the U.S. and could be masquerading as Greta. We've just started our investigation and, if you're not a Russian asset already, you can help us determine the truth. Hence, our discussion."

An emotionally torn Kevin mulled over his options.

I could tell this Brad guy to go to hell and keep dating Greta without ever knowing the truth. Or I could break up with her and wonder forever if I made the right decision.

Neither option seemed very palatable. But, if Kevin cooperated, he'd not only learn the truth, but be in a far better position to prove Greta's innocence. So, he decided to help, but only up to the point where he knew, one way or another, who she was.

He asked, "What do you want me to do?"

"Not much right now. Just go back to your ship, do your job, and proceed on to Vietnam," the Intelligence Officer answered. "Don't tell anybody about our conversation, especially Greta, and we'll be in touch."

"Aye, aye, sir."

"Oh, and by the way, what did you tell her when you were together in Honolulu? Anything we should worry about?"

Kevin tried to remember. "I talked to her about our collision at sea. Was that confidential?"

Brad wrinkled his nose. "Maybe. Did you tell her the name of the other ship? Or where it was headed?"

"Not that I remember," Kevin replies. "Honestly, I didn't know where they were headed anyway. I did tell her that we were going to Vietnam eventually."

"Hmm. Well, that's hardly news," Brad mutters. "Every ship on the West Coast is headed for Vietnam eventually. And the collision is a matter of record. So, no harm so far."

Brad made a few notes in the small notebook, making Kevin uneasy. Then, after a moment of scribbling, Brad looked up, a sober expression on his face. "Did you say where in Vietnam you were going?"

Kevin was surprised. "I don't know where we're going. So, no."

"Nothing about why you were going there, or what you would be doing?"

Sheepishly, Kevin brought up the one subject he's been most worried about, "I did mention a photo shoot we're supposed to be part of when we leave Subic Bay."

Suddenly Brad's expression changed dramatically. The more-serious Brad had reappeared. "What photo shoot?" He asked.

"From what I understand, when we reach the China Sea, all the ships in the area are going to be brought together for one big aerial shot," Kevin explained.

"Some kind of PR stunt?" Brad asked.

"Or maybe to scare the Viet Cong or the Chinese," Kevin said. "What do I know? It's hard to guess what the big brass are thinking at times."

Brad nodded and scribbled some more.

"What else did you say about the photo shoot?"

"Nothing really," Kevin answered truthfully. "The fact that we were going to do it kind of slipped out. I tried to cover it up after that."

Brad got a condescending look on his face. "I doubt you were very successful, especially if she's a trained spy. But nothing we can do about it now. Anything else you might have talked to Greta about?"

"Not that I can remember. She asked about our ship, what weapons we had on board, and the like. She saw our helicopters when she came to the ship to meet me."

"What helicopters."

"We have experimental drone anti-submarine helicopters on board, but I pled ignorance about them."

Brad smiled. "Your ignorance may be our best weapon. Keep faking that."

Kevin smiled, knowing he wasn't really faking it.

"I still don't believe Greta's' a spy. It makes no sense," he protested.

"She might not be," Brad acknowledged, "but that's what we need to find out, together. It's not unusual for Russia to use attractive women as operatives, believe me. It's one of their favorite tactics."

Kevin remained unconvinced. "But I still don't understand why she'd choose to spy on me."

Brad clarified, "I doubt she did the choosing. Some higher-ups must have approved the operation. Maybe she was intending to go to school anyway, but her handlers learned that the Navy Supply School was nearby and thought they could kill two birds with one stone. The Russians are very opportunistic that way."

"I'm still not convinced she's a spy," Kevin repeated.

Brad shrugged, and responded, "Look. Vietnam is the focal point of our fight against Communism. Nothing is as important, to us, or to them, at the moment. And the Navy is where the action is. Any officer headed there could be a target for their intelligence services. Even a lowly supply officer, as you called yourself."

Kevin is still dubious. "It makes no sense. Every officer on our ship knows more than me about what's going on."

'So I ask, Kevin, did you come across any Russian subs or Russian trawlers between Hawaii and here?"

"Well, I didn't actually see them, but yes, my roommate Joe told me they were all over the place."

"Ever wonder what Russian subs or fishermen are doing out there in the middle of the ocean?" Brad asked. "I'll bet those fishing boats have more electronic gear on board than your destroyer."

"OK, I get it," Kevin interjected, "Of course, the Commies are interested in what we're doing in Vietnam. I still don't think Greta's involved. At least, I hope not. But there's not much I can do immediately. I'm headed to Vietnam for the next few months."

"We'll see about that."

******

The *Buck* left the Philippines with most of its crew regretting what they did there.

Kevin was an exception. He stayed on base, never crossing the garishly painted red, orange, and yellow wooden bridge over to the tawdry liberty town of Olongapo. Not even once.

But, from what he heard, there wasn't much to see. Unless you like loud dance halls that featured watered-down drinks and overly-made-up teenage Filipino girls. With thugs and robbers lurking around every corner. On balance, the *Buck* was luckier than most other ships during their few days in the Philippines. Only three sailors got beat up and a dozen more lost their wallets, both statistics way below the Navy average.

Kevin spent his time getting supplies on board, catching up on paperwork, and preparing for what the *Buck* faced next, which was independent duty off the coast of Vietnam, far from any supply lines or other ships. Kevin only got to the Officer's Club in Subic Bay once, to have drinks and dinner with his supply officer buddy Mitch and try to explain his bizarre behavior that first day in port. He was only halfway through the bullshit story he had concocted when Mitch cut him off mid-sentence. "Listen, Kevin. I don't know why you were there, but knowing you as I do, there was probably a good reason. Let's just forget about it and enjoy what might be the last civilized dinner we have together for a very long time."

Kevin breathed a sigh of relief, trusting that the subject would never come up again. That's the kind of friend Mitch was to him.

There's nothing more valuable than a good friend, Kevin reminded himself, *with the bizarre goings-on that happen in the Navy every day, friends are worth their weight in gold.*

******

As the *Buck* glided slowly, and silently, out of the Subic Bay Naval Base, on its way to the South China Sea and eventually the coast of Vietnam, Kevin was once again on the main deck, still marveling at the lush beauty of the Philippine shoreline and wondering if the coast of Vietnam might look similar. Or will the battle scars of decades of war be clearly visible.

It's amazing what happens to a country's natural beauty, Kevin mused, *when human beings decide they have to "tame" it. Or start a war to occupy it. Greta could be right about Vietnam. Maybe we should have minded our own business. But, with Communism on the march in the world, would that really keep us safer? I think not. But it isn't my decision. And I've got a job to do.*

A few hours later, after the food stuffs they picked up in port were appropriately stashed, the parts inventoried, and the books balanced, Kevin found a place on the aft deck, out of sight from the crew, took off his shirt, and pulled out *The Fountainhead,* a book containing the provocative ideas of a controversial author named Ayn Rand. A friend of his from Supply School had suggested he read it.

But, within minutes, he figured out that her ideas, interesting as they were, couldn't compete with the beauty all around him. He felt a slight breeze on his face, but the gray-blue ocean looked incredibly calm. There were only gentle waves, much like those Kevin experienced on the lakes back home in Kansas. Nothing like he had experienced on the way to Hawaii. Then, as had become more frequent with him lately, Kevin's mind drifted back to Greta, and the paradox she now represented.

The woman Brad described, the one who's so duplicitous, can't possibly be the Greta I've been with in San Diego and Hawaii, the one I'm in love with. That Greta is so innocent and forthright and loving. She does ask a lot of questions, but, surely, that's because of her interest in me and my life.

Still, Kevin could believe that Greta actually came from East Germany rather than West Germany. That's something she might have wanted to hide while she was studying in America. Also, she could certainly be older than a typical grad student, although he had assumed her maturity came from her varied European life experiences rather than her age.

But a Russian spy? Greta? No way. He would have figured that out by now.

Suddenly, Kevin felt the engines slowing, the ship beginning a wide turn to port, and he noticed there were other Navy ships on the horizon. Thinking that Operation Photo Shoot must be underway, Kevin tucked his book under a tarp, put his shirt back on and climbed the two ladders up from the main deck to the bridge of the ship.

"Hey. Where's the captain?" Kevin asked Buddy Penn, who was serving as OD.

"Probably sleeping," Buddy answered. "He needs to be ready when the action begins."

Looking at the running lights of other ships, seemingly everywhere, Kevin was surprised. "We haven't started yet, Buddy?"

"Lord no. The shoot isn't until daybreak tomorrow, so I suspect we'll be getting into formation starting some time well after midnight. But a lot of ships are here early, just milling around."

Kevin recoiled slightly. "After midnight? That doesn't sound very smart. The most Navy ships ever gathered in one spot and they're going to try to get in formation in the middle of the night. It could be chaos, right?"

"Good word for it, Kevin," Buddy agreed, "But that's not my concern. I'm just trying to avoid a collision before the chaos. After that, it becomes Captain Riley's problem." Then, he turned to the helmsman and gave the order, "Hard right rudder, Come to two, two, zero."

Realizing he wasn't helping Buddy at all, Kevin decided to grab some shuteye before the big show was to begin. As the safety officer, he needed to be alert, if only to observe.

A few hours later, a well-rested Kevin was back on the bridge, a few paces behind the captain, with an expansive view of the sea, now cluttered with lights and boats. Normally, there were few experiences like being on or around the bridge of a ship, late at night, under the glow of a relatively full moon, with the salty air dampening your face, and the chug of big diesel engines pulsating underfoot.

It can be spiritual. The green glow of electronics, both on the bridge and in the Combat Information Center, reflecting off the faces of the men manning them. And, moonbeams dancing across the waves, making them luminescent. Add a gentle sway to the deck, like a baby must feel when its mother rocks it in her arms, and everybody on board feeling a perhaps misplaced confidence that everything was going to be all right.

But, with Operation Photo Shoot well underway, the scene on the bridge was nothing like that. It was shockingly hectic. There were people everywhere, running around, gesturing, and trying to converse, seemingly all at once. The radar screen in CIC was afire with blips, moving in multiple directions, all at different speeds, with Kevin's roommate, Joe, trying his best to make sense of things. He would watch the blips bounce around on the screen and use his maneuvering board to try to calculate the speed and direction of anybody who might be considered a threat.

The only calm person on the scene was Captain Riley, which obviously was why he was in charge. He seemed to see and hear everything but reacted only when necessary. Because of his vast experience, he seemed to sense what other ships were doing or, even more importantly, what they were going to be doing, even before his officers watching the radar did.

He was like a maestro, calmly directing an orchestra, although the "music" coming out all around him was hardly harmonious. He watched the running lights of ships that were shockingly close to the *Buck*, without concern. He strolled confidently from the starboard side of the ship to its port side, calmly surveying the chaos. Occasionally he adjusted an order just enough to slide harmlessly by a ship that had been a threat seconds earlier.

The captain was born to do this, Kevin realized, *like Wilt Chamberlain was born to play basketball.*

Kevin glanced out over the ocean again. It was lit up like a pinball machine, with the bobbing, weaving lights of dozens of ships trying to get into position without hitting each other. An ocean that was calm hours before was churning with the wakes of dozens of ships, like a mini storm, making the navigation job that much harder. Then, amazingly, right before daybreak, things calmed down considerably. Most of the ships were on station and all were sailing a parallel course at the same speed.

Then, just as the sun rose, one of the spotters yelled out, "What the hell is that?"

He was pointing off the starboard bow at an improbable and disturbing sight. There, in what could very well be the center of the formation, nestled between two large, imposing gray Navy cruisers, sat a tiny Russian trawler, bobbing along on the same path, and at the same speed, as the formation of massive U.S. ships around it. The crew of the trawler was laughing and waving up at the photography plane, as if their boat was the star of the show, which, in a bizarre way, it was.

Damn, Kevin gasped to himself, *Somehow the Russians have positioned a spy ship right in the middle of our formation. Not a good look for a military public relations photo. Too bad. There goes that PR guy's promotion.*

"What the hell?!" the captain shouted. "Where did those assholes come from?"

Immediately, the radio near CIC crackled and an uncoded message came through from the Admiral's staff to break formation as quickly, and as safely, as possible.

"All ships should head back to their assigned duty stations, and await further instructions," the message concluded.

"Good luck with that," Kevin mumbled under his breath.

What ensued made the pre-photo maneuvering before seem like child's play. Ships took off in a hundred different directions, as if their only goal was to get away from the fishing trawler as quickly as possible. Kevin noticed that the Russian crew was no longer waving. Instead, they were trying desperately to keep their tiny boat afloat as large waves, created by the sudden course changes of dozens of cruisers and destroyers, threatened to capsize them.

As for the *Buck*, the captain called for an immediate hard turn to starboard. Then, he slid across the wake of the few other ships near him, earning the *Buck* the distinction of being the first ship to fully clear the area, reinforcing his reputation as a master seaman.

As things calmed down a little, Captain Riley noticed Ensign Boyce for the first time and shouted, "Kevin. For God's sake. What the hell are you doing here? Get your ass up to the Crypto Shack and see if we're getting any messages. I need to know what happened here."

The captain's order was hardly welcome at first, but then Kevin realized that, after such a fucked-up operation, there's probably no more entertaining place to be. He'll be the first to see all the handwringing and recriminations coming from the higher-ups, maybe even the Chief of Naval Operations (CNO) or the Secretary of the Navy.

So, for the next few hours, Kevin deciphered dozens of messages flying around between the *Buck*, the other ships, fleet command, and Washington, D.C. It was clear that the top brass was pretty steamed about what was being characterized as a "major security breech."

Nobody could understand how a small fishing boat could slip into a formation comprised of so many U.S. Navy ships without being detected. Even more amazing was that they did it at night, secretly, without lights or electronics. But the big question everybody was asking was, how did the Russians know about the operation in the first place?

CHAPTER 7

When the *Buck* reached its eventual posting in the Gulf of Tonkin, Kevin was especially busy with both his supply and crypto responsibilities.

The ship was now in what is considered a war zone, making General Quarters a common occurrence, which, for Kevin, meant three or four hours a day manning the crypto machine. As a result, next to the captain, and perhaps Joe Thrasher, Kevin knew more about what was going on than anybody else on board.

He knew, for instance, that the very ship they were relieving, the *Turner Joy*, had been strafed by North Vietnamese gunboats a few days before. The damage was slight, and no one was hurt, so the higher-ups believed that it was probably a one-time event. No reason to panic just yet. Then, the *Buck* was also attacked. The bullets kicked up puffs of water around the ship and a few clattered across her deserted decks without hitting anything.

But, to Captain Riley's mind at least, there was no longer any doubt that the war had begun, and he was no longer waiting around for orders. First, he called the crew to General Quarters. Then, he began taking evasive action, varying the

Buck's course and speed every few minutes or so, to make any future attack more difficult. Black-out orders were put in effect and all the weaponry on board…guns, depth charges, torpedos and the like…were activated, and made ready for use.

As Crypto Officer, Kevin was processing ten times the normal number of encrypted messages and had a front row seat on what could be the event that would result in the United States officially entering the Vietnam War as a combatant. As he worked, he began to feel sick at his stomach. The needless deaths. The lives affected. The worldwide impact of what, to him, had been a pretty minor event, probably triggered by a couple of trigger-happy gunboat captains. His hands had turned clammy and started shaking, making his typing more difficult.

Holy shit, this is big, he thought as he processed one message after another. *We all knew war was inevitable, but here it is in all of its hideous glory, playing out right before my eyes.*

Once the initial shock was over, Kevin calmed down. His hands stopped shaking. He had a job to do, something important, something only he could do, and now that the ambiguity was stripped away, he was ready to go to work.

Fortunately, the gun boats retreated, the immediate threat subsided but as Kevin learned from the messages flying around, the damage was done. Now, there was no stopping the American war machine from doing what it had been trained to do. Attack. Annihilate the enemy anyway possible. And get this thing over quickly.

******

While cruising around the Gulf of Tonkin, there was no opportunity for the *Buck* to slip into port for supplies or

R&R. Nor was there much direct contact with any other ships. Every few days a helicopter would fly over from the carrier *Hancock* bearing a few necessities and mail for the crew. It was always a big event and, when spotted, the crew members topside would break into the same silly ditty:

The Hancock 'helo's
Comin' across the sea.
Bringing my mail to me.

Then, shortly thereafter, there would be an announcement over the loudspeaker:

"Attention all crew members. Mail call. Mail call. Please gather on the main deck for mail call. That is all."

It was like Christmas, New Year, and Marci Gras, all rolled into one. Letters from home were a huge event, not just because of the love and news they brought but because a pecking order was established on the ship based on how many letters each crew member received. And, largely because of Greta, Kevin was right near the top of the list.

In port, Greta's letters arrived daily, and he read them one at a time, savoring each word. Her written English was so much better than her spoken, but not nearly as charming. A little more British than American, perhaps, and perfectly structured.

Somebody spent a lot of time writing these. I'm just not sure if it was Greta. Especially if what Brad told me is true.

At sea, because of the logistics, the letters arrived in bunches, which made it easier to compare Greta's varying styles. Some were mushy, some racy, and every so often he would receive one that expressed Greta's views on the war, which seemed to mirror the views of most civilians stateside. "What do you think now about America getting involved in somebody else's war so far away?" She asked once, as an example.

His reply was simple and direct. "I don't think about it much. I trust our leaders to make the right decisions. And I'm guessing that, in a few years, Vietnam will be nothing but a footnote in the history books. The Chinese Communists flexing their muscles, and us showing them that we won't stand for it. Then, we'll both find some face-saving way to end the dispute and move on. No big deal."

In her followup letter, Greta's anger was apparent. "Your last letter called the defining war of our generation a dispute. The Chinese don't consider it a dispute and they're not going away. Not when it's happening in their own back yard."

Kevin wasn't convinced that carrying on such a debate through the mail made sense. So, his response was brief but conciliatory. "Greta, I respect your point of view and, given my limited access to information, you're probably more right than I am. This thing may not end soon or well, but given my position, I have to believe my superiors, do what they say, and trust that everything will turn out okay in the end."

That long-distance debate ended amicably, with Greta writing. "Kevin, at times you are so obstinate and naïve, but I love you for it, or in spite of it."

But other letters, mirroring the opinions being sent to most servicemen every day, were harsh and accusatory. Not like a spy, though. More like a caring lover who wanted her man to understand. And couldn't understand why he didn't.

******

A few weeks later, when the *Buck* finally reached its duty station off the Vietnamese coast, Kevin was astonished at what they found there. Everything was peaceful and normal. There were no other warships, just uniquely designed Vietnamese boats, called junks, which were ideally suited for these shallow waters.

Most had just enough room for a fisherman or two to move around, but there were larger ones as well, designed to transport goods, and occasionally, even very large junks, big enough to house families of six, eight, or even a dozen people, all living together in unbelievably crowded and dingy conditions. All of the boats had colorful sails and long steering rudders, designed specifically to navigate these waters. There were hundreds flitting in and out of the various islands and inlets that dot the east coast of South Vietnam, going about their business, their owners oblivious to the fact that America was now in the war.

Except for the presence of the *Buck*.

It must have been jarring for them to see such a large gray Navy ship plowing through their midst, creating a wake almost as big as the boats themselves, and complicating their simple lives. They had to wonder why such a ship, with its towering masts bristling with electronic equipment and its multilayered metal decks, featuring huge guns designed to soften up beaches miles away, was here at all. And to do what?

But the *Buck* was there for a very specific reason that, on the surface, she seemed ill-equipped to do. Or, perhaps over-equipped. As Joe explained to Kevin, "We're supposed to identify any suspicious junks sneaking weapons down from the North. Then, once identified, we're supposed to board those boats, take prisoners, and confiscate the weapons."

To Kevin's way of thinking, it was asinine. A boarding party of two to four volunteer sailors were to go on the enemies' junks, use handguns the sailors were unfamiliar with, possibly shoot it out in close quarters (sort of like in the Wild West,) knowing they were only backed up by dozens of mostly unarmed sailors.

What could go wrong? Kevin asked himself facetiously.

Still, as time went on, the Navy brass seemed happy with the job the *Buck* was doing. Dozens of North Vietnamese soldiers were captured, hundreds of weapons were confiscated, and fewer and fewer junks carrying arms were traveling through the waters patrolled by the *Buck*. Of course, by then, the Ho Chi Minh trail had been opened up as the main thoroughfare carrying military supplies from the north to the south. So, having a junk supply line for weapons quickly became less valuable to the North Vietnamese.

The *Buck* wasn't just searching junks though. Often, the destroyer would "plane guard" behind the *Hancock*, while it was conducting flight operations. Again, the assignment seemed simple. Just pick up any pilots who ended up in the ocean after their plane crashed on takeoff or landing. Kevin assumed that would be a rare event. But he was wrong. A surprising number of combat aircraft would return to the carrier in some state of disarray—a damaged wing, a malfunctioning engine, or even an injured pilot. And then, if the plane did happen to arrive in one piece, landing on a carrier deck was no piece of cake, especially during night ops.

Whenever he could, Kevin liked to go up to the bridge at night and listen to normally calm and collected pilots screech into their microphones as they tried to land.

"I can't see anything," a pilot might say at first.

The traffic controller would answer back, "You're doing fine. Just stay the course."

"But I don't see the carrier." Now the pilot's voice was a little higher.

"You're doing fine. Perfect direction and altitude."

"I can see the ocean. It's right below my wings. Where is the damn ship?" Only the pilot was screaming like a scared little kid then. Because, honestly, that's what they were.

Then, even when things went well, the plane would hit the carrier deck at a ridiculously high speed, hoping to catch the strap designed to stop the plane, which worked most of the time. Occasionally, however, even undamaged airplanes went into the water, and the *Buck's* assignment was to lower her motor whaleboat into the water and find the pilot as quickly as they could.

Another role assigned to the *Buck* seemed really benign. It was to house the leader of the South Vietnamese Junk Force, which happened to be a U.S. Navy officer who looked even younger than Kevin. He bore the stripes of a lieutenant commander, but Kevin suspected he wasn't an officer at all, but an enlisted man assigned to Special Forces.

Every morning, the guy would get out of bed, have a nice breakfast in the wardroom, sling a machine gun over his shoulder, and take the *Buck's* motor whaleboat to shore and roust out his ragtag force of junk men.

When the sailors joined him, which happened some of the time, but not always, he would lead them to some godforsaken island where he suspected Viet Cong soldiers were hiding. A short time later, Kevin would hear the unmistakable sound of rapid gunfire, and occasionally, he would see prisoners being 'escorted' onto junks. Then, by dinnertime, the "officer" was back on board, eating quietly by himself.

What a strange war, Kevin thought, as he enjoyed a lobster dinner in the wardroom.

******

After cruising around for over a month off the coast of Vietnam, the *Buck* finally drew an assignment that fit her armament and the crew's training.

In a Top-Secret memo addressed to Captain Riley, the admiral conveyed a terse but historic message, "3500 Marines to be put ashore near Danang. *Buck* to provide shore bombardment support. Proceed to the area (approximate latitude 16.0, longitude 108.0) and await further instructions."

After decoding, Kevin realized immediately the significance of the message.

We're now in this thing for real, he thought. *We're finally putting boots on the ground. No more pussyfooting around with just air raids and junk searches. Now, we can apply some real muscle and, hopefully, leave Vietnam sooner rather than later.*

But, when Captain Riley read the message, his reaction was quite different. He looked up at Kevin, a resigned look on his face, and said, "This thing is about to get very messy, very fast."

As soon as the Buck arrived on station near Danang, preparations began to get the ship, and its armament, ready for the first real combat they might face since their deployment began. Nobody was afraid. The U.S. Navy pretty much controlled the air and the South China Sea around Danang, so the crew didn't expect any attacks from Chinese warships, or aircraft.

But gun boats might make a run at them again, or an explosive-laden junk could ram them in a suicide mission. More likely, however, was a gun attack coming from shore once the fighting began. Nobody really knew if the Viet Cong had that capability or would even use it in this situation. Just one of many things the crew of the *Buck* would have to learn on the job.

Ah, the fog of war, Kevin thought to himself.

When everybody was finally in position for the invasion to begin, a now-helmeted Kevin climbed up the ladder to the deck where the crypto shack was located, did a couple of deep knee bends, then, positioned himself on his stool, ready to receive the barrage of messages expected to come his way. A junior seaman waited outside the door to run any urgent messages down to the captain, and return with his reply, if any.

The first message that clattered through the machine was decoded quickly and sent down. It read, "Don't fire until you have identified the enemy, or you have been fired upon." Two minutes later, the captain stormed into the crypto shack, his face beet-red, and the message crumpled up in his left fist.

"What kind of horse shit is this?" He yelled at Kevin, as if the supply officer had sent the message. "How can we soften up the beaches if we can't fire until we see the bastards?"

Wisely, Kevin chose to remain silent.

"What do these idiots expect the Viet Cong to do? Come marching out of their machine gun nests to greet us? With flags flying and a band playing? For God's sake, what are these people thinking?"

Then, he scribbled out a terse message which said, "To avoid needless casualties, we will fire before our troops hit the beach." Kevin dutifully coded and sent it.

Almost immediately a reply arrived. "Don't fire until you see the enemy or get permission. Orders of the Commander in Chief."

"What the fuck? Johnson is making battlefield decisions now," the captain ranted, "What kind of goddamn war is this?"

Then, he stormed out, throwing one last comment over his shoulder. "The first time one of those cocksuckers even thinks about shooting our guys, he better duck. Cause we're going to send all kinds of hell his way."

A few minutes later, Kevin felt the now-familiar explosion of the *Buck's* 5"38 caliber guns and braced for the ship's recoil that followed immediately. The explosions continued for fifteen minutes or so, and then quit, probably because the Marines had reached the beach and were directly in the line of fire. Or maybe the resistance had melted away. From his cubby hole, Kevin couldn't tell.

The crypto machine remained silent throughout the whole operation so, after a couple of hours, Kevin decided to go over to the bridge to find out what had happened. Nobody knew much, except he could see the beach was littered with jeeps and equipment, so it had to have been secure for some time. Joe rushed by on his way back to CIC and Kevin asked if the invasion was a success. "It seems so," Joe answered. "The marines are already securing the Da Nang airport."

Kevin never had the guts to ask the captain about his decision to begin firing so soon after being told not to, but it must have been justified. At least, that's what Kevin told himself.

CHAPTER 8

After hearing nothing for over a month, Kevin was convinced that the photo op fiasco was well behind him, as was all the nonsense about Greta being a Russian asset.

Another government FUBAR (The acronym for Fucked Up Beyond All Recognition,) he told himself. *The powers-that-be finally figured out what I've known all along, that Greta is no more a spy than I am. She's just an innocent transfer student who happens to love me. That's all.*

Then, out of the blue, Kevin decoded a Top-Secret message from the head of Naval Intelligence himself, addressed to Captain Riley. It said ominously: 'Pls inform your Supply Officer, Mr. Boyce, that a helicopter will pick him up at 0800 hrs. on Thursday to meet with Lt. Cdr. Smith on the Hancock. Should be back on board by 1500 hrs."

It had to be something to do with Greta, and the photo shoot was the most obvious culprit. So, Kevin slept fitfully for the next few nights, anxiously awaiting whatever news Brad had to tell him, and, by the time Thursday finally arrived, Kevin was really on pins and needles, about the meeting, yes, but also about the helicopter ride he had to take over to the Hancock.

One thing that Kevin had learned since joining the *Buck* was that, on a ship, nothing was easy. And getting from one ship to the next often was the most complicated maneuver of all. Whether it was going by motor whaleboat to a large sister ship and having to climb a rope ladder up to her main deck. Or being high lined across between two ships that rock back and forth with the waves, occasionally dunking you in the water. Those were dangerous operations.

But a helicopter ride? That can't be that bad, he told himself. Yes, *the seas are a little rougher than normal, but how hard can it be for a skilled pilot to land his bird on the helicopter deck and just let me hop aboard.*

Don't you wish, Mr. Boyce.

First of all, the helicopter turned out to be much bigger than Kevin expected and, even hovering fifty feet above the deck, the backwash from its rotors almost blew him off the deck. (Not to mention the noise.) And the *Buck's* helicopter deck was way too small to accommodate such a big bird. So, guess what? The crew just dropped a rope, with a harness-like device dangling on the end of it, down to the ship's deck.

"You've got to be kidding," Kevin blurted out, looking around for a sympathetic ear. Fortunately, one of the deckhands heard him and asked, "Need some help, Mr. Boyce?"

"Only if they expect me to get into that damn thing."

"I think that's the idea, sir," he yelled over the noise.

So, the two men crawled out onto the deck, clinging to anything they could as the rotor back wash hit them, and eventually Kevin was snapped into the harness. A few seconds later, when the ship rolled unexpectedly, Kevin found himself dangling five feet above both the sailor and the ship and, when the ship came back up, riding a surprisingly large wave, it gave Kevin one last little tap on the ass.

Thank you, Buck, for that, Kevin thought, *I love you, too.*

When the helicopter finally ascended, with Kevin hanging beneath it, he was treated to a spectacular view of not only his own ship, but several others on the horizon. Not that Kevin noticed any of it, with his hands clasped tightly onto the ropes and his legs flopping about in the backdraft of the helicopter's rotors.

Are they just going to take me all the way to the carrier dangling like this? He asked himself.

Fortunately, a crewman on the helicopter then pulled Kevin up with a winch, somebody grabbed him by the armpits, and he was dumped unceremoniously onto the deck of the bird. Then, everybody went back to whatever they were doing.

"Where's the stewardess on this flight?" he yelled, but fortunately, his words were drowned out by the noise. Nobody seemed in the mood for a wise ass remark. Kevin should have realized that.

When he finally checked out his surroundings, Kevin was underwhelmed. On the *Buck,* everything was always stowed or lashed down. Ship-shape, as the crew liked to say. But not so on the chopper. The only unoccupied seat was piled high with several fleece coats and a couple of life jackets, held loosely in place by the seatbelt. And nobody seemed inclined to move them to give Kevin a place to sit. In fact, nobody was paying the supply officer any attention at all. They were all too busy talking about whether, and where, they could get laid in Saigon.

So, Kevin just grabbed a strap that was hanging down from the overhead and braced himself against the bulkhead.

Then, he looked out a tiny back window to see the *Buck* disappearing over the horizon. A speck in a vast ocean.

By contrast, the *Hancock* carrier came into sight a few minutes later. From the air, with its flight deck, conning tower, and fighter jets lined up for takeoff, the ship was an impressive picture of military size and muscle. And, although now aging and soon to be replaced by even larger, nuclear-powered carriers, the WWII carrier still looked pretty formidable, especially from the vantage point Kevin was seeing her. Before, he had thought of the *Hancock* as kind of an old friend, rather than a lethal warship. But no more.

Fortunately, landing a helicopter on the deck of a carrier wasn't nearly as scary as landing a plane, but the experience still caused Kevin some angst. Luckily, the pilot knew his stuff, and the landing was incredibly smooth. Once the rotor blades stopped turning, the crew motioned for him to disembark, and Kevin breathed his first comfortable breath in quite a while.

Then, he hopped out and saluted the officer there to greet him.

"Welcome, Mr. Boyce," the guy yelled over the ambient noise. "A Lieutenant Commander Smith is waiting in the wardroom for you. He tells us that he won't need to talk to you very long, but you'll probably have lunch afterwards. So, we'll see you back up here on the flight deck around 1330 hours. Then, we'll take you back to the *Buck*, if that's all right."

"Yes, sir," Kevin said, "I'll be here."

The nausea Kevin felt during his helicopter flight over from the Buck had dissipated, now replaced by dread over what he might hear from Lt. Cdr. Smith once he reached the wardroom.

As soon as Kevin's helicopter was lowered below decks for storage, a fighter plane started its approach, and Kevin decided to watch it land, close up. He'd seen landings before, of course, from the bridge of the *Buck*, but, upfront and personal, it was way more impressive.

Once the plane was secure, the pilot hopped out of the cockpit onto the wing and lowered himself to the ground, all in a matter of seconds. He looked like a pilot right out of central casting, and when he took off his helmet, a shock of surprisingly long, curly red hair sprang loose. His face was freckled and very young looking. But, still, he looked confident, if not cocky.

"Just send the paperwork down to the wardroom, Jenkins," he commented over his shoulder. "I'll be there with a big mug of mud. It was a pretty hairy ride."

"Too bad you can't lace it with whiskey or something, Lieutenant," the sailor joked, knowing that normally alcohol was prohibited on Navy ships.

"Yeah, too bad," the raffish redhead said, smiling in a way that made Kevin think there would be whiskey in the pilot's immediate future anyway.

The pilot headed over to the ladder leading below decks, on his way to the wardroom. With some effort, Kevin managed to stay with the guy, and they reached the wardroom together. It was much larger than the *Buck's*, almost obscenely so.

What wouldn't I give to be living like this? Kevin thought to himself.

Brad Smith was sitting at the head of a large, polished teak table, cradling a cup of coffee and looking very much out of place. He had a stern look on his face.

"Fancy meeting you here, sir." Kevin said, in an attempt to lighten the mood.

Brad didn't smile. "Not my choice, I can assure you. We have things to discuss,"

The intelligence officer led Kevin through a hatch, down a passageway, and into an office that, by the size of it, probably belonged to the captain. Avoiding the desk, they both chose studded, leather chairs on the opposite side of the room and faced each other across a weather-worn, wooden coffee table.

"So, tell me about Operation Photo Shoot," Brad began.

"Well, the photographer got a hell of a shot. Just not the one he was looking for," Kevin responded, hoping to break the tension. "He might be able to sell it to a Moscow newspaper, though. I'm sure the Russians would get a kick out of it."

Brad rolled his eyes, leaned forward and responded in a tone not at all in keeping with Kevin's levity. "How the hell could a Russian trawler navigate its way into the center of a Top-Secret operation, without anybody on our side knowing about it?"

"Damned if I know," Kevin responded.

"Not good enough. Best guess?"

"Well, it was a complete shit show," Kevin began to speculate. "I doubt anybody was paying much attention to what running lights, or radar blips, came from what ship."

"It was a little fucking fishing boat," Brad replied. "I doubt they had running lights, or any other distinguishing markers."

Kevin smiled in a totally inappropriate way. "There you go. Answered your own question. I guess nobody noticed because the Russians didn't want anybody to notice."

Brad cringed. "Rather than why we missed it, the real question, of course, is what the hell was it doing there in the first place?"

"Might've just followed one of the ships," Kevin speculated. "Or—"

Brad was done pussyfooting around the issue. "I think your girlfriend tipped them off."

The blood drained from Kevin's face, and he felt dizzy.

The moment of truth. This guy was once again accusing Greta of being a spy. Based only on circumstantial evidence. But it was pretty damning evidence.

"And I think that, obviously, you're the source of the leak," a still-somber Brad continued. "Quite a coincidence, don't you think? You mention it to Greta and a Russian boat shows up at the exact right place and time," Brad argued, his face flushed.

"Coincidence, yes, fact, no." Kevin wasn't budging. "I didn't give her any specifics. Remember?"

"You gave her enough, Kevin," Brad pointed out. "You said your ship would be photographed on the way from the Philippines to Vietnam. Not that hard to figure everything else out, is it?"

"Damn, Brad. How the hell was I to know that a stupid photo shoot would be something the Russians cared about."

Brad shook his head; a disbelieving look on his face. "They care about everything, Kevin. Don't you get that? However, it doesn't really matter at this point. Nobody but the two of us know that you told Greta about the photo shoot. And nobody else is going to know it. I'll bury your involvement in this mess, but, in exchange, I need your help."

Kevin looked puzzled. "I'm all ears."

"A position has opened up for an assistant supply officer at the Naval Air Facility in El Centro, California. And I want you to apply for it."

"Why would I do that?" Kevin was aghast. "I love my job. The *Buck* is operating on the front lines of what is now a bona-fide war. I've earned the crew's respect, and, unlike the supply officer before me, I've got a great support network."

"Good for you."

"Not to mention, I've earned the captain's respect. I like my shipmates. I have a good crew. And, if I had wanted to be a fucking assistant supply officer, I wouldn't have studied so hard at Supply Corps School. I had the goal to be a department head, not an assistant, and I've earned that right. Not to mention that I don't even know where El Centro is, or why the Navy is there."

"It's a hell hole actually, two hours inland from San Diego, in the desert. Gets up to 120 degrees, in the shade, on a nice day."

"Well, that clinches it then. I'll stay on the *Buck*, thank you."

"Look, Kevin, let me be perfectly clear," Brad said, the smile no longer on his face. "Staying on the *Buck* isn't an option at this point. You can either be relieved of your duties because you're facing espionage charges, which I think you'll beat, by the way. Or you can be transferred to a place where you have the opportunity to help America more than you ever would on the *Buck*. Those are your two options. There are no others."

"How does being the assistant supply officer at an obscure base in El Centro help America more than what I'm doing?"

"Well, first, because you'll be working for Naval Intelligence undercover, for me actually. That's the good news."

Brad's smile was back but it resembled a smirk. "And second, and even more important, El Centro is home to the Naval Aerospace Recovery Facility, whose secret mission is to help with the moon landing."

"Shit. Really. They're working on the moon landing in the middle of the desert?"

"Not the landing on the moon part, but the recovery part," Brad explained. "The Naval Aerospace Recovery Facility (NARF) is there, and that unit is charged with getting the astronauts, and whatever samples they can collect, back down to earth safely,"

Kevin was intrigued, but still skeptical about his role in all of it.

"And third, we believe that, if Greta truly is a Russian asset, she'll want to follow you there. And then, we can prove conclusively that she's a spy."

"But maybe she'll want to follow me there, whether she's a spy or not."

"Because you're so good-looking, Kevin? Such a catch? And did I mention El Centro's a hellhole that most would avoid no matter what?"

"How long do I have to stay there, in that hellhole, as you describe it?" Kevin asked.

"No more than a year. Maybe less. Depending on how useful she is to us."

"And if I prove she's not a spy?"

"Then, we're all square, and you can get on with your life, advertising, was it?" Brad responded, hoping to close the deal.

But Kevin wasn't yet convinced.

"One other thing. Kevin. If you help us out here, you'll get an early promotion to Lt. J.G., which you can celebrate with your shipmates at the *Buck's* next port of call, which is Hong Kong, by the way. Then, we'll get you on your way to El Centro from there."

"Okay, I'll do it," Kevin finally agreed, knowing that turning down Brad's offer wasn't really a viable option anyway. "What's the next step?"

Brad leaned in as if to avoid somebody overhearing. "You need to tell Greta about your transfer to El Centro, explain that it is part of the top-secret moon landing project, and ask her if she wants to join you in El Centro."

"I doubt she'll agree but, if she does, where will she live?"

"It's all arranged. You're going to be assigned a brand-new duplex on the base, and she can live there with you."

"A little early in our relationship for that, don't you think?"

Chapter 9

Everybody who has been to Hong Kong has given it rave reviews and yet, when the *Buck* sailed into the harbor just after sundown, Kevin was still blown away by its beauty.

You're not in Kansas anymore, he told himself. *This is a very special place.*

It wasn't just how the city presented itself, with its jagged skyline of magnificent buildings tumbling down to the water. But it was also the energy, with boats and cars and people, both in and around the city, all seemingly on their way to somewhere important.

The place throbbed with a vitality unlike anything Kevin had ever seen.

Like most of the *Buck* crew, Kevin was standing on deck, mouth agape, as the ship glided silently through the picturesque harbor on its way to its assigned anchorage. Those around him were seasoned salts who had been to Hong Kong often, and yet, the wonder on their faces was the same as his. Everybody was in awe as they gazed at a spectacle unduplicated anywhere else in the world. And, as the glittering skyline slid slowly past, Kevin wondered, *Could God be staging this just for me?*

"Almost makes it all worthwhile, huh?" A grinning Hertz said, leaning on the lifeline next to his boss.

Kevin turned toward the clerk, beaming as well, "Yes, it does, worth going through a typhoon, that's for sure."

"Probably not a collision at sea, though, huh boss?" Hertz joked.

"Probably not," he answered, laughing with the storekeeper who had become a good friend as well as a great assistant.

Looking back at the skyline, Kevin made a mental note. *The best way to discover Hong Kong is by boat. And I'll be back someday, on my own yacht, perhaps with my wife, Greta, after we get this little spy misunderstanding thing cleared up.*

The *Buck* anchored well out in the harbor, all alone. Then, Kevin went back to the supply office, and said, "Welcome to Hong Kong, guys. One of the great cities in the world. Let's get our work done quickly so we can enjoy it."

Normally, of course, the two most hectic times for a supply officer are just after arriving in port, and just before leaving. Add to that the fact that Kevin's replacement was due to arrive here in Hong Kong and Kevin was even busier than normal. His books needed to be impeccable for the transfer to come off without a hitch, which Kevin now wanted more than anything.

After giving it much thought, he was looking forward to playing a role in exposing Greta or better yet not exposing her. It was the uncertainty that had been killing him and, if he could move things along at a faster pace, he wanted to do that.

Also, he was beginning to accept the fact she might very well be a Soviet agent. The fact that she was chasing him from port to port seemed to suggest it. And her letters? They could have been ghost-written by somebody else, or, given the surprising variance in tone and style, maybe even several other people, and there were so many letters, at least one a day, with so many questions, as if they were manufactured to keep the relationship going, yes, but also to gather intel.

After a restless night working and fretting, Kevin still rose early to see the sun rise over his new favorite city. He was out on the aft deck of the *Buck* before going to work, with a fresh cup of coffee, just taking in the breathtaking view of a skyline like no other..

No wonder the Chinese want it back, he thought to himself..

Then, Kevin reflected on how lucky he was to have been to exotic places like this, as the Navy promised, and to do it with shipmates who will be life-long friends. His only regret was not finishing the *Buck's* deployment and together achieving the military victory he's sure will happen, sooner rather than later.

Still, Brad was right, Kevin admitted. *If Greta goes with me to El Centro, I can influence the outcome of this war more by feeding her misinformation than anything I might have done on board the Buck. So, I need to get my replacement settled in and begin the next chapter of my life on a high note.*

Kevin's replacement was Ensign Edgar Jenkins, who hailed from Cincinnati, Ohio, and was transferring from shore duty at the Naval Supply Center in Norfolk, Virginia. His performance reviews there had been excellent, with high scores in dependability and leadership. So, it should be an easy transition.

Kevin was putting the finishing touches on his books when Edgar arrived and poked his head through the supply office hatch. He was massive, well over six feet tall and pushing 250 pounds. He had a broad, jowly face, with beady dark eyes set a little too close together. His smile was big, but inauthentic as he requested permission to come aboard, in a lame attempt to lighten the moment. Then, he ceremoniously saluted Kevin, as if the fellow ensign were a senior officer.

"No need for formalities here," Kevin said as he rose from his chair and shook the young officer's hand, "Although I probably do outrank you by a day or so. What class were you in Supply Corps School?"

"One behind you, sir."

"Please, drop the 'sir.' We're all equal on the *Buck*. Well, except for the captain. He's one stripe below God."

"So I've heard. Can't wait to meet him," Edgar lied.

Then, Kevin began the introductions, first to Hertz and Wade who were there in the office, then, to the other storekeepers and cooks and finally, the two chief petty officers who would be critical to the young officer's success.

"You've got big shoes to fill, sir," Chief Denton said, "but, if you can figure out which hat to wear to inspection, I think you'll be all right."

A puzzled Edgar just ignored the comment and introduced himself to the two men, saying, "Just call me big Ed."

Not the smartest move, Kevin thought. *Not only is it presumptuous to give yourself a nickname, but protocol requires enlisted men to call officers by their last name. Something Big Ed will learn over time.*

"Yes, sir, Mr. Jenkins," the Chief said.

As soon as the copious supply officer crammed himself into the only leather desk chair in the Supply Office and buried himself in paperwork, Kevin started thinking about the rest of his day and night. He'd already been promoted to Lt. J.G. The captain did that in his in-port cabin while the *Buck* was at sea. But the celebration of the event was planned for later that night, at a small English pub on the second floor of a shabby hotel in downtown Hong Kong.

Every officer on the ship was expected to be there, except the Captain and Mr. Jenkins. It promised to be a very special event, but a little sad for Kevin. Nothing bonds shipmates together like adversity, especially in the heat of war, and that had certainly been the case with Kevin. He will always have a warm place in his heart for his fellow officers and, hopefully, he can get that across at the party.

But, first, during the afternoon, Kevin had important things to do. Fun things, that can only be done in Hong Kong. He needed to visit a Hong Kong tailor to get the new half-stripe sewn onto two of his uniforms, and to get measured for a civilian suit as well. It needed to be something special, befitting the advertising executive he intended to be when he was once again a civilian. Then, he planned to shop for a high-end camera, and a small hi-fi player. Maybe even buy some pearls for Greta.

Normally Kevin wasn't a big spender. But the money that had been accumulating in his bank account for almost three months, ever since the *Buck* left San Diego, was just screaming to find a home in Hong Kong where everything costs about half what it would back in the States. So, as soon as the *Buck's* motor whaleboat returned from dropping the captain off, Kevin and three of his buddies commandeered it to take them right to a pier in downtown Hong Kong where they could gawk and shop.

They were in a joyous mood, freed of their Navy responsibilities for a few hours at least, and on their way to enjoy one of the greatest cities in the world. The closer they got to the city the more Hong Kong engaged them, in an unfamiliar but exciting way.

From the boat, the first thing they saw were the bright colors of giant signs with Chinese characters and just a few English words and brand names interspersed here and there, looking a bit out of place. The closer they got, the pleasant harbor full of fishing boats, yachts, and ocean liners gave way to a bustling downtown area with sleek skyscrapers looking down on streets peopled by both well-dressed businesspeople and sandaled peasants in rags, some selling their wares in open-air shops and others begging for handouts.

It was a remarkably stark and disconcerting contrast of 'haves' and 'have-nots' for Kevin, who had never been in a large international city before. He was intimidated by the noise and diversity of all that was going on; the hundreds of people, cars, and rickshaws, scurrying about in all different directions, obviously in frantic pursuit of something or other. In the chaos, nobody seemed to pay much attention to the small, gray boat, with *U.S.S. Buck* stenciled on its bow, that slid carefully into a slip between two extravagant yachts.

Nobody except the rickshaw runners on the pier looking for a fare. For them, it was an opportunity to make good money off the casually dressed young Americans that disembarked.

Kevin and his buddies were approached by, no, more like accosted by, a mob of older, mostly small, Asian men, who were chattering loudly at them in Chinese, and waving their arms around as if all the noise and activity would help the Americans understand what they were trying to say. Kevin looked around for a taxicab or bus or any other vehicle that could more comfortably get them where they wanted to go. But no luck. *Oh well,* he told himself, *When in Rome...*

So, the young officers just climbed in the closest rickshaws they could hire, and, within minutes, they were ducking in and out of traffic, and racing down incredibly narrow streets, hopefully on their way to the address they had given the drivers, which was a tailor's shop that had been recommended to Kevin. The Asian men jogged in front of their personal rickshaws, lugging their valued fares behind in a kind of foot race, gesturing and talking to each other, maybe debating what they should charge.

Even though the destination was the same for all of them, the rickshaw drivers often separated for a few blocks, sometimes taking dark, narrow alleys, which of course worried the officers no end. They were sitting ducks for muggers or robbers, and Kevin knew that, if they got robbed, describing the men, or their rickshaws, to the authorities would be an impossible task.

So, we might as well just sit back and enjoy the ride, he thought, *we're on liberty in one of the most exciting cities in the world. What could possibly go wrong?*

They did all end up at the same place, thank God, outside a remarkably nondescript shop with a small sign in the window saying in English, "Shirts and Suits sized while waiting." The tailor was outside to greet them personally, grinning and nodding, although it was pretty obvious to them that he didn't understand a single word they were saying.

His enthusiasm was evident, though, as he chattered away in Chinese and even tried to measure anybody who was standing near him. Eventually, though, the tailor took Kevin's uniforms and, best Kevin could tell, promised to deliver them back onboard ship by the end of the day, a remarkable feat if he could pull it off.

With their only chore behind them, Kevin's three friends headed off in different directions, each determined to spend their money on some kind of frivolous activity, because, as one of them said, "You can only see Hong Kong for the first time once."

Then, Kevin went back into the tailor's shop to get fitted for a new suit, knowing that, in a couple of years, he had to somehow look like an advertising executive, and he couldn't think of a better place than Hong Kong to make that happen.

That evening the friends gathered again for the planned festivities of the night, The hotel bar where Kevin decided to "wet down" his stripes was tiny and authentically British. The officers had reserved a private room but, given the size of the place and how many people were already there when the officers arrived, the party promised to be anything but private.

In fact, the Brits crashed the party as if they had known Kevin for years.

"Cheeky bloke if you ask me," one said. "Beats me at darts . . . four times in a row. And him a bloody American."

"Everybody beats you at darts," another Brit said. "I could go get the old Chinese beggar woman on the corner, have her join us and she'd beat you at darts."

The defeated one replied puckishly, "You mean the blind one?"

The second Englishman managed to keep a straight face. "That's the one."

After the laughing died down, there was a pause before the first man speaks up again. "Probably not four times in a row, though, like this bloke did." The room exploded in laughter again, fueled perhaps by the staggering amount of beers that had been consumed already.

Kevin's plan was to have a brief ceremony, down a couple of pints, and for everybody to go their separate ways shortly thereafter. But the friendly Englishmen had other ideas. They wanted to keep everybody there if only for their own entertainment.

Soon there were matches going on all six dartboards, most featuring an American challenging an Englishman. The competition was fierce, loud, and patriotic. In fact, after a while, teams were organized and a large scoreboard mounted behind the bar, with UK scribbled above one side and USA above the other one. A scoring system was established, and everybody got into the act. They were all either playing, watching, or betting on the outcome. And, as is English custom, the loser of each game bought the winner a beer, fueling a kind of drunken camaraderie.

"I love Hong Kong!" Joe shouted out to nobody in particular. "Love, love, love this place."

"That's so American," a Brit responded. "Why can't you be more reserved, like us?"

"You call it reserved," Joe answered, "I call it boring."

At another time or in another place, that might have precipitated a fight. But not tonight. Everybody was having way too good a time. The "offended" party just went over and gave Joe a big bear hug, saying, "We may be boring, old chap, but we're lovable."

And the competition continued.

Finally, around midnight, Joe tapped on a glass and rose a little unsteadily to speak. "Well, the fun is over," he began, "and the bullshit starts. Does anybody have anything nice to say about Kevin?" Then, he answered the question himself. "I didn't think so." And he sat down.

One of the British lads piped up, "Who cares about this Kevin chap? Let's have another beer."

"Wait a minute," Buddy held his hand up, palm outward. "I have something important to say. Kevin's not that bad a guy." Then, he sat down briefly. and popped up again to add "for a Pork Chop." All of the *Buck* officers laughed.

"What's a Pork Chop?" one of the Brits asked.

"He's kind of like our servant," Adam said. "Whenever we want anything, he gets it for us. Food, money, cigarettes, laundry. You name it."

"How do I get a Pork Chop of my very own?" the Brit responded.

"You can have Kevin," Buddy said. "We're done with him anyhow."

Kevin laughed as hard as anyone, his slightly askew smile and rosy cheeks giving testimony to the fun he was having. When the frivolity died down a bit, Joe rose again and said, as seriously as he could given his condition, "Honestly, Kevin. We all love you, man. Congrats on your J.G. stripes. Well-deserved. Let's raise our glasses to our beloved shipmate, our very own Pork Chop, Kevin Boyce."

And they all guzzled a big swig of beer.

Then, the XO rose and said, "I bring best wishes from the Captain, Kevin. He's sorry he couldn't be here tonight, but he had other obligations, and hoped he wouldn't be missed."

"You got that right, Elmer!" somebody shouted, and others joined in.

"Here's to the Captain not being here." somebody shouted, and everybody laughed again.

Then, Lt. Cdr. Bess tapped on a glass and waited patiently for silence. He was wobbling a little. Then, he continued, "Kevin, you were there for me when I needed you, as you have been for many of your shipmates, and I want you to know that we've noticed."

A smattering of applause followed. Then, Mr. Bess continued, "I'm genuinely pleased, both for your promotion and your new assignment. And I'm sure your replacement, Big Ed, will be fine over time, but one thing is already clear. He's no Kevin."

Heads nodded in approval.

"So, to our shipmate, Kevin, a toast," Elmer concluded, "Until we meet again, buddy, when the sun is over the yardarm." And everybody, Brits included, downed what was in their glass.

Then, one of them whispered, "What the hell does that mean?"

"You should know that," Joe answered, "because it's an old sailor's saying that originated with the British Navy. Loosely translated, it means, "until we meet again to enjoy each other's company."

Adam then piped up, "Kevin, you should say something to your adoring fans."

So, after rising and waving his palms up and down, Kevin spoke. "Thank you, Elmer, for your remarks, and your support. You've been a great XO."

The *Buck* officers applauded in agreement.

He paused briefly, then continued, "This has been a wonderful evening. Lots of inane remarks and stupid comments, yes, but incredibly good fun, which is what I will miss the most. I've been lucky to be part of such a great wardroom. I'm blessed to have all of you as friends. And no better time to let you know it than now."

Kevin paused to get control of his emotions. His cheeks were damp, and he made a half-hearted attempt to wipe a tear away with the back of his hand. Then, he stared off into space for a good ten seconds, before continuing in a voice now surprisingly steady and strong.

"They say adversity doesn't build character. It just reveals it. I saw that in our wardroom. With every last one of you guys. We've come through a lot together. That's for sure. But the job isn't done, and I must say that, right now, I feel like I'm abandoning ship."

A few voices objected, but an emotional Kevin shushed them as he tried to keep his composure and continue. "Just know this. Wherever you go next, I'll be with you in spirit. Sail smoothly and safely. Love you guys."

And he sat down, his face now awash in tears that he made no attempt to wipe away. There was silence for a few seconds. Then, an Englishman at the back of the room started a slow, rhythmic clap. Others joined in and the room broke into a long round of applause. When the noise finally died down a bit, one of the Brits says, "Who's up for a game of darts?"

And Kevin bounded out of his chair shouting, "Count me in."

An hour or so later, he looked around and realized he was the only American still in the place. Everybody else had gone, headed back to the ship, or elsewhere. He glanced at his watch and was shocked to see that it was almost two in the morning.

Luckily, one of the Brits recognized Kevin's dilemma and offered to drive him to the dock, where he hired a boat to transport him back to the ship.

"What a night," he mumbled to no one in particular as he climbed aboard the *Buck*. "A wonderful night, indeed." Hopefully, there will be more to come in El Centro.

CHAPTER 10

A few days later, mail call arrived while Kevin was packing up his gear for what promised to be an agonizingly long trip back to the mainland. There was a letter from Greta that was very chatty and loving.

"Congratulations on your promotion. Excited about your new assignment. Hope things are going well in Hong Kong…etc."

No questions or debate points or indication when he might see her again. All of which would have been wonderful had he trusted her like in the old days. But, with the information Brad gave him, it was unusually vapid. His response was the same, with the relevant part being, "I will be stateside on Thursday, and will call you then to see if we can make arrangements to see each other sooner rather than later. All my love, Kevin."

Then, he drafted a telex addressed to Sally Thomas that said, "Would love to see you again. I'm staying at the Grant Hotel over the weekend. Will call when I arrive. Hopefully, we can have dinner somewhere near my hotel. Kevin."

Kevin took his formal departure from the *Buck* more seriously than many would have. He didn't want to just disappear into the night like his predecessor did, but instead, chose to shake as many hands as possible, and thank everybody for their support over what had been a very eventful eighteen months. So, he wandered around the ship to spaces he'd never visited before, such as the engine room, both fore and aft gun mounts, the crew's living quarters. He even went into the chain locker, deep in the bow of the ship where the anchor is stored. There, he found a ruddy-faced young sailor cleaning up the mess the anchor caused when it was hauled up from the bottom of Hong Kong harbor. Kevin couldn't remember the sailor's name, but the guy seemed to know Kevin well.

"Hey, paymaster," the sailor said. "Have fun in El Centro while we're dodging gun boats in the South China Sea."

"You guys'll be fine," he assured the sailor, "Just fine, indeed."

"You'll sure be missed though, Mr. Boyce. You've been a godsend when we needed some supplies down here in the 'pits.' We always knew you had our back."

"I'll miss you guys, too," Kevin replies, "Glad I could help."

"Lieutenant Boyce," a sailor called the ladder to Kevin from the main deck. "Your departure has been moved up. There's a plane available to fly you to the mainland right away, but you need to get to Barber's Point ASAP." So, Kevin cut his goodbye tour of the ship short and hustled back to after officers' quarters to gather up his gear.

Waiting there was his old buddy, Joe Thrasher, who gave Kevin a long hug. The two soulmates had already committed to reconnect as soon as the *Buck* got back to its home port of San Diego, which was probably in a few months. Then, when Kevin reached the aft deck where he was to board the motor whale boat taking him into Hong Kong, surprisingly the Captain and XO were on hand to officially "pipe him ashore."

"You've been a great shipmate, Kevin," the Captain said as they exchanged salutes and shook hands. "Sorry we got off to such a shitty start."

"It's not important how you start but how you finish, Captain. And we finished well, didn't we? It was a pleasure sailing with you, sir."

"What bullshit this transfer is," Lt. Cdr. Bess said. "We just get you broken in. You're doing a great job, and the idiots in Washington do this to us. We need you with us in Vietnam, if only as a kind of security blanket."

"I've been called worse things, believe me." Kevin joked, then, continued, "I really wish I could stay. I didn't ask for this, believe me."

The XO nodded knowingly. "Well, I hope that whatever they have you doing in El Centro, it'll be more important than what you could have done for us here."

Yes, Kevin told himself facetiously, *I'm going to be on an undercover operation, sleeping with a gorgeous girl. What could be more important to the war effort than that? Uncle Sam needs me…in her bed.*

****

The flight back to San Francisco wasn't exactly First-Class. Kevin was strapped into the only seat rigged up in the cargo space of a smelly C-47. It was a hot, bumpy ride that, including a brief refueling stop in Pearl Harbor, seemed to go on for days, giving Kevin lots of time to think.

I'm closing one chapter, an authentic Navy experience that I'll cherish the rest of my life, he ruminated, *and opening a complicated new one that could end badly. Who knows what the future holds for me, but it promises to be interesting.*

When the huge, cumbersome cargo plane finally lumbered to a stop at the Alameda Naval Air Station in San Francisco, Kevin was surprised to find an armed sailor waiting there to escort him over to the San Francisco Airport, where he was to board a commercial flight to San Diego.

Evidently, I'm now precious cargo that the Navy feels needs protection, he gloated to himself. Which turned out to be more true than he imagined. When the two uniformed Navy men entered the commercial airport, they were immediately accosted by angry protestors.

Signs saying things like "Leave Vietnam Now," and "I Won't Go," were everywhere. Long-haired young men in bandannas and tie-dye tee shirts were jumping in the way of the servicemen, provocatively mouthing obscenities and trying to incite an altercation.

Fortunately, two burly men in civilian clothes stepped through the crowd, pushed a couple of hippies away, and cleared a small path for Kevin and his escort to move toward the gate of Kevin's next flight.

"We're Navy Shore Patrol," one of them whispered, "Don't worry, sir. We'll take over now and get you safely on your way. No reason to aggravate these boys any more. Just ignore their taunts and do what I say."

Kevin was more than happy to do that. After the uniformed escort was dismissed, the largest of the patrolmen, who was obviously in charge, got between Kevin and the protesters. As he did that, Kevin felt a solid metal object in the guy's jacket and was strangely comforted.

Several months in a combat zone and the first time a handgun is needed is when I arrive home. What a bizarre world we live in now.

As Kevin neared the departure gate, most of the protesters faded away, apparently looking for another serviceman to accost or a cameraman to give them air time. The three men settled onto a bench where they were approached immediately by a PSA ticket agent, who addressed the escorting bodyguards, "We'll take it from here, gentlemen. Since we only fly domestically, nobody will bother us. And I'll have this supply officer escorted on board before any of the other passengers. I promise he won't be bothered."

The two shore patrolmen looked at each other, nodded, and left. No backward glance. No chance for Kevin to thank them. Fifteen minutes later, an attractive PSA stewardess arrived and approached Kevin, her hand outstretched, "Hello, officer. I'm Ann and I'm here to escort you aboard, if that would be okay."

More than okay. Kevin thought to himself.

After Kevin's months at sea, she was a vision of loveliness, with her natural blonde hair and peaches-and-cream complexion. An angel of mercy here to rescue him. She took his arm, tucked it under hers, where it was pressed up against her breast, and marched him on board first, apologizing that she couldn't seat him in first class, but promising to make up for it when they were in the air.

The girl knew exactly what she was doing. She was welcoming him back and thanking him for his service, without ever saying it. A real classy move.

Before the plane took off, the girl was back, Bloody Mary in hand, and sat in the center seat next to Kevin. She presented the drink to him with a flourish, then, whispered, "I'm not supposed to do this, but the pilot wanted me to stay with you until we're in the air. Says he's an ex-Navy pilot, and wanted to show his respect for what you did for us over there."

After takeoff, she got up to attend to the other passengers, and whispered, "Welcome home, sailor boy," which reminded him of the time Greta said something similar in Hawaii.

God works in mysterious ways, he reminded himself.

Later, when the pilot cautioned the passengers to buckle up for the landing, Kevin opened the shade to look out the plane window and was staggered by the panoramic views of downtown San Diego spread out beneath him.

First to come into view was Coronado Island, a funky and fun-filled beachfront community located on a peninsula just across the bay from downtown San Diego. He could see the historic Hotel Del Coronado, largest wooden structure in the world, sporting a cantilevered, red-tiled roof with dozens of cupolas and dormer windows.

To Kevin's mind, there was no more authentic, or beautiful, hotel in the world.

Next to appear was Balboa Park, with its world-famous zoo. And just barely visible beyond it, was the "old town" of San Diego, a well-preserved Mexican village, with its distinctive plaza of shops and restaurants.

The plane was enveloped by the city as it lost altitude and Kevin could see, on one side a glistening blue bay, dotted with sailboats and motorboat and, on the other, Kevin could look into the floor-to-ceiling windows of Mister A's, a new rooftop restaurant near the landing path of the plane. Some diners put down their forks and waved.

Welcoming me home, perhaps, Kevin thought to himself, *because I will surely live here again in my life. I just love this place.*

*****

When Kevin checked into the Grant Hotel, he tried to reach Greta, but there was no answer. So, he left a message, "I've arrived back in the states safe and sound and am staying at the Grant Hotel. Please call as soon as you can."

Then, he called Sally and arranged to have dinner with her at Anthony's Fish Grotto, a waterfront restaurant not far from his hotel. Kevin arrived a half-hour earlier than the reservation so he could walk around the pier a bit before meeting Sally.

But, when he arrived, she was already there.

"Great minds," she said. "I decided to arrive early and soak up the sights and sounds. Wow, just smell that salty sea air."

"Reminds me of when we used to walk around Potter's Lake back in school."

"Exactly, except that you could skip a stone across that water," Sally responded. "And the air smelled more like wheat fields than the sea."

"Other than that, though," Kevin acknowledged

Sally pulled off her corduroy sailor cap to let the sea breeze blow through her blonde hair, then turned back toward Kevin and commented, "This is better."

"You got that right."

So, they walked over to the ferry landing, then, out onto Broadway Pier before finally reaching the restaurant. The sun was still out but the heat of the day had dissipated, and a wispy fog bank was rolling in. The pier was mostly deserted, with only a handful of fishermen milling about discussing their day and their catch.

Kevin and Sally didn't talk for a few minutes, which they could do, one of the nice things about their long-time relationship. They found a bench and just sat there, enjoying the ambience and the moment.

"So, what are you doing in San Diego?" Kevin asked.

"I'm working for Avon in sales promotion. My job is to motivate our sales reps."

"I'll bet you're very good at that."

"Hope to be. Right now, I'm just learning the ropes. Nothing like what you've been doing, though. What was it like for you in Vietnam?" She asked.

Kevin smiled. It was nice to be questioned about his feelings rather than the specific questions Greta asked. And he didn't have to be as careful with his answers.

"Better than you might imagine," he answered. "On a ship, everyday things seem dangerous, just going up and down ladders, or handling ammunition, or getting onto a helicopter, but we were hardly ever fired on, or threatened in any way."

"That surprises me."

"It did me too. In many ways, I was expecting a different kind of war, more like WWII, with submarines and planes attacking, and us responding with torpedos, depth charges, and our deck guns. But, it wasn't like that at all."

"I'm glad."

"Don't get me wrong. Vietnam is like any war, just not on the sea right now. In the air, it's a different story. Our fighter squadrons are losing a third of their pilots every time they deploy. And, on the ground, I think it's going to be be even worse. Still, with our air and sea dominance, we should be able to win this thing easily and quickly. I sure hope so."

When they finally circled back to the restaurant the sun was setting over the bay. It was spectacular. "Best show in town," Kevin remarked. "And the best part is that it's available to everybody, for free."

They just stood there on the pier, holding hands, and gazing up at the pastel colors spreading along the horizon.

Which, of course, made them late for their reservations, but it didn't matter. As the hostess said with a smile when they finally checked in, "This isn't the first time the sunset has screwed with our reservations."

After ordering margaritas, the two old lovers began to talk again. "Are you glad you did it? Joined the Navy, I mean," Sally asked, her head on her hands, and gazing into Kevin's eyes.

"Hell yes. If you had arrived in Hong Kong by water, like I did, you wouldn't even ask that question."

"Are you sorry you had to leave the *Buck* early?"

"Yes again, But duty calls. I have some important things to do in El Centro." Kevin said, before realizing he'd ventured into dangerous conversational waters.

"Like what?" She asked.

Let's see. I can't say I'm going to be undercover, living with a beautiful Russian spy. Nor can I say we're working on the moon landing. Time to bull shit just a little.

"El Centro is an important training ground for pilots," he answered, "And they have some support issues I need to clean up, which seemed more important to them than just 'plane guarding,' which was what we were doing at the time,"

Sally wrinkled up her nose, and asked, "What's 'plane-guarding'?"

"It's when we cruise behind the carrier while they are conducting flight ops and pick up any pilots that accidentally go into the water."

"Did you pick up many?"

Kevin hesitated before answering, "Surprisingly yes. It's not easy to take off from the deck of a carrier. Even harder to land on one, especially at night. So a few went in."

"Don't they have lots of lights to guide them when it's dark?" Sally asked.

"Yes, normally they do," Kevin answered, "but not in war time. To avoid being a target, the carrier is blacked out until the last second. So, the planes are being guided in by a single deck controller, with a laser light, that's turned on at the last possible second."

"Landing a plane on a ship you can't see, in the dark, sounds pretty hairy," Sally agreed.

"You have no idea," Kevin explained, "Up close, carriers look huge. But, from the air, in that vast ocean, they are actually shockingly small"

She asked, "Why would anybody want to take such a risk?"

Kevin arched his eyebrows, confused by the simplicity of her question. "You got me, Sally, maybe adrenaline," he answered, "Or because somebody told them to, I suppose."

Sally looked puzzled at first, then grinned. "Do you do everything you're told to do?"

"Shockingly, yes," Kevin answered, "you can't imagine how many times I've said to myself, 'You've got to be kidding.' when I'm given an order to do something that seems crazy dangerous."

Sally cocked her head. "But you go ahead and do it. That's interesting."

"Yes, well, it turns out I can do crazy, dangerous things if I'm ordered to."

The waiter interrupted the discussion by delivering their entrees, the fish special for her and shrimp for him. They sampled a few bites, then, a reflective Kevin continued. He was enjoying the chance to talk about his experiences with somebody who was interested for the right reasons.

"I used to hang around the bridge and listen to the pilots as they approached the carrier after a mission," he said, "They always sounded so calm and collected. But the closer they got to the carrier, the more nervous they got."

"How could you tell?" Sally wondered.

"Well, their voices got louder and squeakier as they said something like 'I can see the waves, but I can't see the ship. Are you sure I'm okay?' At times, they sounded like little kids, pleading to their mommies."

Sally smiled at Kevin's impression of a scared pilot, then asked, "Did anybody ever crash into the side of the ship?" she asked.

"Not that I saw," he answered, "The couple of pilots we picked up missed the tail hook and kept going, right off the ship, into the ocean."

Her mouth gaped open. "Oh my God. That would be awful. I can't imagine."

Kevin paused for a second, and looked up at the ceiling. He was thinking about a friend, a fellow supply officer, who had that experience. He was just hitching a ride to Saigon in a Skyhawk fighter plane when the plane went directly into the ocean on takeoff. Fortunately, because he was a college swimmer, he made it to the surface relatively unscathed. Physically at least. But mentally, not so much. Kevin heard the guy slipped into a catatonic state that eventually got him released from the Navy, a little factoid he decided not to share with Sally.

When the waiter came to deliver the bill, the guy lingered for a while until Kevin saw he wanted to say something. Given his long hair, scraggly beard and red eyes, Kevin worried he might be a strung-out hippie protestor, kind of like Kevin encountered in San Francisco.

"Hey, man. I couldn't help but overhear. Were you in 'Nam?"

"Just got back. Why do you ask?"

"I served one tour there and it was hell. Started out fine, in Saigon. Beautiful city. But then, the skirmishes and bombings started. And you couldn't tell who was on your side. At times, it seemed like everybody was either Viet Cong or a sympathizer."

"I wasn't on the mainland," Kevin interrupted, "I was offshore, on a ship. So, my experiences were different than yours."

"Yea, I overheard you backed up a carrier," the waiter responded. "I wanna say thank you. Your pilots saved our asses. Without their skills and courage, we wouldn't have stood a chance over there."

"Wasn't me. I just picked up a couple of pilots when they went into the drink."

"Everybody had their role, man. Except maybe those candy asses who went to Canada, or the ones who stayed just to protest. What bullshit that was. We had a job to do, and then they yell at us for doing it."

"Well, I appreciate you doing your job," Kevin said, handing the guy an extra five bucks on top of the tip. Then, his eyes suddenly wet, the waiter bent down and gave Kevin an awkward hug. "We veterans got to stick together, ain't that right man?"

CHAPTER 11

The next morning, Kevin tried to reach Greta again, but was unsuccessful. So, he called Naval Intelligence at the San Diego Naval Base, and asked for Brad Smith. It was time to get his marching orders.

"Lt. Cdr. Smith speaking. What can I do for you?"

"This is Lt. J. G. Boyce reporting for duty, sir," Kevin said, a bit facetiously. His relationship with Brad had developed to the point where he felt could have fun with the guy without offending him. They both had a sharp, but slightly warped, sense of humor. That, along with being co-conspirators in what was turning into quite a spy caper, bonded them into an unlikely friendship.

"I wondered when I'd hear from you. Did you enjoy your days off?"

"Day off, to be exact, Brad, and yes I did."

"Well, your fun is over now, Mr. Boyce. Did you talk to our friend yet?"

"Left word but she hasn't called back. Maybe she has bigger fish to fry, so to speak."

"Maybe, but I'm thinking you're her biggest fish, and I mean that in a nice way."

"Is there a nice way to tell somebody they're a fish?"

"Good point. When do you plan to report to El Centro?"

"My orders say Monday, but I thought I'd drive over tomorrow and get settled in before the fireworks start. There, I'm to report to a Lt. Cdr. Bob Higgins, by the way. Does he know about my undercover work?"

"The only guy on the base who knows anything is the commanding officer, a Captain Sims, and he doesn't know much," Brad answered. "Just that, in addition to your regular duties, you'll be working for us and, to be effective, you and your wife will need your own quarters."

"My wife?"

"Oh, I forgot to tell you. According to your amended file, you and Greta are now married. A belated congratulations, by the way."

"What do I tell Greta?"

"I'll leave that up to you, buddy. Just finesse it."

"Not my strong suit."

A few minutes after Brad hung up, the phone rang, and coincidentally, it was Greta. She talked about how delighted she was that he was back in one piece, and that she missed him, and wanted to see him somehow.

"That's why I wanted you to call, actually. I'm driving out to El Centro, tomorrow, and I'd like you to join me there."

"To visit?"

"No. Actually, to live with me," Kevin explained, "I was able to get a unit on the base that's normally reserved for married officers. We'll have to pretend to be bored with each other like other married couples are, but it'll be good practice should we ever decide to go in that direction."

The moment of truth. Spy or not, it's a big ask. Not only the living together part, but pretending to be married as well.

Kevin could feel the hesitation before she said,,"That's a little difficult, Kevin. I finally got my master's degree, and I've been looking for some kind of a teaching or administrative job out east."

"There are several colleges in or around El Centro. You should have no trouble finding a job out here. In fact, they'll probably welcome you with open arms."

"When were you thinking I'd join you?"

"About a month or so. That'll give me a little time to settle in."

"So, living together, huh?"

"The place has three bedrooms, so it could be like living in a dorm, if that's what you want. Besides, it'll be a great way to see how compatible we are."

"Don't you already know that?" She teased.

"Seriously, Greta, being thousands of miles away from you doesn't work for me. I figured that out on the ship. Loving you by mail is just not the same in person, and you can blame your sensual side for that. Being with you in San Diego and Hawaii was highly addictive for me."

Another long silence.

"Kevin, I'm not sure I'm ready for such a big commitment, but let me think it over. I'd have to rearrange a few things to make it happen."

I'll bet you would, and get your handler's permission as well, he thought. *Hopefully, when they figure it out, the moon landing will be a big enough draw for them to want you to come.*

"Greta, you're not really committing to anything that big. If you come, and don't like it, you can get onto the next flight back to the east coast, or Germany, or wherever you want to go. There are no strings attached here, although obviously I'm hoping things head in that direction."

"You make a compelling case. Let me get back to you."

After hanging up, Kevin called Brad right back. "She's thinking it over."

"Probably weighing her options, intel-wise," Brad mused. "And her handler will be checking out the base in El Centro."

"They won't like it," Kevin suggested.

"When they learn about the moon landing part, they'll love it. I guarantee you that. The Russians are trying to launch their own space program, and because of that, where you're going is an intel-rich environment for them. They just have to figure that out for themselves."

******

The only highway from San Diego to El Centro is Highway 8. It wends its way through mesquite-covered foothills for several miles. Then, it begins to rise up into forested mountains, the air cooling dramatically with each elevation change.

Kevin's Ford Falcon was struggling with the conditions, not only because of the inclines but also because of the winds whipping through the canyons, sometimes reaching over fifty miles per hour at times.

I remember reading that, in the County of San Diego, there are more climate zones than any other place in the world, and it seems like I'm experiencing all of them on this drive, Kevin thought as he tried to keep the small car on the road.

The temperature was in the sixties when Kevin left the beach community of Del Mar. Then, it climbed into the nineties as he crossed the arid plains before reaching the foothills and mountains beyond, where it dipped back down into the low forties. All within about an hour. And Kevin expected it to rise quickly into the hundred-degree range in the desert areas surrounding El Centro, a difference of sixty degrees over a two-hour drive.

Given that it was a Sunday, there was little traffic on the road, just those trying to escape to the mountains, or a few hard-core outdoor enthusiasts looking for a desert experience.

Kevin passed a group of motorcyclists pulled over at a scenic overpass near the summit of the last mountain. They were encircled by a yellowish cloud of smoke that Kevin assumed was some kind of marijuana haze. Not good. So, he sped up, not so much to outrun the smoke, but to reach the bottom before these crazy, medicated bikers came pummeling down the mountain toward him. Handling the treacherous mountain hairpin turns was hard enough without motorcycles roaring up from behind to harass him.

Fortunately, Kevin did get off the mountain before the bikers arrived. Then they whooshed by on both sides of the car, spinning out a bit as they did so, with their mouths flapping and middle fingers waving. But they didn't slow down, thankfully.

Within a few seconds, Kevin was alone again, on a silver ribbon of road that stretched ahead for miles, straight as a ruler, right into the vapors of an overheated terrain that looked very inhospitable. The car's air conditioner was spewing out warm air, which was doing nothing to prevent beads of perspiration from popping up on Kevin's forehead, and then, sweat was wiggling its way down, across his nose, and onto his chin, from which they dripped into a gathering pool of salty liquid in his lap. The bleak landscape never changed as Kevin pushed the struggling car forward, hoping its radiator wouldn't boil over, stranding him.

This is pleasant, he thought. *Who wouldn't want to live here? Hell, Kansas is paradise compared to this place.*

Then, out of nowhere, a sign whizzed past on the right, and Kevin barely reacted quickly enough to read it. It said, "Welcome to El Centro. Home of the Blue Angels."

"I'll be damned," Kevin said to nobody in particular. "I'm home."

But where is the town? Or the base? And what the hell are the Blue Angels doing out here in the middle of nowhere."

Then, upon reflection, he answered his own question. *Same thing you are, Mr.Boyce. Just following orders. We go where the Navy sends us. Sometimes it's Hong Kong, sometimes it's Vietnam, and sometimes it's El Centro.*

Long before there was any evidence of a town, the entrance to the Naval Air Station appeared on the left. It looked like what you might find at military installations all over America, with a sign sporting the naval station's blue logo, with a winged crest, beneath which was the slogan, "Home of the Blue Angels." Next to the sign, there was a gate, a small security building, and a Marine guard, sporting a light tan helmet, desert camouflage gear and holding an M-15 across his chest.

Well-guarded for a place nobody wants to go, Kevin pondered, *well, except maybe for me, and Greta.*

When Kevin had crossed over the left lane into the entrance road, the guard stepped forward, and motioned him over to the side. His expression was gravely serious, probably because Kevin wasn't in uniform. Or maybe because Kevin's small car was beginning to smoke profusely from overheating.

Hardly an auspicious arrival for the new assistant supply officer.

"Your papers, please," the guard said sternly, his face a steely mask.

Then, surprisingly, after reviewing them, the guard snapped to attention, saluted, and said, "Welcome to El Centro, Lieutenant Boyce. We've been expecting you."

Kevin returned the salute, a tad embarrassed that he didn't dress more formally for the occasion. "Who's 'we,' sailor?" He asked.

"Well, me and your boss, Mr. Higgins, sir. He's waiting for you at the Officer's Club."

"I wasn't supposed to be here until Monday," a surprised Kevin clarified. "Why would he be waiting for me now?"

"You'll have to ask him that, sir. I just know what he told me."

******

The Officer's Club was located in a Quonset hut metal building just off the base's main drag. The only thing that distinguished it from all the other nondescript buildings was a small sign, in the front of an immaculately maintained front lawn, that said, "Officers Only."

When Kevin opened the door, a frigid blast of cold air attacked him much the same way the desert heat had an hour or two before. He was stunned for a second, by both the temperature and the darkness.

"Hey, close the door. Were you born in a barn?"

The faceless voice came out of the darkness in the very under-lit room. Kevin glanced around, trying to make out the guy who spoke. His eyes hadn't fully adjusted yet but, as they did, he saw a few Naval officers, both uniformed and not, sitting alone at wood-topped tables near the back of the room, nursing their drinks. The voice he heard hadn't come from those guys.

Then, he noticed several men sitting on barstools at the formal oak bar to his right. They had returned to what they were doing, which wasn't much. One of the men, a small, portly, bald-headed lieutenant commander, looked up again and then seemed to recognize Kevin. He approached the supply officer amicably, a big smile on his jowly, flushed face, and a glass in his left hand.

He extended his right and, as they shook, whispered, "Don't mind that guy that bitched when you came in. He's a little into his cups. Made lieutenant commander last week and thinks he's hot shit. I'm Bob Higgins, by the way. I assume you're Boyce."

"That's right, sir, the guard told me to meet you here."

"Good, good," the base supply officer responded, "Please call me Bob, by the way."

"Yes, sir. Bob it is."

"I wanted to welcome you to El Centro and give you a little run through on what you might be facing here. It'll probably be different than you expect."

"I appreciate that, sir. Frankly, I never heard of this place until I got orders here. It's a little off the beaten path, especially for a Navy base."

"Not many ships around here, I admit. But we're pretty important to the Navy, nonetheless."

Kevin was surprised by the charm of the older man, especially given that he had probably been in the club for a while now. He seemed lucid, and aside from his watery and red-rimmed eyes, perfectly normal. Just a friendly guy trying to help out a fellow supply officer.

"Let's go over to that back booth, Lieutenant. You might need a drink when I tell you what's actually going on here," Lt. Cdr. Higgins said.

"No thanks to the drink, but I'm all ears," Kevin answered as he followed Higgins to the booth. He was genuinely curious to hear how Bob would handle the moon landing project. But, first, Bob went off in a different direction.

"You may not know it, Mr. Boyce, but this is a cursed base," he whispered, his eyes intense and his brow furrowed.

"How so?" Kevin responded.

"I don't know why but bad things just keep happening here. I suppose you read about the air show accident we had a year or so back."

"I vaguely remember something about that. Didn't remember it was here though."

"It sure was. Very tragic. Killed nine people and injured twenty-two. But that was just the latest tragedy we've experienced on this base. For some reason, we've lost a number of pilots, most of whom just crashed their planes into the desert floor."

"Suicides?"

"Who knows? Folklore has it that the spirits around here don't like the Naval Air Facility much."

"That's a bit of a stretch, don't you think?" Kevin queried, "Probably just a run of bad luck.".

"Well, something is pretty weird about this place. Maybe it's the desert heat, but people do strange, irrational things. For instance, the officer you're replacing 'borrowed' $50,000 out of his safe and took it to Mexico to bet on a horse."

"Didn't turn out well, I'm guessing."

"Not so well. That's right. He's now in the brig, poor guy. I don't know what he was thinking."

Then, Lt. Cdr. Higgins leaned in so close to Kevin's face that Kevin got a whiff of his alcohol breath, mixed in with an aftershave smell. It wasn't pleasant. Nor was the affable Bob anymore.

He can go from sweet to scary in a nanosecond, Kevin thought, *I don't know who the real Bob Higgins is…if there is one.*

"Even stranger," Bob went on, "the assistant supply officer before him just plain disappeared. He was vacationing in Mexico, and never came back."

"My God. That is strange."

"Captain Sims thought I should mention these things to you before you check in, just in case you want orders elsewhere. That can be arranged."

"You know, Mr. Higgins. I'm not the type to worry about a curse or stealing money or me disappearing. So, I think I'll just give it a go, but thanks for the warning."

A scowl crept onto the senior officer's face, as if he half-expected Kevin to be scared off, but it quickly disappeared, and the fake, friendly smile returned.

"I'm glad to hear that, Mr. Boyce, because the Navy really needs you here right now. We have a lot at stake on this base." Lt. Cdr. Higgins paused then continued in a conspiratorial tone. "We're doing some heavy-duty shit here, and we need a guy like you to help us out, somebody with a Top-Secret clearance who knows how to keep his mouth shut."

You can trust me, Kevin thought to himself. *Whatever you tell me, Bob, is just between the two of us …and Brad, of course…and Greta. So, just you, me, my boss, and a Russian operative who's been sent here to spy on us. And, oh yes, probably her handler…and the Kremlin, of course. But that's it. I promise. Just the dozen or so of us.*

"You will be secretly working on the space program, the moon landing, to be exact."

"Not sure what you mean, Bob," Kevin said, already fed up with his boss's inflated perspective of things. "We're just supply officers, right? We will be paying, feeding, and delivering supplies to the people who are working on the moon landing. Is that correct?"

Bob's face turned beet-red, and there was saliva dribbling out of the side of his mouth. "Look, young man. I'm serious. If we don't do our job, guess what? No men on the moon."

Talk about delusions of grandeur. I hope it's just the booze talking, because if this guy actually believes this bullshit, it's going to be a long few months for me here.

"I apologize, sir," Kevin responded in as contrite a tone as he could muster under the circumstances, "I take what we do very seriously, and plan to give it my all. Sorry if I gave you the wrong impression."

"I hope so, Mr. Boyce. We have to work well together if this thing is going to succeed. I'll do my job and you just do yours, which, in the beginning is to manage disbursing and the storerooms. I'll keep the food and beverage operations, and all the other service activities, including the clubs."

Makes sense that Bob would keep food and beverage. He seems to be an expert on both, Kevin acknowledged to himself.

After exchanging a few more pleasantries and shaking the older man's hand, Bob returned to his post at the bar, and Kevin left the club. Once outside, when contrasted with the chilliness of the conversation he had just had, the heat was even more oppressive than before.

Holy shit, Kevin thought to himself. *I need to talk to Brad. Cursed base? Pompous ass for a boss? This isn't what I signed up for. Working undercover is one thing but putting up with this nonsense as well? I don't think so.*

A distraught Kevin got into his car and drove around the base looking for the administrative offices where he could check in and get the keys to his quarters. The whole base seemed deserted, which, given it was Sunday and insufferably hot, was probably not surprising.

But it was pretty eerie just the same.

Kevin decided to park and wander around on foot, hopefully finding somebody in or around the buildings. He traversed the immediate area, through hangars, warehouses, and even went up to a few planes sitting outside the hangars, totally unattended. Nobody was around, and the lack of security was appalling.

Naval Intelligence should have me plant 'fake' bombs here, he told himself. *I've never seen a place more susceptible to espionage, or sabotage.*

But then, after getting back in his car and driving several blocks away from the main road, Kevin stumbled onto another base, a sort of base within the base.

A small wooden sign identified the small fenced-in compound as the Naval Aerospace Recovery Facility (NARF,) where all the secret moon landing stuff was supposedly going on. And, not surprisingly, it was buttoned up tighter than a drum, with an armed guard warily watching Kevin pass by.

Then, ominously, the patrolman moved out onto the street, a rifle cradled in his arms, just to make sure the Ford

Falcon kept moving. Which it did, of course. Kevin saw no need to announce himself to the guard at this point.

Getting secrets out of NARF and spinning them into misinformation that can fool the Russians, won't be as easy as I'd been told, Kevin admitted to himself. *To make Greta believe I'm a valuable source for her, I'll have to either find some way to get inside that facility or befriend somebody who works there.*

Glancing down a side street, Kevin saw a large metal building which seemed to have some activity in and around it. There were several cars in the parking lot, and a flashing *Budweiser* sign in the window. After parking, Kevin got out of his car and heard the unmistakable sound of bowling balls rolling over wooden alleys, then the clatter of scattered pins, all of which made him feel more comfortable.

There is life on this planet, he assured himself, *maybe even with human beings.*

Once inside the building, after his eyes had adjusted, he saw the inside was smaller than he expected. There was a Formica counter where patrons could check out equipment, a spartan bar with six stools in front of it, four bare wooden tables, and six bowling lanes, only two of which were were in use. Not much of a gathering place for a base this size.

Lounging around on the benches fronting the two alleys were a dozen or so young men, drinking beer, smoking cigarettes, laughing, and occasionally throwing a ball haphazardly down an alley. One or two guys looked up, wondering if a friend had entered, but, seeing Kevin, they went back to what they were doing.

After a minute or two watching the festivities, Kevin approached the skinny, pimple-faced kid nearest to him and asked where the base administrative building was.

"Go back to the main street, sir, turn right, then it's the first building past the roundabout. But nobody's there."

"I need to check in somewhere today. I'm reporting for duty."

"On a Sunday?" He asked, but before Kevin could answer, a voice from behind him piped up."Good luck with checking in today, sir. Are you Mr. Boyce, by any chance?"

Kevin turned around to see a tow-headed, friendly-faced young man coming toward him.

"I'd salute but that would be awkward," the guy said, a lop-sided grin on his his face. Instead, he offered his hand saying, "I'm Tommy Adams, one of your storekeepers, and I'd like to officially welcome you to the base, sir."

"Thanks for that, Tommy. So far, that's the friendliest greeting I've received today."

"Probably the only one, but it's genuine. I'm really happy to see you. It was beginning to look like we'd never get another supply officer here. For some reason, the others all backed out before reporting."

I met Mr.Higgins and I think I know the reason, Kevin thought.

"I was hoping to check in and get the keys to my place." Kevin explained.

"I don't think that's possible. Most everybody here flees the heat on the weekends, up to the mountains or over to the beaches of San Diego," Tommy said, "We're here because we have some kind of duty. I'm in charge of the storerooms for the weekend, not that anybody will need replacement parts, and my buddies are cooks, who drew weekend duty in the kitchen."

"Any chance of me getting my keys from the guard at the front gate."

"I doubt it, but you could try. However, if you're unsuccessful, you could crash with us in the enlisted men's quarters."

Kevin made a face and Tommy went on, "But I doubt you'd be comfortable there. A better alternative is a motel about three miles down the road, a little closer to town. It's not fancy but it's a lot better than anything we could scrounge up for you here."

"Okay, Tommy, that's what I'll do. Thanks for the suggestion."

"No problem. And seriously, I'm glad you're here. We need somebody to watch over us."

CHAPTER 12

Kevin found the motel easily and, within fifteen minutes of checking in, was fully immersed in its relatively small pool. The water wasn't as cold as he hoped but it was still a welcome respite from the 100-degree desert heat, and a perfect place to contemplate his situation.

My new boss is a disappointment, although maybe I just caught him in a not so sober moment. Still, he didn't seem to want me around, or anybody else for that matter. I wonder why? And then, there's this whole rigamarole about the base being cursed. What the hell was that all about?

Kevin got out of the pool and started to towel himself off, but the dry heat did the job for him better than he could have himself. Once dry, he flopped down on the chaise lounge, positioning himself so the metal wouldn't burn his skin, and drifted off to sleep, wondering what the hell to expect next.

An hour or so later, Kevin woke up, still hot and tired, but now hungry as well. He remembered then that, in the flurry of his mostly boring non-activity, he'd skipped lunch.

Guess that Mr. Higgins character threw me off my game, he posited to himself, *But I saw a bar and grill on the way here, Sammy's something or other, and a hamburger might be just the ticket to get me energized again.*

After retracing his route, Kevin found the place he had seen earlier and settled onto a stool at the bar near the front door. He glanced around and saw only two other people, a boy and a girl, nestled together in a back booth. The décor was understated, but the boozy, fried food smell of the place made him feel right at home. And it turned out he was right about one thing. The hamburger was just the ticket to make him feel better, although it took some fries, and a few beers, to finish the job.

While he was enjoying his meal, Kevin struck up a conversation with the owner, Sammy, and quickly learned that Bob Higgins was right about people thinking the base was cursed. For a decade or more, at least one unfortunate pilot per year had died crashing into the desert floor during training exercises.

"But I heard there was a psychological explanation for it," he explained. "It's called it 'target fixation.' Evidently, pilots hone in on a target set up on the desert floor and get so fixated on it that they keep going right into the center of it. According to experts, something about the monotony of the terrain makes them lose track of where they are."

"That wouldn't explain the air show crash though, would it, Sammy?" Kevin countered.

"No, it wouldn't, but I think that's just law of averages. With the Blue Angels practicing dangerous stunts every day, and given all of the air shows staged here, a tragic accident was bound to happen sooner or later. Plus, let's face it, those pilots aren't exactly the most stable individuals, are they? Why else would they be doing what they're doing."

"So, you don't believe the base is cursed."

"Not really, but I don't think it's a great place to work either."

Kevin pondered the remark for a minute, which seemed to confirm his feeling that, to him, the place felt creepy. But was there more to it?

"I have to work there. I'm reporting in tomorrow," he admitted, "What makes such it a bad place?

"I don't know," Sammy went on, "The few people who wander in here from the base seem very unhappy. They say there's high turnover rate, partially caused by bad vibes that you can sense when you've been there awhile."

"You don't even need to be there awhile. I could sense it right away just wandering around."

"Plus, everybody leaves on the weekends," Sammy continued, "which is kind of creepy."

"I guess that's what I experienced."

"And they say the place is populated with a lot of arrogant pricks, pilots and parachutists and the like. Of course, I'm hearing this mainly from enlisted guys. Officers rarely come in here. We're not fancy enough for them, I guess. The only officer I get in here regularly is the base supply officer."

"Bob Higgins?"

"That's him."

"What's he like?"

"Seems like a nice enough guy. Family man. Slew of kids. Elder at my church. Boy Scout leader. The enlisted men call him the Godfather because he takes good care of them. But, boy, can he drink."

"During the day?"

"Most of the time, here, it's during the day. But occasionally he'll have dinner with three tough-looking Mexican dudes. They sit in a back booth and talk business."

"What kind of business?"

"Who knows? But whatever it is, I wouldn't want to be doing it with those guys. They're not exactly friendly types. Just saying."

******

The next morning, Kevin arrived at the Naval Air Facility around 7 a.m.and was surprised to see a whole line of cars waiting to get in and, once he was on the base, a hubbub of activity, with sailors and civilians going every which way as if it were mid-day. In marked contrast to the day before.

"What the hell is going on?" He asked the guard, who responded with a dumbfounded look. So, Kevin clarified. "Why are there so many people here at this time in the morning?"

"This is normal, sir. We start work at daybreak and then quit early so everybody can get out of the heat. We call it 'desert hours.'

"So, this is my first day here, and I'm already late to work?"

"I guess so, but you're an officer, so I doubt anybody will call you on it. Are you Lieutenant Boyce by any chance?"

"One and the same, sailor. I suppose I should check in at the administration building."

"Probably, but first, I have a telegram for you. The office sent it over. If you'll just sign here acknowledging receipt, I'll get it for you."

Kevin wondered who would be sending him a telegram on his first day, but it turned out to be from Greta. When he tore it open, her message was short, but sweet.

My darling Kevin.

Thanks for the surprising invitation and, yes, I will join you in El Centro by the end of the month. See you then.

Love, Greta.

Kevin had mixed emotions. The next chapter of his inauspicious spy career was about to begin, and he really didn't know whether he was ready for it. It was one thing to 'fake' a romance in letters, quite another doing it face-to-face.

Also complicating things for Kevin was the whole Bob Higgins dilemma. He knew when he agreed to come to El Centro that he'd probably have a boss looking over his shoulder, but a delusional drunk who fancied himself some kind of base godfather? That was unexpected, and complicating.

******

Kevin parked in front of the administration building and entered through the double doors, surprising the secretary sitting there. Obviously, they didn't get many visitors. The woman was middle-aged, hair in a bun, looking more like a librarian than a secretary.

"May I help you," she asked, one eyebrow arched.

"Yes, ma'am," Kevin answered in his best midwestern drawl. "I'm Lt. J.G. Kevin Boyce reporting for duty. Is this where I report and fill out the necessary paperwork?"

"We've been expecting you, Mr. Boyce. A little late this morning, aren't we?"

"I didn't know about 'desert hours', ma'am. Sorry about that."

Her displeased look spoke volumes. Obviously, a woman to be reckoned with.

"I'm Ethel Haynes, the Captain's secretary," she offered, her hand now extended, "and the captain asked me to send you in as soon as you arrived."

Kevin gulped, and started to ask why, but thought better of it. This was reminiscent of when he reported to the *Buck*. Better to keep his mouth shut.

Just then, a small, rotund, red-faced Captain Jack Sims burst out of his office, and did a dramatic double-take, obviously not expecting an unfamiliar officer in the waiting area. "Whoa, what have we here?" he asked his secretary while giving Kevin the same once-over she had given him a minute or two before.

"This is Mr. Kevin Boyce," the secretary clarified, "the supply officer we expected earlier this morning."

She just won't turn loose of that, will, she?

The captain hesitated for a second, then smiled in recognition, and said, "Oh yes, of course, Mr. Boyce. I've been looking forward to your arrival. Please come in." He gestured toward his office door, then reached out and shook Kevin's hand a little too aggressively perhaps, as if he wanted to greet him, and get rid of him, all at the same time.

"Follow me," Captain Sims tossed over his shoulder as he turned and led Kevin into his surprisingly sumptuous office, shut the door behind them, and turned around, a conspiratorial look on his face.

"So, I understand you'll be doing a little extra curricular work while you're with us, Mr. Boyce. I just want to assure you that you'll get my full cooperation on whatever it is."

"I appreciate that, sir, but I'm hoping I won't need anything on that score. As for my job as a supply officer, I'll keep you posted."

"Of course. Of course. No problem. I get it. Hush hush," the overweight officer said as he gestured for Kevin to sit in the chair across from him. Then, he settled his ample rear end into a swiveling leather desk chair that seemed to have been widened and fortified to handle his heft.

"You know, Kevin, Bob Higgins has all the supply stuff well under control, so I can't really help there. He's a great officer and, if you just do what he says, everything'll be fine,"

Captain Sims then lowered his voice, and looked around the empty office as if it might be bugged. "But, seriously, Kevin, I'd like to know why Naval Intelligence sent you here. Is there a problem with how I'm running this place. Something I need to know, or somebody to watch out for. Because, if there is, I'm all ears. You can trust me."

"Captain Sims," Kevin said, smiling broadly in an attempt to soften the mood, "What I'm doing for them is extremely confidential, as I'm sure you understand. But I don't think I'm disclosing too much by saying it isn't about you, or this base."

"You do know we're working on the moon landing, right?" Captain Sims whispered.

"Bob said something about that."

"Oh. So, you've met Bob?"

"Briefly," Kevin replied, "I'm looking forward to knowing him better. In fact, I should get over to the supply office soon. He's probably wondering where I am."

"Yes. Of course," Captain Sims agreed. "But remember, I'll help any way I can. It's not often we get somebody from Naval Intelligence stationed here."

"I'm not Naval Intelligence, sir. I'm just a supply officer that's been asked to do some work for them. Keeping things here running smoothly is my top priority, I assure you of that."

******

Fifteen minutes later, Kevin was in the supply office introducing himself to the dozen or so sailors working there.

"Hello, men, I'm Mr. Kevin Boyce and I'll be working with you all on managing our financial accounts, inventory and warehouses. Incidentally, I come from the *U.S.S. Buck* a destroyer currently deployed in the Far East."

"Were you in Viet Nam, sir?" one of the sailors asked.

"Yes. And the Philippines and Hong Kong."

"What was the war like? Did you see any action?"

"That's a subject for another time. But yes. Not like the Marines though."

Tommy Adams, the storekeeper Kevin met at the bowling alley, piped up, "Were you the only supply officer on board, a department head?".

"Yes, Tommy, I was. But it was a very small ship, with not many officers."

"Still, why did you come here, sir? Isn't this quite a step-down?" There was a nervous tittering.

"Not really. This is a far bigger operation, as you know, and I'm here to help Mr. Higgins in any way I can. Where is he, by the way?"

"He's in Mexico," somebody in the back answered, "Tying up some loose ends on next year's food contracts."

"We buy food from Mexico?" Kevin asked.

"Yes, sir. Saves us quite a bit of money on certain kinds of meat, and vegetables as well."

"I'm just wondering about the quality. Do you do the Q.C. here?"

"We spot check, yea. But most of the heavy-duty inspecting is done at the plants. Mostly by Mr. Higgins and Chief Eliot. Not much different than when you bought food from vendors in the Far East, right?"

"Yes, of course. But we bought mostly fresh items that we couldn't get from the Navy reefer ships," Kevin replied. "Here in El Centro, I would think you can get anything you want from San Diego, fresh, within hours. But what do I know?"

"Mr. Higgins has been dealing with one major vendor in Mexicali for years. He trusts them implicitly, and we have their trucks coming in and out every day. Along with the food we get from our regular Navy channels in San Diego."

"Well, enough about that," Kevin changed the subject. "As I said, I'll be working on disbursing and stores. Today, it'll be disbursing. Is the disbursing clerk here?"

"Yes, sir. Right here. I'm First Class Petty Officer Jones at your service."

"Great. We'll start by counting the cash on hand, Mr. Jones, and going over last month's receipts and disbursements. And tomorrow, Mr. Adams, we'll begin inventorying the storerooms as part of the 'change of command' protocol. Please put a team together to help us, and we'll start at daybreak."

"Aye, aye, sir."

"Expect to work long hours for a few days, gentlemen, and, hopefully, we'll be back on a regular routine in no time at all."

Kevin started to dismiss the men, then stopped, got a big grin on his face and said, "Oh, and it's great to be on board. Look forward to working with you guys."

In response, there was a murmur of welcoming voices as well, although given the work now ahead of them, the sincerity might have been questioned. Still, all in all, Kevin was pleased with the response, and the interchange, except perhaps for the information about food coming from Mexico. That was a new one to him and he made a mental note to stop by the loading docks soon and take a look at what's in the supplier's trucks.

Something about that whole deal doesn't smell right, he admitted to himself, *and I'm not talking about the food.*

******

That night, Kevin moved into the new digs he would be sharing with Greta on the base.

It was a brand-new duplex with living room, dining room, kitchen, and three bedrooms, everything a young couple in their twenties would want but could ill afford. It was only available because NAF El Centro had overbuilt their married officers' quarters in anticipation of an expansion that had not yet materialized, and Brad had told the housing authorities that Naval Intelligence needed one unit as a base for its operations.

Greta will be thrilled, Kevin told himself. *Maybe not with the base. Or El Centro. Or the weather. But with the accommodations I was able to get. And the casual lifestyle we'll have here, just like any other American couple, except we're unmarried, and, oh yes, spying on each other.*

******

The next day, Kevin was up at four a.m., and in the office by five. He liked to be present when his men arrived, which was going to be more difficult with the base on 'desert hours.'

The team that was going to help him with the inventory was already assembled and, based on the number of locations they would have to cover, it could be a long day. On their way to the first storeroom, Kevin noticed a dilapidated reefer truck go by with 'Productos Frescos' stenciled on its side in big green letters.

"That's the first truck this morning delivering food products from Mexico," Tommy said. "We get several a day, most of them half-full. I'm not sure why we don't just schedule one full shipment a day, but that's Mr. Higgins business, not mine."

"Have you ever asked him?" Kevin asked, followed by some smothered giggling.

"You don't ask Mr. Higgins that sort of thing, Mr. Boyce," Tommy replied. "The general mess is his baby. Well, his and Chief Shaw's and Petty Officer Smith's.' They are highly protective of their domain. We just focus on ours, which is now yours too, sir."

When the crew broke for a late lunch, they still had two more storerooms to inventory. So, instead of going out, they stopped by the mess hall to pick up sandwiches. It was a converted hangar, with a small buffet line, dozens of unoccupied tables, and, scattered here and there, a few sailors eating alone. It was cavernous and uncomfortably unoccupied for a lunch hour.

"Where is everybody?" Kevin asked.

"I don't know. I never eat here," one of the crew members answered.

"Why not? It's so convenient."

"Well, for one thing, the food isn't that great. And second, most of us start work at five a.m. and get off at one. You know, 'desert hours." So, it gives us the whole afternoon free. Few of us want to stick around to get a bad meal."

"Is that typical? I see fewer than a dozen people here today," Kevin asks. "And what about dinner? More people eating here in the evening?"

"Even fewer. The only people who eat dinner here are those on duty. You have to understand, sir, with the temperatures as high as they are, and cooler temperatures two hours away in San Diego, or one hour away in the mountains, who wants to sit around on base? To do what? Play cards and sweat until we go to work again."

"I see ball fields, and gyms, and a bowling alley."

"Live here for a while, Mr. Boyce, and you'll see what we mean," Terry chimed in. "One hundred twenty degrees is very different than ninety. You don't play ball in it. Or even bowl, for that matter, unless, of course, that's all that's available."

"Even in air conditioning. I don't get it."

"You will. You officers have the O Club, which has great food and drinks for reasonable prices, and it's packed every afternoon. But, for most of us, our best alternative is to take a six-pack into the mountains and chill out. Or go fishing in a mountain lake. Or find some hiking trail, in sixty-degree weather, only an hour away. That kind of stuff is far more enticing than bad food at the General Mess."

Kevin couldn't argue with Terry's logic, and he didn't want to. His mind was now on why a base food operation that serves so few meals a day has so many trucks coming and going all the time. It didn't compute.

******

As it turned out Kevin was a little ambitious in believing they could finish the inventory in one day. The inventory wasn't completed until ten o'clock the next day and, to reward the crew who had worked much of the night before, he gave them the rest of the day off.

He had an ulterior motive, however. Kevin wanted time to follow up on a hunch.

After going home to change into blue jeans and a tee shirt, Kevin drove his car to the mess hall and parked a few blocks away. From there, he meandered through an alley, around some packing boxes, and approached the building from the rear.

Fortunately, nobody saw him, although he probably wouldn't have been recognized anyway.

There were two trucks parked at the dock, one, an official Navy vehicle with its doors wide open, and its cargo bin empty. And the other with the now-familiar logo of the Mexican supplier scrawled across its side.

Although the second truck's battered doors were lashed together by a chain, Kevin could loosen it enough to see clearly that the cargo space was fully loaded with food stocks. Either it had not been unloaded yet, or, as Kevin was beginning to suspicion, the truck was ready to leave with stolen Navy food supplies, intended for customers in Mexico.

Then, Kevin heard voices and just barely had time to scurry behind an adjoining building where he could clearly see two Hispanic men get into the truck and drive away.

Suspicions confirmed, Kevin told himself smugly, *the churchgoing, Boy Scout troop-leading Lt. Cdr. Higgins is running a food-smuggling operation that comes in from Mexico with trucks half-full, and leaves fully stocked, maybe even with food that was stolen from the Navy truck sitting beside it.*

But, I have to check out one other thing to be sure.

CHAPTER 13

The following morning Lt. Cdr.Higgins was back in the office and welcomed Kevin with open arms. All animosity from their earlier meeting at the Officer's Club seemed gone.

"Kevin, my boy. I understand you've already completed your inspections and are ready to assume responsibility for disbursing and the stores," he bellowed in a voice loud enough for everybody in the office to hear. "I'm really pleased. This will be the first time in years that we have a real supply officer in charge of those areas. I did my best to cover, but there's nothing like somebody focusing on them full-time."

"Before officially taking over, Bob, I wonder if you could show me around a little. I'd like to see the general mess, the Officer's Club, the commissary, laundry, you know, maybe look at the books, and meet some of the people who report to you."

"As you know, those are all my areas of responsibility, but, sure, let's do it," Bob answered.

"Any chance of touring NARF as well?" Kevin asked as they exited the supply office into the heat of the day.

"I'm really interested in the work we're doing there on the moon landing."

Mr. Higgins arched his eyebrows and frowned, wrestling around with how to tell Kevin something he suspected the guy already knew. "Technically, that unit doesn't report to us, but I'll be happy to arrange a visit. Let's cover all of the other areas first. OK?"

"Sure, boss," Kevin answered in the friendliest tone of voice he could muster.

When they reached the mess hall, Kevin finally had the opportunity to see the books and confirm his suspicions. The log showed hundreds of meals being served every day, at breakfast, lunch, and dinner. But Kevin knew for a fact that those numbers were inflated by a factor of two. And when he met Chief Jeff Shaw and First-Class Petty Officer Richard Smith, Kevin couldn't even look them in the eye. *These guys have to be complicit in the scam or, even worse, they are running it themselves without Higgins' knowledge,* Kevin speculated to himself. *Whatever the case, they are the scum of the earth and deserve to be taken down. Which I will certainly do.*

A few hours later, Kevin was back in the office of Captain Sims, not as a courtesy visit this time, but to report a crime. He asked for the door to be closed and methodically outlined the facts that made him conclude there was something nefarious afoot at the general mess.

The CO listened patiently but his face was a sea of emotions as Kevin presented his arguments. At one point Kevin wondered if Mr. Sims might be involved, which would make coming here a terrible mistake, but an arched eyebrow here and there, coupled with an occasional wide-eyed look of amazement, convinced Kevin that the senior officer was hearing most of this for the first time. Still, his response was surprising.

"Why are you talking to me?" The captain asked.

"Because you're in charge of the base. And because Mr. Higgins reports to you. And mostly, because I thought you needed to know so you could do something about it,"

"Like what, Mr. Boyce? What would you have me do?"

"Confront him. Arrest him. Throw him in jail," Kevin pleaded, a look of disbelief on his face. "Whatever bosses do in this kind of situation."

"I can't do that just on the basis of what you are claiming," Jack Sims countered, "But what I can do is call in my head of security, ask him to investigate, give me a report. All of which would alert Bob of our intentions and put him on notice that we are investigating. Not to mention his cohorts down in Mexico."

"Well, do that then, sir."

"But I have a better idea. Why don't you talk to your Naval Intelligence boss? You guys are experts at conducting clandestine operations, and that's what we need here. Not some goon security guy asking questions and banging heads."

Kevin remained silent. He was surprised at the depth of the captain's thinking, and a little ashamed he hadn't thought of it before. This operation required a kind of finesse the captain and his team probably lacked.

"We have no idea how deep this goes, or even whether Bob is involved, or just incompetent," the captain went on, "but we need to find the head of the snake and cut it off, or it'll resurface somewhere else, probably in another unit of the Navy."

Kevin nodded. *I was so intent on putting Bob Higgins behind bars that I couldn't look beyond my own vengeance.*

Maybe the Mexicans are running this show, and maybe Bob is just a pawn, who's asleep at the switch, or has been blackmailed or something. Maybe his underlings are orchestrating the whole thing. Who knows?

"Naval Intelligence already has you embedded in the perfect place to dig up information," Captain Sims went on, "They can build a case far better than my head of security can. And, wherever that information leads, they have the resources to prosecute and make the charges stick. It's a no-brainer."

"Okay, sir. You make a good point. I'll talk to my contact."

"Do that, and I'll bet he'll consider this case way more important than that 'tiny' thing you're already working on."

I wouldn't bet on that, sir, Kevin mused.

One week later, Brad drove over to El Centro from San Diego for a kind of summit meeting with Kevin, and to discuss what the supply officer had discovered. They met in Kevin's quarters.

Brad started by saying. "I'd love to hear about this food smuggling operation you've uncovered, but first we have to strategize what we're going to do with Greta. She'll be here soon and I'm not sure how you plan to use her."

"If you're not sure, we're really in deep shit," an angry Kevin responded, "Because I have no clue. You're the one who set up this whole operation, remember. Your idea was to exploit my relationship with her before arresting her. So, let's exploit, shall we?"

"Look, Kevin, we don't have any definitive proof that Greta's really a spy. Or at least anything that'll hold up in court. So, we need to set up a trap to confirm her guilt."

"Like what, Einstein?"

"That's what we have to figure out. Have you made contact with the NARF supply officer yet?"

"I've been a little busy, Brad, in case you hadn't noticed. Contrary to what you told me, this place is a shit show. A crooked boss. A cursed base. And the supply areas I've been assigned to haven't had any attention in months, if not years."

"Let me be clear. Your number one responsibility, Kevin, is the undercover work you were brought here to perform. Got it?"

"Yes, of course, boss. And I understand we need something from NARF to set the trap. Luckily their supply officer, and his family, will be living right next door to Greta and me. So, when she gets here, my part of the operation can get underway."

"Good. Find out all you can, about launch date, the mission's objectives, what kind of recovery vehicles they are using, samples they may bring back. Also, I'm thinking we could make up a fake 'capsule recovery' test out in the desert and see who shows up. If the Russians monitor it, that will prove our girl's guilt beyond a doubt."

"Okay. I guess that could work."

"But let's wait and see what information you can glean from the NARF guy first. We want any misinformation we use to be as authentic as possible."

"Okay. Now, can I tell you about the situation I uncovered here?"

"Of course."

Which Kevin did, in copious detail, surprising Brad with how sophisticated the food smuggling operation appeared to be. And how long it had been going on.

"Maybe it's not as 'small potatoes' as I thought," a grinning Brad concluded, and Kevin just groaned. His boss continued,

"Why don't you focus on Greta while I find out more about the Mexican guys that Bob's been hanging out with?"

*****

A few days later, Kevin picked Greta up at the San Diego airport.

She looked especially lovely coming off the plane dressed in a form-fitting, kelly-green, silk dress that hinted at what was underneath rather than advertising it.

Any red-blooded American guy would be proud to have such a girlfriend, he thought, *but I have to remember that no matter how much she seems to love me, it's all part of the act. And I mustn't fall for it.*

Not that easy, especially when, after deplaning, Greta rushed over to Kevin, threw her arms around his neck, and gave him a long kiss that was incredibly convincing.

It had been a few months now since those torrid days in Hawaii, and Greta was bursting with questions about his life since they last talked. "How was Subic Bay? As bad as you expected. Did you see any action in Vietnam? Any more typhoons? Or collisions? Did you go ashore?" And on and on…

Of course, her questions weren't as innocent now as they seemed before Brad told him she was actually a Soviet spy.

The photo shoot, for instance.

"How did that go?" She asked, her brown eyes wide-eyed and innocent, "Did the PR guy get his shot?"

"It was as fucked-up as I expected," he answered carefully, "Hundreds of near collisions. Then, a Russian trawler showed up to spoil the picture, which, to be frank, made me happy. The whole idea was bad from the get-go. I'm glad it blew up in the PR guy's face."

Surprisingly, Greta had no follow-up questions.

Her disinterest is curious, although I imagine that's what a skilled spy does, he told himself. *Her operation was a success. Why gloat about it and draw more attention to herself?*

All the way from downtown San Diego, through East County and into the mountains, Greta was surprised, and blown away by, the beauty of everything. When she visited San Diego before, she had spent most of her time at the Navy base or downtown, both of which were a little too tawdry for her taste. But she had no idea that there was such a different kind of topography directly east, only minutes from San Diego, with mountains and valleys and even, on occasion, refreshingly chilly weather.

"This is such a diverse and wonderful place to live," she commented, echoing Kevin's thoughts when he first drove over the mountains to report for duty in El Centro.

But we're not living here, sweetheart, he thought, *let's see how you enjoy our new hometown when we get there.*

"Home sweet home," Kevin whispered when they arrived at the front gate of the Naval Air Facility, and he lowered the window to show his ID card to the guard. The heat flooded in, overpowered the car's air conditioning, and made Greta recoil as if she was feeling the blast of a furnace.

"It's only for a few months. How bad can it be?" She said to Kevin once he raised the window and let the cool air fill the cabin once again. "I'm just going to lean into the whatever I find here, weather included, and enjoy it. You should do the same, sweetheart."

Good luck with that, sweet pea, Kevin thought. *Just wait until the first time you can't open your car door without getting third-degree burns on your hand. Then, we'll talk about your positivity.*

Greta's mood improved when she saw the base, and especially the duplex they were to live in. It was a brand-new one-story adobe unit, with a beautifully maintained lawn, and flower gardens all around, like a painting, just framing the house in color.

To her, it looked adorable and spacious and wonderful.

As they walked up to the porch, Greta noticed something on the stoop that seemed out of place. It was a freshly baked apple pie covered in cellophane, and next to it, a six-pack of beer in still-frosted bottles, both obviously placed there just minutes before Greta and Kevin arrived.

There was a note on top which read, "Welcome to your new home. Alex and I couldn't agree on what might please you the most. So, we each contributed something we thought might be appropriate." It was signed Binkie Hankins.

Kevin looked quickly over to the other duplex unit and saw a rustling of the curtains. Obviously, the two of them were peeking out, and Kevin motioned them to come over.

There was a wave back and Greta whispered to her 'husband,' "Do they think we're married, Kevin? I'm just curious."

"I suppose so, and there's no reason to disabuse them of that thought."

"What if they ask?"

"I guess we lie. Are you able to do that?" It came out unexpectedly.

"I'll do my best, darling," she said with a sweet look on her face.

The Hankins came out of their unit and walked sheepishly across the lawn, apologizing profusely as they came.

"I told Alex to let you get settled in first, but that's just not his style," the woman said with a slight East Coast accent, and extended her hand, "Hi, I'm Margaret Hankins, but everybody calls me 'Binkie.' And this is my husband Alex,"

She was a relatively tall young woman, dark-haired, wearing cut-off jean shorts and a bright tee shirt that read *Sunny San Diego*. She had long legs, walked like a fashion model, and the expression on her pale face was welcoming but serious, with a furrowed brow and judgmental dark eyes, peering over a regal nose, underneath which was a tight-lipped smile.

Overall, she looked imperially attractive, like she was royalty or something.

Certainly not a 'Binkie,' Kevin thought.

Alex was the opposite. He was a down-to-earth, happy-go-lucky guy with an impish, gap-toothed face that reminded Kevin of *Mad Magazine's* Alfred E. Neuman. He had red hair, big ears and a wide, lopsided, non-threatening smile that made him look as affable as his wife appeared not to be. He wasn't handsome in the traditional sense but was open-faced and friendly, the kind of guy you'd like to have a beer with.

"Hello, Kevin," he said, a big grin spreading across his face, "I'm the NARF Supply Officer, sort of your counterpart on the other side of the fence. Welcome aboard, and to you as well, Greta."

She nodded but said nothing.

"I'm pleased to meet you finally, Alex," Kevin replied, "I had planned to come over for an official visit a week or two ago but I've been up to my armpits in alligators."

"I know. We've noticed you working very long hours. 'Binkie' wanted to come over earlier to pay a social call just on you, but I convinced her to wait until your wife got here."

He looked back at Greta, and added, "And, boy, am I glad we did."

She felt a little uncomfortable with the comment, but Alex was so wide eyed and innocent-looking that she couldn't take real offense. He was the kind of guy who would just let fly with whatever comes into his mind and worry about the consequences later.

And Greta seemed OK with that.

"Well, we'll let you get to it. We just wanted to say hi," Alex said, taking a step back, obviously uncomfortable with having intruded.

"Can we offer you something? A beer, perhaps? Or a slice of pie?" Kevin joked.

"Thought you'd never ask," 'Binkie' replied immediately.

So, Greta toured her new home for the first time with people who lived in an identical unit next door. They were quick to point out what was great about the place, almost as if they were real estate agents working on commission. But the place didn't need to be hyped. Greta was genuinely blown away by everything she saw; the number of rooms, their size, how fresh everything was. To her, the duplex was like a wonderful blank canvas, crying out for her special touch to make it special.

When the Hankins left, Kevin seemed a little apologetic about the place. "I know it looks sparse, Greta, but I told them we didn't need much furniture to start, so the living room, dining room, and kitchen have furniture, but only one bedroom does. On the plus side, we have a nice patio with a barbecue grill, if it ever cools off enough to enjoy it. But it sure looks nice out there baking in the sun, don't you think? We can cook hot dogs on the lid if you want."

"Oh, darling. I love it. Love, love, love it. We'll pick up some things down in Mexico to make it homier, but it feels comfortable already. You did a great job. I love it and love you for getting it for us."

"Maybe we should give our new bed a trial run," Kevin suggested. Greta smiled sweetly at him and answered coquettishly, "I'm sure it's fine. Besides, I've got better things to do."

"Like what?"

"I don't know. Is there a crossword puzzle around somewhere?"

"Maybe down here," he answered, trying to reach down the top of her dress with his right hand. She wiggled away and turned her back to him, as his left hand crept up her leg.

She deftly pushed him away and shimmied a little, dropping her dress to the floor in one obviously practiced motion. She wasn't wearing a bra, and her light-green panties sort of matched her dress, not that Kevin was in any mood to notice the fashion statement.

Greta darted away, going from the front hall to the only bedroom with a bed in it, in record time. Kevin wasn't far behind, though, admiring her swinging ass as it disappeared around the corner. And, by the time he reached the bedroom, Greta was already testing the bed, bouncing up and down like a teen-ager, her panties now on the floor.

Kevin found himself in catch-up mode as he made a frenzied attempt to remove his trousers and underpants together, leaving them in a ball on the carpet. His shirt would have to wait, he decided, as he plunged under the covers, thinking she might wiggle away from him again. But she didn't. Instead, she leaned into him, lower body pulsating with passion, and it didn't take much touching and caressing on his part until she shuddered to a sudden climax.

Then, Kevin ripped off his shirt, and laid back against the headboard, hands behind his head, and just enjoyed the show as she grabbed his member, settled her crotch down onto it, and began moving around until he had climaxed as well. And then, when she had dismounted, and moved to her side of the bed, he kidded, "Couldn't find that crossword puzzle anywhere, but maybe I'll look again later."

Kevin watched her sit up in bed and gaze around the room, obviously pleased with everything she saw, and he couldn't help but notice how appetizing she still looked, with her tousled brown hair tumbling over her eyes, and her full, well-rounded breasts now fully exposed.

A spy? It's hard to believe, he told himself, *what she just did couldn't really be faked, could it?*

He looked at her innocent face, her smile so beguiling and sweet, in stark contrast to her tempting body, to which his eyes said yes, and his spent member said no.

"I think this bed will do," Kevin finally said, patting the heap of tangled bed coverings, "I really like it.".

Greta answered, "I'm not so sure, sailor boy. Maybe we need to test it again. You can't be too sure about these things." And, to make the point she reached for Kevin one more time. "Whoa," he said, "I agree that we shouldn't jump to snap decisions. But me and my little friend here need to rest up first."

CHAPTER 14

K evin was finishing his second cup of coffee the next morning when he heard a high-pitched toot from his driveway. It sounded strange, like somebody playing the kazoo. Turned out it was Alex on a small red scooter. He was here to take Kevin on the tour of NARF he had promised the day before.

"I'm not hopping on that death trap," Kevin shouted as he came out of his house.

"Here's your seat, buddy," Alex explained, patting the small leather seat behind him.

"Not on your life."

"You want to see what we do at NARF, right?" Alex asked. "This is your only option."

Kevin looked around, then shrugged and somehow balanced himself on the tiny passenger seat just behind the driver's seat.

"Keep your hands to yourself," Alex ordered.

"In case of emergency I'll just grab ahold of anything I can."

"If you can find it."

Touring the small NARF base on a motor scooter seemed crazy to Kevin, but it was so Alex. The guy had a wild, rebellious streak in him that was very uncommon in a supply officer.

He was in uniform, yes, but just barely, with an open shirt and regulation khaki shorts suitable for this base, perhaps, but only this base. He was lid-less, and his red hair curled over a silk scarf that was wrapped around his neck, topping off a look that was a little European, and a little ridiculous.

"We'll start with a spin around the facility," he said, "and then spend some time back at my office while I tell you about this place. As you know, I'm just the supply officer here, so I can't tell you much about operations. I know to the penny what these guys get paid, for instance. But what they do? Not so much."

"I understand that very well, Mr. Hankins. We all have our jobs to do."

On the surface it seemed that Alex wasn't a serious guy. Everything about him shouted frivolous and fun. But Kevin learned as the morning went on that nothing could be further from the truth. The guy's cartoonish grin and cavalier manner hid a deep-seeded ambition and a deceptively sharp mind.

Still, his wit and insights aside, the facility tour wasn't much.

There were only two things of interest; the parachute tower, where various recovery devices were tested, and, next to it, the so-called "engineering lab" which was housed in a large warehouse building that looked just like any other hangar on the base. But both of those facilities were locked up tight as a drum when they arrived.

So, Alex promised to get Kevin in later in the week.

The tour ended in Alex's office which, though messier than Kevin might have expected, looked like any other office on the base. Nothing special, including the paperwork Kevin could see, which was similar to what he had back on his own desk.

"So, what do you want to know?" Alex asked as he leaned back in his chair, fingers intertwined behind his head, a big grin plastered on his face.

"I don't know, Alex," Kevin responded. "Maybe what NARF does would be helpful, and how it's different from NAF, or NASA for that matter."

"At NAF, you fly things, and sometimes crash them. More often than you would like, in fact. We're the opposite. We recover things and do everything we can to keep them from crashing."

"Very insightful," Kevin responded.

"Our mission here is different than NASA in that we're trying to find a safe, error-free way to get the astronauts, and their contraband, back to earth after they've been uncoupled from the rocket. That's it," Alex said. "And NASA handles everything else."

"So you don't interact with those guys?"

Alex sat up in his chair. "Not as much as you'd think," he answered, "They just tell us how big and how heavy the recovery capsule will be, and we pretty much take it from there. We have all the best pilots, engineers and parachutists in America, right here, within one hundred yards of us. With the models they construct, we know how to get things down to the ground in one piece."

"Why isn't NASA working with the Army or Air Force on that? They would seem like more appropriate partners," Kevin asked..

"Well, Mr. Boyce, the answer to that is quite confidential, because, frankly, nobody has been officially told where the capsule will land," Alex replied. "But I'll bet you can figure it out."

Kevin stroked his chin facetiously, and guessed, "The ocean?"

Alex feigned surprise, his eyes wide and palms skyward. "Wow. They told me you were smart. But I had no idea."

Both officers smiled at Alex's sarcasm.

"So, yes," he went on, "They'll land in the ocean. Which is the Navy's bailiwick, of course. And our mission is not only to get the capsule back from the moon and safely landed in the ocean but also to get the astronauts out of the capsule before they drown, and then back to shore."

"How can you test that in the desert?" Kevin asked.

"Again, very perceptive. Although you see hundreds of parachutes in the sky every day, all with interesting types of boxes, containers, and what not hanging from them, the experimentation that involves the astronauts actually takes place offshore."

This piqued Kevin's interest. Maybe he and Brad can use this. "Do you know where?"

"Of course not. Like you, I'm just a desk jockey, with no "need to know." But, the pilots know, and therefore, anybody who hangs out at the O Club probably knows," Alex replied. "Loose lips sink ships, as the Navy preaches but that doesn't apply to airplanes, I guess. Because oiled pilots love to talk."

"I'll bet our enemies would enjoy talking to them," Kevin offered.

"I agree. As far as space goes, the Russians are very much in a catch-up mode. So, anything we're doing here would interest them greatly." Then, Alex added, "So, that means we have to protect our secrets. I'm only telling you all this because I'd like to be friends, and oh yes, you have a 'Top Secret' clearance."

"You know I have a 'Top Secret' clearance?"

"Of course. Everybody on the base knows that by now. We didn't all grow up in Kansas, for God's sake," he answered, a shit-eating grin on his face, "Not that that's a bad thing."

Later that afternoon Brad joined Kevin in his office to find out what the tour of NARF revealed.

"So, what did you learn about the moon landing?" he asked, after a perfunctory hello. "Anything we can use?"

"Not much. Alex was pretty tight-lipped and, for some reason, we couldn't get into any of the facilities," Kevin ventured.

"I'll bet there's a reason for that," Brad interjected.

"Why don't you just go to NASA and get the authorization you need? Why try to get it surreptitiously from Alex."

"It's not that easy to cross agency lines," Brad replied. "The red tape is incredible. And you'd be surprised at the lack of trust. Look, Kevin, I'm not asking you to actually spy on our own operations. Just find us something that we can twist into misinformation. That's all,"

Kevin didn't have to think very long. "I did find out that a lot of the capsule recovery testing is being done off the coast somewhere, and not here. They're actually dropping units into the ocean in order to calibrate their survivability and buoyancy."

"Do you know where off the coast?" Brad asked, "Because I'm thinking we can learn from their photo shoot playbook."

"No, I don't, but what do you mean?"

"Give Greta a fictitious location and see if any Russian trawlers show up."

"That could work."

******

The next Sunday, Greta and Kevin took a field trip to visit the marketplace in Mexicali, which had been described to them as a "must see."

They were surprised to find, not the quiet Mexican square they had envisioned, but hundreds of booths, and hordes of people, in a large section of downtown Mexicali that was cordoned off for the day. Immediately, their senses were assaulted by sights, sounds, and smells that, to Kevin at least, were pretty overwhelming. Yes, it was friendly, festive, and fun. But a little depressing as well.

There was a kind of a honky-tonk, carnival atmosphere to the place, with grubby-handed beggar kids flitting in and out of the crowd, and a few disheveled women sitting cross-legged on the pavement, some with babies on uncomfortable display, hands out, pleading for any scraps of food or money that the passersby might give them. The crowds were suffocatingly large, so large in fact that it wasn't easy to comfortably browse the booths.

This is not the experience I expected, or wanted, Kevin told himself, *Something to do once, maybe, but not to be repeated.*

Still, Greta seemed to love it. They wandered around and through the booths as best they could, looking at trinkets, art, and pottery that might spruce up their duplex. But, finding nothing of interest, Kevin cautiously asked, "So, you ready to go?"

Greta's jaw dropped, and she blurted, "Are you kidding, Kevin. We just got here, and I haven't bought anything yet. We need to elbow our way up to one of these booths so I can spend some of our hard-earned money. It's the American way."

It was Kevin's turn to be surprised, "Greta, we came to see the sights, right? It's all about the experience."

"Speak for yourself, sailor boy," she responded, "I need a, how do you say it, oh yea, souvenir. That's what I want, a souvenir. And just look at that gorgeous embroidered blouse?"

Kevin shrugged. "Hardly a souvenir. But, if you want it, let's get it, and then go?"

Greta frowned and stuck her tongue out at him, effectively communicating her displeasure. Then, she bought the blouse, and began looking for a matching skirt.

Kevin gave up on the idea of leaving any time soon. Another half-hour or so later he asked, "Can we at least find somewhere to sit down?"

Greta nodded, and they wandered down a deserted side street where they found a small park with an unoccupied bench. It was a pleasant respite from the chaos and noise, so the two of them just stretched out their legs and said nothing for several long minutes. Then, Kevin broke the silence. "So, this is more like it. I can even hear some birds chirping."

Greta leaned forward and began to talk. She said it looked like she might get a job at Imperial Valley College just outside the city. And she seemed thrilled about it, although she will be sort of a receptionist to start, then, maybe some administrative work, with a little substitute teaching tossed in "to add spice."

Then, she asked about Kevin's work, and he was able to flow into the script he and Brad had prepared, that

NARF was working on the moon landing, "but a lot of the testing is taking place off the coast of San Diego."

Greta was surprised to hear that. "There are planes and parachutes in the air every day. What are they doing?"

"Mostly testing parachutes. But the actual recovery part is being done out at sea."

"Do you know where?"

"I suspect south of San Clemente Island, away from the normal shipping lanes. That was our favorite place to test DASH when we didn't want prying eyes to see what we were doing."

Greta cocked her head, then changed the conversation back to something they had been discussing a lot lately, which was Vietnam, and how arrogant she felt it was for America to gallivant around the world 'freeing' everybody from their own circumstances.

"Recently, you said something that bothered me," she started, "About America being the land of opportunity. As if the rest of the world isn't. Do you really believe that?"

"Of course, I do," he responded, "Because we provide more opportunity and more upward mobility, for more people, than anywhere else in the world."

"I'm not sure what that is, upward mobility. Most people just want the chance to grow their crops, feed their family, and be left alone."

"They can do that, of course, but there needs to be a thriving economy around them creating markets for what they want to grow," he argued, a little too-cocky smile on his face. Kevin was in his wheelhouse.

"None of us exist in a vacuum anymore. Societies have to grow, and flourish, in order for its people to grow and flourish."

"Nice thought," Greta countered, "But, the people have to grow and flourish equally. Therein lies the rub."

"And who's going to control that?" Kevin interrupted, "In America, we give more people a chance to succeed, no matter where they come from. That's our idea of equality. And as people better themselves, they grow the economy, making everybody better off. Growing the pie is more important than dividing it equally."

Greta's back stiffened, and she got up to walk around. Then, she turned around and got in Kevin's face. "Honestly, darling, I'm not a big fan of your whole free enterprise system bullshit. Without some government oversight, it's inherently unfair. Too many people falling through the cracks. And too much poverty."

Kevin leaned in toward her, and countered, "Less poverty than anywhere else in the world and we have programs, like social security and welfare, to help those in need."

"Inadequate, in my opinion," she spat out, a pinched look on her face, "because, in such a rich country, there shouldn't be so many in need." she says. "You have the resources to take care of everybody, but the wealthy in America keep too much of it for themselves."

Kevin hesitated for a second, thinking he should steer the conversation to safer ground. Then, *what the hell*, he thought, and waded in with both feet. "You like to attack the wealthy, and I get that. They're a handy target. But they're also the ones who invest the money, create the business activity, and drive the whole economic machine. Honestly, those of us who benefit from their investments in our economy should be kissing their feet."

Greta visibly recoiled. "Kissing their asses is more like it. That's what the poor have to do to get anywhere in your country."

"That's a little unfair, isn't it, Greta?"

"Look, if America is such a shining beacon for economic success, what about your aging infrastructure? Your roads. Your trains. Your cities. Where does the money go that should be allocated to those kinds of things? I'll tell you where it goes. Back into the hands of your coveted rich people."

"Believe me," Kevin responded, "enough money is collected in taxes to rebuild our infrastructure several times over. It's a matter of priorities."

"Look, our disagreement here is pretty simple," Greta was softening her tone, "You trust the wealthy to do the right thing and I don't."

"That's a discussion for another time, Greta, but, if you're saying the wealthy are driven by self-interest, I agree with that. But so is everybody else. It's how people are wired. And, if you're saying that government has an important role to play in controlling that self-interest, I agree with that as well."

"So, you're saying I'm right."

"I'm just saying you're not all wrong."

"I'll take that as a win," Greta responded sweetly.

"OK. For now, you win," a seemingly contrite Kevin responded, "But to be continued."

"Yes, of course," Greta responded. "I enjoy our debates, sailor boy, and one thing is abundantly clear to me. You're a patriot, and I love you for that, even if you're often misinformed, and occasionally confused."

At just that moment, there was a loud explosion, and rising above the buildings across from the park was a fireball. It was as if a boiler had just exploded. People started running in every which direction, some toward it but most away from it.

"Let's just wait here," Greta said. "Our car is parked over that way, and we probably can't get out anyway until the emergency vehicles clear the area."

So, they talked about Greta's job and Kevin's and how he was embracing his new responsibilities.

"To be honest, it's a little boring," he admitted. "Not only do I have much more help than I had on board ship, but my responsibilities are considerably less. And my boss is highly protective of his areas. So, even though I know a lot about the operations he's in charge of, I have to hold my tongue."

Kevin didn't feel comfortable going into his suspicions about Bob's nefarious goings-on until Brad finished his investigating. After all, it could just turn out to be nothing.

Fifteen minutes later, with the sirens now quiet, and most of the streets deserted, Kevin and Greta walked hand-in-hand toward where the explosion had occurred. When they turned the last corner, there were still emergency crews clearing debris from what appeared to be a car bombing.

"What happened," Kevin asked an English-speaking bystander.

"Looks like some kind of gang-related violence," he answered, "Probably trying to send a message. Nobody was in the car and there were no injuries, thank God."

Then, Kevin got a closer look at the crumpled metal that used to be a car and slowly realized that it was, or used to be, his beloved Ford Falcon.

******

"Anything monumental happen on your trip to Mexicali?" Brad casually asked when he and Kevin got together at Sammy's on Monday.

"Not really. Greta and I discussed capitalism again, she bought a dress, and, oh yes, somebody blew up my car."

"What? How did that happen?"

"The police called it a random act of violence that was meant for somebody else. Evidently, there are two or three gangs in Mexicali now, and they're fighting over turf. There was another bombing elsewhere the same day. And two gang members were murdered the day before."

"Holy shit. Just bad luck, huh?"

"I don't know," Kevin answered, "You tell me. How much have you been digging around on the food smuggling thing."

"I just did a stakeout on Sammy's and identified the Mexicans Bob meets with regularly. Also, I talked to a friend of mine, a DEA agent who's familiar with the gangs in the area. He said he might be able to identify them from my description but would prefer a photo, which I said I would try to get."

"Did you tell your friend about me."

"Not by name, no," Brad answered, "I just mentioned I was working off a tip from somebody on the base."

"Okay," Kevin responded, "It just seems curious that we start investigating a Mexican gang and my car gets firebombed a week or two later."

"I agree. But, I assure you it's just a coincidence. Now, tell me about your conversation with Greta."

"She's not a big fan of capitalism, that's for sure."

"Of course not. No Russian is."

"Remember, she's not Russian. And just because she feels the same way many young Americans do these days; that doesn't necessarily make her a spy."

Brad countered, "She's attacking who we are at our core."

"So do I at times. Don't you?"

"No I don't, Kevin," a frustrated Brad replied, "And you shouldn't either. I joined the Navy to travel the world spreading our gospel of freedom, liberty, and self-reliance. And I assume you did, too."

"Yes, of course, but not blindly," Kevin answered, "Frankly, I don't think our system is perfect all the time. Elections can be messy. And capitalism isn't always fair. Some people get screwed, and some get left behind."

"That's true for every country on the planet," Brad countered, "But, in a lot of places on earth, people don't just get lost in the system. They get oppressed and killed. By their own government. You realize that, don't you?"

Kevin nodded. "I know, Brad, and I agree that, with all of our faults, our system is far better than anywhere else in the world? That's why I'm willing to put my life at risk to protect it."

Brad shrugged, and conceded, "So she hasn't turned you yet. That's good. It's hard to get a true patriot to turn, by the way."

"That's what Greta called me. A patriot. In fact, that's how she ended our discussion."

"Well, good. But, don't fall victim to her arguments. Just appear open-minded. Keep the conversations going. We want her to think she can turn you at some point,"

"Aye, aye, sir," Kevin responded sarcastically.

"Now, tell me. How did the conversation go about the testing we're doing?" Brad asks.

"I said exactly what you told me to say," Kevin replied, "That there was testing south of San Clemente Island."

"Okay, we'll see how the commies respond to that information. Anything else going on?"

"I hear there's a big parachute drop here on Thursday," Kevin responded, "They've suspended the normal Blue Angel practice session to clear the skies around El Centro. Should be quite a show. The sky will be filled with multicolored chutes."

Brad was mildly interested. "I'll watch for that. Anything else?"

"Some scientists are visiting. Alex asked if we could prepare a special dinner for them Thursday at the Officer's Club."

"Wonder what that's about?" Brad queried.

Kevin shrugged and replied, "I really don't know. But it probably has something to do with getting the moon specimens back safely."

"Can you ask Alex about that?"

"Actually, I can't," Kevin answered, "There's absolutely no reason for me to care about what the scientists are doing."

"Yes, but Greta will care," Brad argued, "and her handlers will care. It's a good opportunity to draw them out into the open."

"Brad, you're going to have to trust me on this one," Kevin replied, crossing his arms across his chest. "As you well know, Alex is no dummy. If I ask him too many suspicious questions at this point, he's going to clam up. Or worse, talk to somebody in authority about me.

Brad rubs his chin ruefully. "Okay, Kevin, but we need to keep trying to draw Greta out somehow."

CHAPTER 15

A couple of weeks later, Kevin received orders to an inventory control school in San Diego and, for him personally, the timing couldn't have been better. The *Buck* had just returned from Vietnam and Kevin wanted to get together with his old shipmates anyway. So, he asked some of them to meet him at the hotel where he would be staying, and they agreed.

The drive over to San Diego from El Centro was uneventful and Kevin checked into his hotel right about the time they had agreed to meet. Seeing nobody in the lobby, Kevin took the elevator up to his room on the third floor where he dumped his overnight bag on the lumpy-looking bed, then opened the drapes to enjoy the view. Instead of the bay or the skyline, though, he was treated to a close-up look at the San Diego airport terminal. Not that inspiring. Still, the room price was right.

Then, after freshening up, he went down the back stairs and exited into the lobby, excited to see his friends. But they weren't anywhere to be seen, just heard. Among the most recognizable voices was Buddy Penn's hearty and unbridled laughter coming from the bar off the lobby, and

Adam West's shrill voice as he finished some probably inane story that still set off a crescendo of laughs from the already tipsy Navy officers.

Kevin managed to slip in unnoticed, and surprised everybody by asking in a loud voice, "Hey, sailors, is the sun over the yardarm yet?"

Joe Thrasher came forward, and answered, "It's been over the yardarm for hours now, Pork Chop. Where ya been, buddy?"

Kevin looked at his watch and responded, "I'm right on time."

"Not *Buck* time, especially when there's partying to be done. We've been here for over an hour, buddy."

Then, they all came forward to shake the supply officer's hand or clap him on his back. Everybody was grinning and seemed thrilled to see their old friend again. One face though was unfamiliar, and he introduced himself to Kevin, "I'm the new deck officer, Tom Jenkins. I've heard a lot about you, Pork Chop."

Kevin grimaced, then glanced around the room asking, "By the way, where's the supply officer who replaced me? What was his name? Big Ed, as I recall."

"Big Ed is no more," Joe replied, "A moment of silence, please. He didn't last two months under Captain Riley, who of course was used to your impeccable, kiss-ass service. So, right now we're without a supply officer and, frankly, things couldn't be better."

"I'm sure," Kevin responded, "Who needs to be fed and paid anyway?"

Adam chimed in, "Apparently, we do, because the captain tried to get you back. He said the higher ups wouldn't even consider it. I wonder why?"

"What *are* you doing now, by the way?" Buddy asked. "Last I heard you were headed to a deserted airfield out in the middle of nowhere, to do not much."

Kevin paused, wrestling around with exactly what to say.

"Well, that's not far off. I'm stationed at a naval air facility in El Centro, California. It's not deserted but appears to be at times."

"Never heard of it," somebody piped up.

"Isn't that a couple of hours inland," Joe asked, "In the Imperial Valley?"

"That's right, only it's hardly the kind of valley you're picturing. It's a desert, about 120 degrees in the shade right now. No ships but lots of airplanes, boiling in the sun, like the rest of us."

"So are you the senior supply officer?" Joe wondered.

"No. I'm an assistant, in charge of disbursing and stores."

There were confused looks until Adam posed the question, "I don't get it, Why the hell was that more important than what you were doing for us?"

"You'll have to ask the guys in Washington. I'm just their pawn."

"You're nobody's pawn, Kevin. But I won't probe further. I'm sure they had their reasons."

"Thanks for that. So, how were things in Vietnam after I left?"

"About the same, although things really heated up for the Marines we put ashore. Those guys are still suffering. It's certainly not the cakewalk we thought it would be."

In an attempt to lighten the mood a bit, Joe interrupted, "Enough about the war. Let's update Kevin about how we pranked the Captain in Yokohama."

"I'll handle that," Buddy Penn chimed in, "Well, knowing the Captain's wife was going to be meeting the ship there, we all pooled our money and hired a young Japanese woman, along with five little Asian kids, to greet him when he disembarked. They all came up to him hollering 'Papa-san, Papa-san,' right in front of Mrs. Riley. She wasn't pleased."

The room exploded in laughter, although Kevin was the only one hearing it for the first time. "I wonder how the Captain talked his way out of that one.".

"He's probably had to explain worse," somebody added.

Then, Joe talked about the time a reserve officer came onto the ship by helicopter. He was there for summer duty. But he got seasick immediately, ran to the nearest head, which was in the captain's in-port cabin and threw up on the captain who was on the throne quietly reading a book.

"As you know, Kevin, when we're at sea, Captain Riley is always in his cabin, up on the bridge," Elmer Bess added, "He's never in his in-port cabin. So, I sent the poor guy in there, feeling there was no risk. Big mistake."

"What was that guy's name again?" Joe asked.

"Who cares?" several guys answered in unison.

When Kevin finally left the party, he was so jacked up, he hoped he'd be able to rest. Fortunately, he slept OK, woke up early, and even stayed awake during the highly entertaining lecture explaining the LIFO (Last In, First Out) method of efficiently managing inventory.

Ain't being a supply officer the best, he said, mostly to convince himself. *Can't wait to get back to my real job, which is Greta.*

*****

When Kevin got back to his office there was an urgent message that a Lt.Cdr. Smith wanted to meet him for lunch at Sammy's Bar and Grill. When he arrived right on time the place looked, and smelled, exactly the same as when Kevin was last here, and Sammy himself was tending bar again.

So, the wise ass in Kevin looked around dramatically, then nodded toward the bar and commented, "Very nice Sammy. I like what you've done with the place. Did you remodel or something?"

"Not since 1940," was the reply.

"We'll, it's nice, very retro."

"That's what we were shooting for," the bartender responded, with a smile on his face. Kevin always liked to kid around with Sammy after entering, if only to give his eyes time to adjust to the dark. When they did, he saw Brad in a corner booth, glaring at him.

"Long time, no see," Kevin greeted the intelligence officer as he slid in across from him, "Did you miss me?"

But Brad wasn't in the mood for levity. He immediately confronted Kevin. "Where the hell have you been?"

"At a school in San Diego. Why?"

"Never do that again, pal. I'm your boss and I need to know where you are at all times. This operation always takes priority.You got that. No more schools, or trips to Mexico, or whatever, unless I approve it."

Kevin recoiled, surprised by the intensity of Brad feelings. He was right, of course, but the strength of his emotions, and how much control he wanted, was surprising. Obviously, Kevin should have told him about the school. That was inexcusable. But, having to get permission for anything he did in the future seemed a bit too much.

"We need to touch base regularly now. There's too much happening right now," Brad explained.

"OK. I'll bite. What's happening?"

But Brad was still mumbling about coming over to El Centro and having his undercover agent leave for San Diego for a week. He couldn't turn loose of it.

"Please, Brad. What's so urgent?"

"Well, for one thing, this food scandal thing is much bigger than even you imagined. The Mexicans that Bob meets with regularly are leaders of a drug gang headquartered in Mexicali and, yes, I believe they are paying Bob for excess food from your General Mess. They bring in trucks half-empty and leave almost full. How Bob covers the shortages I don't know."

"I think I do," Kevin interrupted, "He just pads the number of meals served."

"What do you mean?"

"At this base, because of a thing called 'desert hours,' very few people eat lunch or dinner in the General Mess, but his records probably show a healthy attendance. I'm going to check that out," Kevin explained. "And, then, he sells the Mexicans the leftover food."

"I'll leave the proof of all that up to you," Brad said. "But here's the kicker. When the trucks enter the United States, they're about three-quarters full of food, but when they reach NAF El Centro, they're only half full."

"No big deal. They probably have other customers."

"They don't. The trucks stop at a nondescript, out-of-the-way warehouse in downtown El Centro before going on to NAF. They are delivering something to that warehouse."

The implications were beginning to dawn on Kevin. "Who owns the warehouse?"

"The ownership records are complicated but we believe a title search will reveal that it's owned by the gang itself, and they are unloading smuggled goods there, probably drugs."

"Holy shit," Kevin reacts viscerally, "You think Bob is involved in a drug smuggling ring on top off the food scam?"

"I didn't say that. He might just be making money on the food and totally oblivious to the rest, but we need to figure out his level of involvement before proceeding any further."

"What do you want me to do, boss."

"Nothing, Kevin. I'm now officially working with my friend at the the Drug Enforcement Agency and I suspect we'll jointly interrogate Mr. Higgins at some point to see how much he knows," Brad answered.

"So, them bombing my car in Mexicali? That could have been a warning?"

"I just don't believe that. They would have gone after my DEA friend, or me, or Bob first, but you? That doesn't make much sense."

"Okay. But your assurance doesn't make me feel any safer."

"Well, this news might. No Russian trawlers showed up at the location we gave Greta."

"Meaning what?"

"Maybe she's not a Russian agent after all."

******

A week later, Tommy Adams rushed into Kevin's office. No knock, no salute. Just a torrent of words. "Did you hear that Mr. Higgins killed himself this morning?"

"Holy shit, no."

"What a shock. I was with him yesterday. Seemed perfectly normal. In a good mood…"

"Slow down, Tommy. Are you sure about this?"

"It's all over the base now. Carbon monoxide poisoning, they say. He hooked up a hose up to his car's exhaust. Also, burned some papers in a trash can. But, no suicide note, as far as anybody knows."

Kevin's eyes opened wide, his jaw dropped, and his mind began racing.

To most it would make no sense. Bob had a wonderful wife and six adorable kids. Seemed to be respected both on and off the base. But, if he was about to be exposed as a thief, or worse, well, that could have triggered his action. I wonder if Brad and the DEA confronted him yet.

But first, before calling Brad, Kevin needed to talk to Captain Sims, and find out what the plan was for the department going forward. The CO answered on the first ring.

"Kevin. Thanks for calling. I feel terrible about Bob. Just don't understand why. It's really tragic."

"I agree, Captain. Shocking. On the surface he seemed to have it all."

No reason for Kevin to bring up the food smuggling scam again. Better to touch base with Brad first, and figure things out from there.

Then, appropriately, Captain Sims assumed control of the base situation. "Of course, Kevin, you'll take over the department for now. You need to gather the Supply Department staff together as soon as possible to comfort them and discuss responsibilities going forward. I know Bob had responsibility for all of the food and beverage operations. Right?"

"Yes sir. General mess, clubs, bowling alley, etc. I manage disbursing and all of the store rooms."

"OK. So, as soon as possible, you need to initiate change-of-control procedures, including an audit of everything Bob had control of, inventories and the like. I want you to sign off on everything by the end of the week, so we can go into the new month fresh and clean.

Fresh and clean, Captain Sims? Really?.

****

The next day, Kevin was busy at his desk when he got a call from the guard at the front gate.

"Mr. Boyce. There's a woman here to see you," he dutifully reported, "Name's Sally Thomas. Says she knows you from college or something. Should I let her in."

Oh, oh. Fortunately, Greta's at work, but I'll have to be discreet anyway. Wouldn't want anybody to see Sally and tell Greta, especially at this point.

"I'll come meet her. Thanks."

Kevin couldn't believe Sally was actually here, in town, at the base.

Who comes to El Centro? he asked himself. *I've talked to Sally a few times since our date in Del Mar, and she never hinted she would visit. Although that could be exactly the kind of sanity check I need right now. Sometimes God works in mysterious ways.*

Kevin took her to the Officer's Club because, well, there was nowhere else on the base they could go. The old standbys were there, undoubtedly lamenting Bob's passing. Also, clustered over in the corner were a dozen or so civilians, most likely the technicians from NASA he had heard were coming to the base. So, he guided Sally to a table on the other side of the room, far away from their commotion, and signaled the bartender that they wanted two draught beers.

"So, what brings you to El Centro?" Kevin began the conversation with the obvious question.

She smiled coquettishly, "You, silly. You're why I'm here. I was offered the opportunity to run a motivational meeting for our sales reps, and I jumped at it."

"Not much competition, I suspect."

She grinned, her dimples prominent, as the bartender set down two frosted mugs.

She's really an attractive woman, Kevin acknowledged to himself. *She has managed to mature gracefully without losing any of her girlish charms. Maybe when all this nonsense is over..."*

"I've missed you," she said, the beer foam still on her upper lip. "We had a lovely dinner in San Diego. Then, a few phone calls. Then nothing. What gives?"

What gives? How to answer that? This is one of those situations where, if I want to keep Sally in the picture, the truth won't work.

"I'm sorry, Sally, but I've been insanely busy, first trying to get my arms around things here, and now, well, my boss committed suicide yesterday."

"Oh my God, I'm so sorry Kevin. And then, I show up to complicate things."

"You're showing up may be just the tonic I need, Sally."

"I hope you're not just being gracious, Kevin," she pondered, "I can go anytime you want. This was just a spur-of-the-moment thing, and we can easily postpone it."

"And leave me to wallow in my self-pitying thoughts? No, you need to stay. I don't have many friends on the base, and I need one right now. You've been elected."

"Talk away. I'm listening."

So, Kevin told her about his troubled relationship with Bob, how he didn't like him, or respect him, and the challenges he'd faced working alongside him. He didn't mention his suspicions that Bob was a drunk, and probably a crook, partially because it would be unseemly at this point. "But, the crazy thing is, I feel guilty about his death. If I had treated him better, would he still be around? That's what I wonder."

"Okay. I get your angst. It's part of the grieving process. But it's rubbish," she responded in a not-so-surprising way. "Don't be like that, Kevin. Blaming yourself for something you had nothing to do with. We both know the guy didn't kill himself because he wanted you to like him."

"It wasn't that so much," he began, but didn't finish. What Kevin didn't know was whether his suspicions about the food smuggling operation played a role in Bob's death, and whether Brad even talked to him about it. But he couldn't talk to Sally about that right now.

"You mentioned not having many friends on the base. Do you have at least one?" Sally asked. "A person who you can discuss your thoughts with honestly."

Kevin thought for a moment. His best friend on the base was obviously Alex, but he can't be honest with him just yet. And his very best friend anywhere, the one he can be most honest with, is surprisingly, Brad, who he talks to regularly but seldom about feelings.

"By the way, there was another reason I wanted to see you today," he heard Sally saying. "We have our annual Avon sales conference coming up. I'm going to be honored at the dinner. No big deal but I'd like you to be my date, if you can do it."

"Honestly, Sally, I can't even think about that right now. There's too much on my mind." Kevin answered truthfully. But, also, given the Greta situation, he can't imagine trying to explain to her that being Sally's date is no big deal. Better to just punt that decision down the field for now.

"Okay, I get it, But it's real important to me. And I plan to follow up in a week or two. So, be ready, Kevin. Okay?"

CHAPTER 16

The next morning, Kevin got a call from Captain Sims. It was short and sweet. "I need to see you in my office right away. Something has come up."

When Kevin walked into the office, he was shocked to see Brad there, alone, sitting in a chair next to the coffee table.

"What are you doing here?" Kevin queried.

"I figured it was time to lay all of our cards on the table. I just gave Captain Sims a quick rundown on our activities, and he felt you needed to be here, too,"

Just then, Jack Sims walked back in and plopped his hefty body on the couch. There was a smile on his face. He seemed to be enjoying whatever intriguing story Brad had just shared.

"So, Kevin," he began, "This Naval Intelligence Officer has been updating me on your activities. You've been a busy man."

Kevin didn't know how to react. He looked at Brad pleadingly, imploring him to clarify things. *How much of the truth have you shared with Captain Sims? And, therefore, how much can I share? Or, maybe more appropriately, how many of your lies would you like me to corroborate?*

"Perhaps it would be best, Captain, if I summarized what we talked about," a pensive Brad finally said."And then, Kevin, you can add to it as you see appropriate."

Kevin nodded in relief. *This ought to be interesting.*

"I told the captain that we assigned you to this base with one very specific objective, which was to entice a Russian spy to come live with you here so that we could use her as a conduit for passing on misinformation to the Russians. It was our intent to milk the relationship as best we could, and then arrest her."

So far, so true, Kevin silently acknowledged.

"But things got complicated when she didn't pass on the information we wanted her to, and then, the informant who had outed her as a spy recanted. Turns out he didn't even know Greta. He was just trying to earn favors from us."

"You mean…" Kevin began.

"Yes, Kevin. Turns out she wasn't a spy after all."

"When did that happen?" Kevin blurted out. "And why didn't you tell me?."

"I found out a day or two ago. I've been waiting for the appropriate time to let you know," Brad answered, "But I've been busy as well. With the help of DEA, we've confirmed that the late Bob Higgins was indeed involved with a gang in Mexico who was using their food contract with NAF El Centro as a coverup to smuggle in marijuana. But probably other drugs as well."

"You know that for a fact, Brad?" Kevin asked.

"Yes, I do. Two nights ago, the Drug Enforcement Agency stopped one of the gang's trucks on its way to deliver food here and found marijuana bricks packed among the canned goods. I was on my way to interview Mr. Higgins about that when I found out he was no longer with us."

"So, he killed himself because he didn't want to meet with you?" Kevin asked.

"Or because he knew the jig was up. Or maybe he didn't kill himself at all."

"What do you mean by that?"

"I'm thinking the gang might have staged his suicide just to shut him up. And, by the way, I now believe the gang did in fact blow up your car as a warning. It's pretty clear they knew you were sniffing around."

Kevin was confused So many thoughts and questions were running through his head, but the main one was self-serving. He asked, "What happens now, and am I safe?"

"That's what Captain Sims and I have been discussing. Now that they're knee-deep in this thing, the DEA will take over the investigation, and we are going to be out of it. A new supply officer will be brought in to replace Bob Higgins. You're to hold down the fort until he gets here, and then be reassigned somewhere else, out of harm's way."

"So, no change of command. No audit."

"It looks like, before committing suicide, Bob burned the attendance records anyway," the captain weighed in. "So, if there was a scam, it might be hard to prove at this point. And do we really need to prove it? The operation is shut down, the main player on our end is dead, and the biggest issue, the drug smuggling part, is in better hands than ours. What's the point of us stirring the pot any more than we have?"

"Good point," Kevin agreed, "But, Brad, what about our operation?"

"We need to talk about that, but let's not waste any more of the good Captain's time. Can we go somewhere private?"

"How about my office?"

****

The forlorn Brad who showed up in Kevin's office fifteen minutes later bore no resemblance to the cocksure Brad that had so effectively controlled the meeting with Captain Sims only fifteen minutes before.

Once seated, he looked up, his eyes red, and surprisingly began to apologize.

"Sorry, Kevin, for dragging you into this mess in the first place. And pulling you away from your ship at such an important time."

"Why? That's the only question I have. As a friend, please explain to me your rationale."

"That's easy. I was fully convinced that Greta was indeed a spy and that she stayed with you just to get intel. All I had to do was prove something I already knew. Of course, now, I realize I couldn't prove it because it wasn't true."

"I was the opposite, as you know, especially in the beginning," Kevin reiterated. "The idea that she was a spy seemed ludicrous to me. What agent would spend hours with a lowly Ensign, romance me even, when I had nothing of value to give her."

"It turns out you were right. But I saw things differently. I knew Russian spy agencies think long-term. I thought they were just developing you as a source and, at times, I even wondered whether they had already flipped you. I was so myopic."

"So what happens now?" Kevin asked.

"I'm being reassigned, but I don't know where or when," Brad answered carefully. "I staked my career on this operation, and I suspect my next posting will be to a desk job somewhere way off the beaten track."

"I'm really sorry."

"Maybe Kansas," Brad asked facetiously. "Is it nice there?"

Kevin shrugged, happy that Brad hadn't totally lost his sense of humor. Then, he wondered aloud, "What about me and Greta?"

"I guess that's up to you," Brad responded with a wink. "She's not after you to get information. That's for sure. So, it must be something else. Maybe she's in love, If so, you're a very lucky man."

"Don't I know it? Still, it'll take awhile for me to fully trust her again."

"I get that, my friend. But, hey, she's worth the effort. Right?"

That's true. Kevin acknowledged to himself. *And knowing that she was an innocent in this whole affair will only make me love her more.*

"Switching subjects," Kevin asked, "do you believe the Mexicans killed Bob Higgins?"

Brad looked down for a minute, either gathering his thoughts or trying to figure out how to phrase his answer.

"You know, Kevin. It's a real possibility. But maybe I wanted to think that in order to absolve me of any guilt. He knew I was going to talk to him. Maybe he just couldn't face up to that."

"Too embarrassed? Too ashamed?"

"It's a possibility. Still, suicide is the worst crime imaginable, because there are so few answers to the questions everybody has, and so many victims."

"So, will I see you again?"

"Highly doubtful, Kevin. I'll let you know where my next duty station is, But I'll probably leave the Navy," Brad replied. "If I do, there's a friend of mine, name of Alexander. He'll always know where to reach me."

Then, he wrote down a phone number on a piece of paper and handed it to Kevin. "But don't call him unless it's really important."

****

Kevin burst through the front door, tossed his lid on the couch, and called out, "Greta, where are you? We're going out."

She came around the corner and deftly sidestepped his lunging bear hug. Then, with her right hand planted on his chest, she asked, "What got into you, Mr. Lover Boy?"

"Maybe you don't recognize it, but this is me in a good mood," he joshed.

"Well, tone it down a touch and tell me what this is all about."

"We're going to an Italian restaurant for a romantic dinner."

"I didn't know there was such a thing in El Centro," she queried.

"The chef might be Mexican, but I'm told the food is excellent, and Alex says it's the best Italian place in town."

"High praise indeed, although it's probably the only Italian in town," Greta responded.

No matter, Kevin told himself, *Alex said it had candles and checkered tablecloths and wine. What more do I need for this special 'apology' dinner?*

He intended for this event to signify the beginning of a new era of trust between the two of them. It's as if a huge weight has been lifted from his shoulders and he was now free to do, or say, anything he wanted to.

The restaurant turned out to be perfect for a romantic 'apology' dinner. It may have been a caricature of what an

Italian restaurant should look like but for Kevin, who had never been to Italy anyway, it was perfect.

Once seated in a small booth beside Greta, Kevin turned to her and said he was sorry, genuinely sorry. Greta had a puzzled look on her face. "For what?" she asked.

"For ever doubting you," he said.

"Okay. Didn't know you did. But I'll certainly accept your apology, as long as it comes with wine and pasta."

"That it will," Kevin confirmed, and ordered a carafe of Chianti. When each of them had a full glass, he proposed a toast. "Here's to an honest and trusting relationship going forward." Greta clinked her glass against his but said nothing.

Kevin was feeling especially loving as he asked about Greta's new job at Imperial Valley College and discussed the new John Wayne movie and the Beatles 'Help!' album, which was all the rage at the time, all safe subjects for a night of frivolity and 'apology.'

Then, as so often happened with them, and a lot of couples those days, the subject turned to politics, with Greta putting Kevin on the defensive quickly.

"Surely you're not one of those Americans who just wraps himself up in the American flag," she posited, her chin jutting forward, "And spouts meaningless slogans without thinking about what's really behind them."

Kevin had a big grin on his face. He'd rather enjoyed their debates in the past but, with knowing she's not a spy, he could now argue his points more freely, and eloquently.

He responded, "Like freedom and justice for all? "

Greta nodded her head emphatically while she downed the last of her first glass. "Exactly. What does that mean? Everybody wants freedom and justice, of course, but there are tradeoffs."

"Like what, for instance?" he asked, refilling her glass.

"First of all, people don't have total freedom in any civilized society. The essence of a social contract is to trade some freedoms for security, justice, and your favorite word, opportunity," Greta answered, a smug look on her face.

"Yes, it is my favorite word, because it's opportunity that sets America apart."

Greta sighed, as if she can't believe what he's saying. "It's incredibly naïve to believe that opportunity exists only in the U.S. In fact, developing countries offer even more opportunity at times, don't they?"

"Look, I'm not saying it doesn't exist elsewhere. I just think that, with our individual freedoms and unfettered free markets there's a much better chance of making it here than in other countries."

"Really? And that's based on your vast experience with other countries and cultures?"

Kevin had no immediate reply. She was right, of course. Much of what he believed came not so much from first-hand experience but from what he'd been told through the years, from his father and uncles mostly, who all served in Europe during the war.

"We may need another carafe with dinner," Kevin offered, in an attempt to lighten the mood. But Greta was having none of it. She moved away from Kevin in the booth and turned toward him, a sure sign the verbal battle was just beginning. Then she started lecturing, as if she was explaining something to a child.

"All the words people use to describe a social contract with a government," she explained, "Democracy. Capitalism. Socialism. Communism. Monarchy. You name it. All of them deal with how much freedom people are willing to give up in order to live a secure and comfortable life. There are no perfect societies or imperfect ones. Not even your beloved America, sweetheart."

Greta paused to finish her glass, and then pointed to it, her way of saying they needed another carafe.

Then, she continued, "All countries have laws and customs based on negotiated agreements through the years, on what their people want, or will tolerate, in order to have a government that gives them what they need."

Kevin ordered the carafe, then, arched one eyebrow, and argued, "Yes, but the people within a society have to agree on what they'll give up, through some form of democratic process."

"Agreed. But, if they choose communism, as an example, like they have in Vietnam, who are you to question their choice?" Greta argued.

"But, Greta," Kevin blurted out, his face reddening, "We've been through this before. The Vietnamese didn't choose Communism. Or, at least, the South Vietnamese didn't. Communism is being forced on them."

Greta rolled her eyes. "Look, Kevin. The fight in Vietnam is a lot like your civil war. They are trying to unify, under one set of beliefs, with a single government who will enforce those beliefs. Like you did with slavery."

"Actually, I think it's the opposite. In Vietnam, the North is trying to enslave the South, not free the slaves, like the North was in our country."

"You don't know what North Viet Nam is trying to do. You're just inserting yourself into a conflict you don't really understand."

Kevin squirmed a little in his seat, knowing there was some truth to what she was saying. Then, he answered carefully. "The South Vietnamese government asked us to help protect their right to be a free, equal, and just democracy. We have an obligation to do that."

Greta moved further away from Kevin and faced him even more directly. "There are those words again." She jabbed the table with her finger to punctuate each of her points. "Freedom, justice, equality. As if you have a monopoly on them."

She seemed to be trying to escalate things, which was the last thing Kevin wanted on this evening of reconciliation. So, in order to keep the peace, he smiled broadly, shrugged, and jabbed his finger onto the table, punctuating each word as he spoke.

"We.....Need....To....Order....Dinner."

Greta grinned but leaned in and asked, "If you were convinced that America had to get out of Vietnam, would you go to Canada to make your point?"

Kevin tried unsuccessfully to keep his eyes locked on hers, but he had to look away. Greta's unblinking and beautiful brown eyes were too disarming for him. Then he looked back up and said, "Probably not."

"Because the Canadian government can't be trusted to give you freedom, justice, and equality?"

"No. Because I'm an American."

Greta smiled wistfully, then, looked away as she said "I rest my case, sailor boy."

"And I rest mine," Kevin replied, "What are you going to order for dinner?"

"I'm thinking about spaghetti and meatballs," she answered.

"Have you tried the veal parmigiana? I hear it's great," he proposed.

There's a brief pause. Then, Greta blurted out, "That's so American of you, Kevin. Even when we're talking about something as European as Italian food, you think you know best."

They stared at each other stonily for a minute. Then, Greta stuck her tongue out and they laughed before playfully embracing.

"Don't get me wrong. I love America," Greta continued, then, with a wink, "just not all Americans."

And, with that, their latest philosophical discussion came to an amicable draw, which Kevin chalked up as a win. At the end of the evening, over two glasses of limoncello, Kevin made a toast, "May we meet again when the sun is over the yardarm."

"I remember that. It's one of those quaint Navy customs," a wide-eyed Greta recalled. "Something about the masts. And drinking. And fellowship."

"Good memory."

"Good custom. I love how you've embraced the Navy, sailor boy," Greta whispered, snuggling up to him. "Almost as much as I love your beautiful sky-blue eyes." And she kissed him passionately, something he wasn't sure was going to happen earlier in the evening.

Then, he remembered another reason for having dinner with Greta. He pulled away enough to say, "There's a big dinner/dance coming up at the Officer's Club. It's very formal and fancy and fun. At least that's what Alex tells me. They want to go with us. You up for that?"

"Of course, Kevin," she answered, "I'd like nothing better. So, look, I understand what 'fun,' is, but what do you mean by 'formal?' And 'fancy?'"

"The whole works. I'll be wearing my dress whites and you should wear your very best gown."

"I would do that, for sure…if I had a 'very best gown,'" she said, pouting like a little girl. "Maybe you need to invite one of your glitzier girlfriends," she teased.

"You're the glitziest I've got," he teased back, "so I'm thinking, maybe we should drive into San Diego next weekend and pick something out for you."

Greta grinned and answered, "I'd like that very much."

CHAPTER 17

So, on Saturday, Greta and Kevin made the two-hour drive through the mountains to San Diego and, after checking into the Grand Horton Hotel, drove down to the May Company department store in Mission Valley, where they began a search for her perfect gown.

It turned out to be an unexpected pleasure for Kevin. He just planted himself in one of the overstuffed chairs near the changing rooms and let Greta put on a spectacular performance modeling dresses for him. Each one she tried on looked better than the one before it. Whether it was a sleek body-hugging number with sequins, or a frilly, feathery one with a plunging neckline, Greta had the body and presence to make them seem crafted especially for her.

But it wasn't just her figure, or her poise. Her face seemed to adjust beautifully to each gown the way the designer might have hoped. Her expression was cool and elegant for some, hot and sexy for others. Eventually, they both opted for a sophisticated, dark-blue, strapless satin dress that, to Kevin's eye, made Greta look like royalty, serene and sophisticated, but also highly approachable, like the girl next door. A next-door Princess, what a killer combination.

******

The weekend of the big party arrived, and Kevin was still playing catch-up at work. However, now that Bob was gone, his primary duty was to oversee all social activities at the Officer's Club, and that included this party. Thankfully, the Officer's Club had built up a sizable financial reserve through the year and Kevin was determined to spend it all on one spectacular evening.

His craziest extravagance was a flower-covered bridge built just for the occasion. It originated in the parking lot, under a huge wreath of flowers, and then crossed over the east end of the lighted pool to the patio beyond. Floating in the pool were islands of gardenias, each sporting a spotlight with rotating multi-colored beams that would shoot off into the night sky. When each couple descended from the bridge they were to be announced to the rest of the party as if they were celebrities.

Then, the couples had a choice.

They could turn right toward the pool, where the bandstand was located, and either dance, or stand at poolside tables sipping fancy drinks. Or they could turn left into the clubhouse itself, where they would find elegant linen-covered tables sprinkled about, each with their own unique, hand-designed, floral centerpieces. Surrounding the tables Kevin had three spectacular bars, all featuring back-lit ice sculptures, and serving Manhattans, daiquiris, martinis, or margaritas. Kevin worked on his masterpiece until fifteen minutes before the first guests arrived and, after a quick look around, hustled back to their duplex to change into his dress whites.

Greta was there, of course, and already dressed for the party. She posed for him when he entered the bedroom, her hands demurely clasped in front of her, like the virginal Princess she definitely was not. *What a beautiful woman,* Kevin thought as he looked at her admiringly. *And she's all mine. No secrets. No complications. We're just going to have the time of our lives tonight.*

Her blue dress looked even more spectacular now than when he saw it on her in the store. Her hair was swept up into a bouquet of curls piled high on top of her head, leaving her neck and shoulders exposed. A pearl necklace completed the look. The highlight, however, was her face, with a well-defined jaw line, lush lips and flawless skin.

"You are . . . a vision of loveliness," he said.

"And you are so full of shit," she replied. "You better stop gawking and get ready. Alex and 'Binkie' are picking us up in fifteen minutes." He tried but when the doorbell rang, Kevin still wasn't close to ready yet.

So, he watched through the bedroom door as Greta answered the front door. Standing there, at attention, in his dress whites, was an almost unrecognizably elegant Alex, with a wicked smile curling up the corners of his mouth.

He saluted Greta and then bowed ceremoniously from the waist, kissing her hand.

"So lovely to see you again, my dear. You look lovely. I'm here in my pumpkin to transport you to the ball."

Greta smiled sweetly, "What a wonderful pumpkin driver you are, Mr. Alex. And more of a gentleman than I'd been told. When one asks for a pumpkin to pick you up these days, you never know what you're going to get."

"Did that piece of crap husband of yours say I wasn't a gentleman," Alex said in mock anger, his palms out. "I will have you know I was commissioned an officer and a gentleman."

"I heard that," Kevin yelled out from the bedroom. Then, he entered, still trying to clasp his highly polished belt buckle. "And it takes more than a commission to make a gentleman."

Although Kevin's stark white uniform was not as dramatic as Greta's gown, he still looked pretty debonair, with his polished brass buttons, and his chest sporting a few colorful medals that effectively advertised he was once in Vietnam. And when he put on his lid, the greased-up brim shimmering in the hall light, the look was complete. The only problem was it would be the same look every guy at the party was going to be sporting. Oh well.

The drive to the party was all of three blocks long but, of course, it wouldn't do to walk there. What celebrities arrive on foot? And, although the two couples pulled up in an old car rather than a limo, it felt like Academy Award night to them. They gracefully exited the car onto a red, carpeted runner, with a few people on each side of it, politely applauding. Then, as an added touch, up stepped a photographer, startling each couple with an exploding flashbulb, just like in Hollywood.

As Kevin and Greta crossed the bridge, the crowd broke out in applause, maybe appreciative of the work he'd put in to make the party special but, more likely, recognizing the vision he had brought as a date. They snuggled together for a second at the top of the bridge, then kissed, after which Greta whispered into Kevin's ear, "This is fantastic. We've come a long way from Athens, baby."

"And Wichita too."

"And Uberlingen."

Each waved one hand back and forth as they came off the bridge, milking every moment, then they melted into the crowd of partygoers, who accepted them with open arms, as one of their own, with everybody laughing, kissing, and toasting anybody who would listen.

"Oh, Kevin, before we sit down, let's dance," Greta pled. "I don't remember ever dancing with you before."

So, she led him to the dance floor, where they were joined by Alex and 'Binkie.' The first song was a ballad, and Greta snuggled up close to Kevin, put her head on his shoulder, and they glided around the floor as if they had been doing it forever. Next up was the band's rendition of the Chuck Barry classic, *Maybelline,* which gave Greta a chance to showcase her moves while Kevin hung on for dear life. She jumped, wiggled, and shimmied across the floor, thankful that her gown stayed in place, although many eyes were on her, just in case it didn't. When the band followed with *Rock Around the Clock,* Kevin begged off and they stole away to the bar to get a couple of Manhattans, a first for both of them.

Kevin didn't know whether it was the dancing or the drinks, but he felt a warm glow, toward Greta of course, but also toward the other revelers as well. It was the best he'd felt in many months, and much of it he attributed to the clarity he finally had in his life,

They were seated with the Executive Officer, and his flirtatious wife, Janet, for dinner, along with the base doctor, Gerry Sutter, and his wife, Hilda. It was a lively table, with anecdotes from the doctor, funny war stories from the XO, and witty repartee from the two women who were meeting Greta for the first time.

Overall, the party was a huge success, far beyond Kevin's expectations, until a sweet-faced, matronly woman came across the bridge and approached Captain Sims. Kevin guessed correctly it was Bob's widow, Alice.

After a very brief conversation, the CO pointed Kevin out to her, and the woman made a beeline for his table. Once there, she paused a second, obviously steeling herself, then launched into a rant, her face a bubbling sea of emotion. She closed with, "You were supposed to help my husband, and take some of the stress off him. But it turned out you just added to it. Thanks for nothing, Mr. Boyce."

Then, she spun around, wove through the tables of gawkers, and left the party.

It was a curious moment for those who heard her. She was clearly laying the blame for her husband's death on the shoulders of the Assistant Supply Officer. But, why?

Kevin stood there kind of shell-shocked for a second. Then, he departed to the men's room to get control of his emotions alone. For several minutes, he just stood in front the mirror, motionless, staring into his own eyes, saying nothing. Then, he spoke to the teary image in the mirror, a person he hardly recognized. "She's right, you know, you sorry son of a bitch. If you hadn't shown up and poked around in Bob's business, she and her family would still have a husband and father to love."

Kevin felt a hand on his shoulder and turned to see Alex Hankins, who, bizarrely, had a big grin on his face. He asked, "You all over feeling sorry for yourself, partner? Can we get back to the party now?"

"I wasn't feeling sorry for myself. I was feeling sorry for Mrs. Higgins," Kevin replied.

Alex scrunched up his face making it look even more cartoonish, and countered, "Well, whatever. I heard you blame yourself, which is ridiculous. Alice had to lash out at somebody. It's all part of the grieving process. And you were just the most handy punching bag around."

"Interesting choice of words, punching bag. I feel like that."

"Who else can she blame?" a persuasive Alex argued. "Her husband? For now, she sees him as the victim. The Captain? He was Bob's friend through everything. Herself? Well, she'll get there soon enough. But, for now, she needed to unload on you. A convenient scapegoat. No matter how irrational it is."

Kevin looked earnestly into his friend's eyes as he ruminated, *Alex has no idea how involved I was, and how I set off the whole chain of events. And I can't tell him.*

"Things were fine until I showed up."

"Nonsense," Alex replied, "Whatever caused Bob to take his own life had deep roots in his soul somewhere. It may have been damaged pride. Or self-loathing. Or guilt. Or whatever. It certainly wasn't you. No way, no how. Now let's get back to the party and enjoy the rest of the evening, for our wives' sake, if not for ours."

Alex was right, as he often was. Kevin vowed to put Alice Higgins' tirade out of his mind, and he was helped in that endeavor by the parade of partygoers who stopped by his table to offer their genuine love and support. What had seemed a complete downer at the time, the dressing-down by Alice Higgins, had actually made Kevin realize how loved and supported he was already by his contemporaries on the base.

By the time Kevin laid his head on the pillow that night, he was feeling just fine, thank you. The booze helped, of course but more importantly, he finally had come to grips with the fact that Bob Higgins was the only one responsible for what had happened to Bob Higgins.

The next morning Greta woke up early and shook Kevin awake. "Are you OK?" She asked, obviously concerned about the after effects of the party. Kevin smiled drowsily and answered, "I was, until you disturbed me, sweetheart."

"Sorry for that but I wanted you to know that I'm going for a swim in the Officer Club pool with Janet," she said. "I'll see you later."

"Why are you doing that?" It was kind of a rhetorical question.

"Janet has had experience with these kinds of things and she guaranteed that a swim and a Bloody Mary will do wonders for my hangover. Now, go back to sleep. I'll be back before you wake up."

"Sure. Whatever," Kevin answered, then, covered his head with a pillow and was back asleep in seconds

An hour or so later, Kevin sat straight up in bed, remembering that Greta had said something about a swim. *I better go check up on her*, he thought. So, he dressed quickly, and walked over to the Officer's Club pool, where he was surprised to see about a dozen of his fellow officers milling around, acting like they were helping the crew clean up.

Kevin asked one of them, "Larry, what the hell are you doing here?" and got a sheepish grin in response. Then, when he looked toward the pool, the answer was clear. There, lying on adjoining chaise lounges, were Greta and the XO's wife, Janet, chatting up a storm, in big floppy sun hats, and bikini bottoms. But no tops

"Holy shit, Greta," he yelled across the pool to her, "What are you doing?"

Her startled expression said, "What does it look like I'm doing?" but her voice was more contrite. "Janet said it would be OK."

And, as if to emphasize the point, Janet tipped her Bloody Mary glass at Kevin.

"Listen Greta," he called out, suddenly realizing all eyes were on him. "We need to go. I invited some friends over for lunch."

Big mistake. He should have told her to dress first.

Greta gathered up her things, put them in a beach bag, and, without covering up, strolled nonchalantly over toward Kevin, obviously in no hurry. Her hips twisted provocatively as she walked around the pool. Her breasts swayed back and forth in tandem. And she held her head high, as if she didn't have a care in the world.

"Greta," Kevin whispered when she was closer, "For God's sake. Cover yourself up."

"Don't be such a prude, Kevin," she answered. "Where I grew up, this is normal, and your friends seem okay with it."

His face contorted, like he bit into a lemon "But I'm not."

Greta made a playful pout. "Okay. Whatever you say, sailor boy. But you're not in Kansas anymore. Remember that."

Then, to the chagrin of the gawking onlookers, she wiggled her body into a full-length coverup, then curtsied, drawing titters from her appreciative audience, and joined Kevin.

As they walked away, he yelled back, "Show's over, gentlemen," to which Janet responded loudly, "I'm not going anywhere, boys. Oh, and come back anytime, Greta. We all really enjoyed your company, didn't we boys?"

Which elicited a chorus of appreciative agreement.

When they get back to their quarters, Greta asked who was coming over to visit, and Kevin had to admit he made that story up just to get her away from the curious eyes of his buddies. She shrugged in a way that expressed her confusion, then, went off to nap while Kevin wrestled with his conscience.

Why am I so upset? I don't own Greta. Not yet anyway. And, if I really want that kind of honest relationship with her, one that can stand the test of time, I need to come clean with my duplicity over the last few months.

So, that night, while Greta was getting ready for bed, he finally screwed up the courage to tell her what he had been doing for Naval Intelligence. "Greta, can you come in here for a minute?" He called out from the sofa in the living room. "I have a confession to make."

She appeared a few minutes later, fresh out of the shower, with a robe hanging loosely around her, and a towel wrapped around her head. She was holding the towel in place with her left hand as she tried unsuccessfully to keep the robe closed with her right. One breast was tantalizingly exposed, making what he was about to do that much harder. He patted the couch beside him, and Greta sat down, a quizzical expression on her face.

"What do you want to confess?" She asked. "Has my quote, husband, unquote, been unfaithful to me already."

Kevin ignored the comment and scooted around on the cushions so he could look directly into her big, brown eyes, and nowhere else. He didn't want to be distracted at such a pivotal moment in their relationship.

"I haven't been entirely honest with you," he began.

"Really? How so?" She answered, wide-eyed with curiosity.

Sheepishly he admitted, "It's difficult to tell you this, Greta, but a while back the Navy asked me to keep an eye on you."

Greta wrinkled up her forehead, trying to process what he had just said. Then, she asked, "An eye on me? The Navy? Whatever for?"

"Well, actually," he replied, "It was Naval Intelligence. They thought you might be a Russian spy."

Surprisingly, Greta seemed unfazed by the revelation. She returned his gaze without blinking and responded, "And what did you think?"

"I didn't believe it at first, not even when they presented intel to back up their claim." Kevin replied, "although it was compelling."

"Like what intel?"

"They said you were born in East Germany, under another name. That you were too old to be a graduate student. And that you weren't even enrolled at the University of Georgia. But, in the end, they admitted they were wrong."

"So, why are you telling me this now?" Greta asked plaintively, her beautiful eyes still fixed on his.

Kevin hesitated, because what he really wanted was to put all the deceptions behind him, get their relationship back back on a solid footing, and maybe ask her to marry him someday. But going there now would probably scare her away.

"You know I love you. I've told you that. And that I believe we were meant to be together. So, with your name now cleared, we can start fresh, with everything out in the open."

"You're such a sweet sailor boy," Greta said, snuggling up close to him, her clean, wet hair under his chin.

"You're not angry?" Kevin asked, a wave of relief washing over his face.

"No. Why should I be? You said you supported me, and only followed orders," she answered, "That's good enough for me."

Kevin was puzzled and pleased. He had certainly expected a different reaction, including, at the very least, a lot more questions. Greta seemed perfectly content with his vague explanations, and she nestled up against him, one hand caressing his face, and the other exploring his body.

Then, once she knew he was sufficiently aroused, she stepped back, loosened the sash on her robe, and let it drop to the floor. She pirouetted in front of him, her nude body still damp from the shower, then, gave herself to him fully, loving him with every caress, yes, but thanking him, too, in a way, for believing in her. Her lovemaking was slower and a little more deliberate than in the past, with Greta getting most of her pleasure out of pleasuring him. Kevin laid there for a while afterwards, his chest heaving, his energy drained, and his thoughts racing.

I did it. I confessed and she forgave me, both in words and deeds. My conscience is clear, and now we can move forward without any hidden agendas.

When he went to bed, Greta was already there, her back toward him, seemingly asleep, and Kevin joined her, soon enjoying the deepest slumber he had experienced in months. He couldn't wait for the next day when he and Greta could start their new life together.

Only, when he awoke in the morning, Greta was gone.

CHAPTER 18

Where is she? He asked himself. *Where did she go? Maybe she was more upset than I thought. Or had a change of heart in the middle of the night.*

He decided to drive over to where she worked, not only to check on her well-being but also to gauge her mental state after hearing that Kevin had been so duplicitous. She seemed fine with it at the time, but was she really?

Imperial Valley College was easier to find than he expected. It was just east of El Centro, near a town called Anza, on a barren piece of land littered with mesquite and sagebrush. Kevin parked outside the administration building, a one-story, sandstone-colored building with an overhanging flat roof. Then, he looked around. The campus wasn't much, just a few modest buildings scattered about, all relatively new, and with lots of acreage for expansion should the need arise.

"May I help you, sir?" a fresh-faced young woman asked him when he entered. She rose to greet him at a small counter that separated the reception area from the office.

"I'm looking for Greta Schmidt," he answered.

"Who?" the young woman asked.

Not the reaction Kevin was expecting or hoping for.

"Greta Schmidt," he repeated, "She works here. I think in administration. She just started a few months back."

"Only Rita and I work here in the office," the girl explained. "Our manager is Teresa Lopez, whose office is there in the back. The other people here are our President, Dick Donovan, and our head of curriculum, Maria Alvarez. No Greta Schmidt. Does she teach perhaps?"

Kevin realized that he didn't know for sure what Greta did at the school. She just said reception or administration, with occasional substitute teaching when the opportunity arose. Anytime he had questioned her about particulars, Greta was evasive and, although he had asked a few times, she had never invited him out to see where she worked. Not once, which was curious in retrospect.

"She may substitute teach, but I was positive she said administrative work," Kevin answered.

"Well, I don't know anybody by that name. Sorry." Then, she headed back toward her desk. But, Kevin stopped her by asking loudly, "Excuse me, miss. Would you mind checking to see if she's one of your teachers then? I'm sure she works here."

"Okay, sir. But I know most of our teachers by name and I don't know any Greta."

While she went into a back room containing the employee records, Kevin sat down on a bench and tried to comprehend what the facts were shouting at him. His mind was telling him one thing and his heart something else.

If she never worked here, what does that mean?

After a few minutes, the girl came back and reported that they had no employees named Schmidt. Not on staff. Not as a teacher. Not as a substitute teacher. .

He went back out into the sun, dazed by the glare, but also the news.

On the drive back to the base Kevin's mind mulled over the possibilities, none of which were very palatable. It was now clear that, not only had Greta fled, but she probably wasn't who she said she was all along, which could only mean one thing.

****

After a sleepless night, Kevin arrived at his office the next day to find an unfamiliar, uniformed officer waiting for him in the reception area.

"Hello Kevin, I'm Lt. Tom Brown with Naval Intelligence stationed in San Diego. Can we go into your office?"

"Sure," Kevin answered as he guided the guy out of the reception area and into his office, shutting the door behind them. Tom had an honest, open face, with hazel eyes, and a cockeyed grin, the kind of person he would normally trust, but not anymore. He was out of the "trust" business.

When they were seated, Kevin behind his desk, and Mr. Brown in front of it, the intelligence officer leaned forward and spoke in a hushed tone. "What I'm about to tell you is highly confidential," he started, "But first, a few questions. How well do you know Lt. Cdr. Brad Smith?"

"Pretty well. He was my case officer until a week or so ago when he was reassigned."

"He wasn't reassigned, Mr. Boyce, but we'll get to that. Have you ever known Mr. Smith to lie to you? Or make strange requests?"

"No, of course not. He's a fine officer, as far as I know. And a patriot."

"We'll get to that soon enough as well."

What is this about? Kevin pondered. *I know Brad thought Greta was a spy and wasted a lot of federal money trying to prove it. And, of course, that mistake would affect his career. But this guy seems to be implying something murkier.*

"Okay. I'm done answering questions," Kevin said as he stood up, "Why don't you tell me what this is all about, Mr. Brown."

The guy wasn't offended or intimidated in the least. He remained seated; his legs crossed comfortably in front of him. He pulled out a cigarette and lit it with a silver lighter bearing the Naval Academy crest. Then, he exhaled, all very dramatic.

"Mr. Smith has disappeared. In fact, you may have been the last person to see him."

Tom then leaned in and looked at Kevin without blinking, which was disconcerting. He continued, "I talked to Captain Sims yesterday, and he told me that, about a week ago, you and Brad left his office to discuss something personal. He hasn't been seen since. What did you talk about?"

Kevin weighed his options, finally deciding to come clean.

"You know about Greta Schmidt, right?"

"I sure do. She was the target of Brad's most important investigation."

"Well, he said that Naval Intelligence had proof Greta wasn't a Russian asset, that he was sorry he dragged me through this, but, mostly, we talked about another case we were working on, a suspected scam going on here on the base."

"Yes. Captain Sims told me about that. Did Brad say goodbye?"

"In a way, yes," Kevin responded, "But, he didn't say he was going to disappear. And, given that we were pretty close. I think he would have."

"Look, Kevin, I reported to Brad for five years," Mr. Brown admitted. "We were best friends. I worshipped the guy. And he didn't tell me anything about going AWOL either. So, there's that."

Kevin is taken aback. "AWOL? That's a strong accusation."

"Not really. AWOL just means 'absent without leave." A stronger and more appropriate word would be "deserter," which I might have used instead."

"You sound angry?"

"You're damn right, and you will be too, when the enormity of Brad's betrayal sinks in,"

Then, he looked down, gathered himself and said with a sigh of resignation. "Anyway, back to the Greta Schmidt situation. You should know that she actually is a Russian spy. No doubt about that. Why Brad told you differently I really don't know. Maybe to cover up for her escape, which I assume has already happened."

"Do I need a lawyer?"

"Look, Mr. Boyce, we know you had nothing to do with Brad's betrayal, and that you weren't complicit in whatever double-agent game he was playing. You were just an innocent conduit for intel flowing from, and to, Greta."

Kevin's facial features relaxed a little, but he wasn't convinced that he was out of the woods just yet. "Okay, I'm glad to hear that," he said, "But I'm a little surprised. I've been involved with Greta longer than anyone, and was pretty supportive of her all along, which you must know."

"Let's be honest. I've seen pictures of Greta, and what red-blooded American male wouldn't have been supportive?"

"There were others like me?"

"Dozens probably, obviously including your buddy, Brad. No, Kevin, you weren't her one and only. Far from it."

"It certainly felt like I was for awhile."

"Well, that's part of Greta's genius, isn't it?"

****

The next few days Kevin kept busy but, because his mind was elsewhere, accomplished very little.

The events of the last few months had been a whirlwind of conflicted emotions for him. First, Brad tells him that Greta is a Russian spy and he needs to keep the romance going while they feed her misinformation. Then, once Kevin settles uncomfortably into that role, Brad tells him that Greta is totally innocent, which thrills Kevin at the time. All ambiguity is gone. But wait. Next thing he knows both Greta and Brad are Russian assets.

The whole thing was way too much for an uncomplicated guy from Kansas to wrap his head around.

Then…luckily…Sally Thomas entered his life again with an invitation for Kevin to accompany her to the Avon Sales Convention in San Diego. Not so appealing back when he and Greta were an item, but, under the new circumstances, a perfect diversion.

This could be my island of sanity in what has been a tumultuous sea of confusion, he thought as he called back to accept.

"Oh, great," Sally responded. "I'm being honored as one of the top sales promotion people in my area, and I'd love to celebrate with somebody I care about. Please understand, Kevin, I just need your friendship and support, nothing more."

"You got it, Sally," he responded, although now, surprisingly, he may want more than that himself. "Just tell me where and when."

Immediately after hanging up, the phone rang again, and it was Captain Sims' secretary summoning him to a meeting. Something about making amends.

Oh great. Just what I need right now, Kevin thought. *Another pity party.*

But no matter the subject, the meeting was still a command performance, as is always the case when a high-ranking officer wants to see you, So, within fifteen minutes Kevin was in the captain's office, acting very interested in whatever his commanding officer had to say.

"Nice party the other night," he began. "Thanks for all you did to make it special."

"My pleasure," Kevin responded, realizing that it actually was his pleasure, the whole thing, from the conceiving to the execution to the enjoying. A great evening. Until Alice arrived, of course. Then, an even better following day with Greta, until she disappeared, of course.

"Look, Kevin. I want to apologize for sending Alice your way the other night." He sounded genuinely contrite. "She just said she wanted to know who Bob's assistant was, and I pointed you out. That's it."

"No problem, Captain. She seemed to blame me for his death which, in a strange way, I guess I understand."

"Well, it's hogwash. I doubt she knew about Bob's side business and, even if she did, she should blame her husband for that rather than you, and for his suicide as well...which I'm sure she will over time."

Kevin nodded but chose not to say anything.

The captain continued, "Anyway, I appreciate how you dug into your new responsibilities after Bob's death. Found another major food supplier. Got rid of the Chief in charge of the General Mess, rallied the troops. All things made more difficult by the circumstances."

Kevin nodded again, waiting for the other shoe to drop.

The captain smiled broadly and continued. "And NARF has been extremely complimentary of the backup support you've been giving them. In fact, their supply officer, I think his name is Hankins, he gave you a rave review as well. So, from a performance standpoint, things are going very well here."

"Thank you, sir," Kevin said tentatively, still not sure where this is going.

"But, honestly, it's time for us all to move on. So, I'll cut to the chase. In addition to bringing in a new base supply officer to replace Bob, we're requesting a new assistant as well…to replace you."

Kevin had expected the news. And, frankly, welcomed it.

"So, actually, Kevin, I think that's the good news. You won't have to put up with me, this place, the weather, or our nonsense, anymore. But there's better news. The new guy in charge of the San Diego Naval Intelligence office, the one who replaced Brad Smith, wants you to spend the rest of your service time working for him there. His name is Tom Brown. I think you know him."

Now, Kevin was surprised, and delighted.

Not only will I be leaving the uncomfortable memories of El Centro, and the threat of gang retaliation, behind me, but I'll be moving to San Diego, a place I truly love, and now consider home…while doing something more interesting than taking inventory and keeping books.

******

The hotel where the Avon convention was being held was in downtown San Diego, and Kevin's room overlooked the harbor, with a spectacular view of Coronado Island. There was also a glimpse of the Naval Station where the *Buck* was tied up, and around it, a panorama of sailboats taking advantage of the incredible San Diego weather.

One could be forgiven for thinking everything was good with the world. But Kevin knew otherwise.

The Vietnam War had become a quagmire. President Johnson was under siege for an escalation that wasn't yielding the results he promised. Russia was in the middle of a leadership change that promised more "saber-rattling," and threats of nuclear annihilation. Protests were rising in number and intensity.

And, for Kevin, his private life was in shambles as well.

But, for one night, he planned to put all that aside to make Sally feel appreciated and supported. After all, she was being honored for her work in making women more beautiful, which can play a role in making everybody feel better about things.

Kevin put on his dress white uniform, with its epaulets and starched white collar, and gave his shoes a quick spit shine. He tried not to think about the last time he wore this uniform, and the cascading events that had followed shortly thereafter.

At his young age, Kevin didn't know what it's like to lose a loved one but losing both Brad and Greta in the same week must feel similar, with the same stages of grief. Kevin was probably still in the denial stage but edging over into anger.

Surprisingly, though, Kevin was much angrier at himself than anybody else. He'd come to grips with Greta's behavior rather easily. She was a spy after all. Brad's betrayal was a little harder. He was a trusted friend who abused their friendship in a stunning way. Still, going back over everything that had happened, Kevin realized that they had both just taken advantage of his naïveté, for which he had only himself to blame.

The loud ring of the hotel phone startled him out of his self-pitying thoughts.

"Kevin," Sally said in an excited voice, "Are you ready? I'd like to get down there a little early and show you off."

Kevin grimaced. He wasn't in a 'showing off' mood. "Give me five minutes. I'll meet you just outside the ballroom, where they're serving cocktails."

"Okay," she replied. "I'm so nervous and excited. And I can't thank you enough for coming."

"My pleasure," he said. "But don't be nervous. With your infectious personality, you'll do fine."

Which was true. Sally had always been a naturally gifted conversationalist, a kind of social savant, young-looking, yes, but surprisingly mature in her thinking, and comfortable in her own skin as well. People naturally liked her and gravitated toward her. So, unsurprisingly, as Kevin was introduced around, all everybody wanted to talk to him about was how talented and special Sally was. She was truly admired, and, in a competitive field like cosmetics, that wasn't always the case.

The dinner conversation was light-hearted and friendly. Nothing about world affairs or Vietnam or politics, even though her co-workers seemed thrilled to have a Navy officer in their midst. Kevin told a few sea stories. Sally talked about his athletic exploits in college, and how they met on a very uncomfortable blind date, where everybody else was 'making out' behind a barn.

After dinner, the meeting and awards ceremony began, and it more closely resembled a pep rally than a business conference. Each winner was ushered to the stage by two tuxedoed young men who were obviously chosen based on their looks. The Avon representatives who were seated at a table with each of the chosen winners whooped and hollered as they walked up, much like they would a homecoming Queen at a college football game.

When it was Sally's turn, she formally curtsied to her two escorts, then bounded up on stage like she owned the place, hands clenched above her head in a triumphant gesture that brought roars of laughter and appreciation.

Her speech, however, was much more modest than Kevin expected. She thanked those who recruited her, and those who helped her along the way. She pledged to take what she'd learned in her training, and make a difference in the world, one pretty client at a time.

Then, as she was closing, she acknowledged Kevin and asked him to stand. And, when he did, she told the audience that he was an old college friend who went into the Navy with the patriotic dream of protecting America's interests overseas. And that he had done that in Vietnam and elsewhere. She asked the audience to bring their hands together, not just for him but for all the servicemen "who are out there on the front lines tonight, keeping the rest of us safe, and free to do whatever we want, even something as seemingly superficial as making women more beautiful."

Then, on cue, the band broke into a short but spirited rendition of "Anchors Away," followed by the three other service anthems. It was an obviously well-planned stunt to whip the audience into a patriotic frenzy. And it worked.

When Sally got back to the table, Kevin gave her a peck on the cheek and whispered into her ear, "You could have at least given me a warning."

"Just be thankful I didn't invite you up to say a few words," she replied.

Kevin laughed, "You should be the thankful one. You wouldn't have liked what I said."

"About *moi*?" Sally asked in a flirting tone.

"Exactly," Kevin fired back.

Later that evening, when the festivities were over, the two ex-lovers ended up in Sally's room sharing a bottle of champagne which they had smuggled away from the dinner. Sally had kicked off her shoes, and Kevin had opened the stiff collar of his formal white uniform.

"That was some party and some meal," he said. "I haven't eaten that much since Thanksgiving at my grandmother's house."

"Avon believes in doing these things up right. Our representatives like to make money, yes, but they like recognition even more, like I gave you there at the end".

Kevin was mock offended. "I'm not a rep, and I don't need recognition, especially when nobody warned me it was coming," he said.

"Oh, that wasn't for you. That was for them. There's nothing like good old-fashioned flag-waving to end the evening. And you were a convenient prop."

"Prop?" he asked, arching his eyebrows.

"Well," she said as she sat down on the couch next to Kevin, "A very handsome, friendly, and lovable prop, but a prop nonetheless."

Kevin thought to himself, *I've just been sucker punched by a Russian agent and abandoned by a good friend. So, being a lovable prop isn't so bad, I guess.*

Then, Kevin shared the good news with her that he was moving to San Diego to finish out his Navy term.

"Are you going back on board a ship?" she queried..

"I wish, but no" he answered. "It's shore duty, working with Naval Intelligence."

"Wow. Doing what?"

"I'm not really at liberty to say, but it'll be little things, ship audits and the like."

"I'm so pleased for you. Hopefully, we can see more of each other now."

"That's the plan," he assured her, a big smile on his face. Sally leaned over to give him a congratulatory kiss, and then, they kissed again, more passionately.

This could really work, Kevin thought. *With Greta out of my life, a romance with Sally makes a lot more sense.*

CHAPTER 19

The transition into the San Diego office of Naval Intelligence turned out to be easier than Kevin had imagined. There was the to-be-expected joshing about letting a Pork Chop into their midst, of course. "Be a darling and get me some coffee please, Kev," and "When will you have the sandwiches ready, Kev?" Stuff like that. But, as a general rule, everybody understood that Kevin could add value in a way they really couldn't.

As Tom expressed it, "We have submariners, staff aides, chief engineers, you name it, all working for us. It's about time we have a supply officer."

And, as if to underscore the point, Kevin's first assignment was to play the role of a fleet supply officer conducting a routine supply audit on a destroyer sitting in dry dock at the Long Beach Naval Station. Pretty standard stuff, except the audit was actually a cover that would allow Kevin unfettered access to the ship's records without drawing undue attention to his real purpose, which was to uncover an accounting fraud supposedly taking place between shipyard executives and a supply clerk on the ship.

The role was perfect for Kevin, and he slipped into it easily, played it to the hilt, and successfully uncovered not only the fraud, but the high-level vice president of the ship-building firm, who was behind it. Appropriately, heads rolled, and when Kevin got back to headquarters, he was greeted like a returning hero, one guy remarking, "Damn it, Kevin. For a Pork Chop you done really good. Who woulda thunk it."

Although a little uncomfortable with the syntax, Kevin couldn't have said it better.

******

It didn't take long before Kevin asked Sally out again, not just because she was the perfect antidote for the Greta hangover he was experiencing but because it was dawning on him that, in some ways, Sally was more fun, and certainly more comfortable to be around than Greta.

For a change of pace, Kevin suggested a fancy restaurant in La Jolla called The Marine Room. He picked her up at her downtown apartment and they drove to the restaurant together, arriving a half-hour before their dinner reservation, again, as was now almost a tradition for them.

As they walked the beach, hand in hand, they talked about the weather, sports, and particularly the conference they attended together. Then, Sally broke the big news that she was interviewing for a high-level executive job in Washington, D.C. Kevin stopped suddenly, as if he'd been knocked down again. He turned to face her; a disbelieving look on his face. "I'm thrilled for you, of course, but not so much for us."

"That's sweet, I think. And I feel the same way. But this is such a good opportunity."

"It's just that I was excited to finally be in the same town with you, Sally. I was hoping we could begin to date regularly, and capture some of our 'old magic.'"

"I was thinking more about 'new magic.' And I'm sure we can figure out how to make that happen, even though we're a whole continent apart."

"Not easy, but we'll work something out. So, tell me about the opportunity. Is it related to what you've been doing?"

"Yes. Well, sort of related. It's with the DSA, an organization that represents direct selling organizations to Washington," she explained.

"A lobbying organization. I'll be damned. Not what I would have expected."

"I'm going to be a lobbyist, Kevin. Can you believe it?" she shouted to nobody in particular. "A goddamned lobbyist."

"Best-looking lobbyist in D.C., I'd daresay."

"Most of them are much older men."

"Exactly."

Once their walk was over and they were seated at a table near a large plate-glass window looking out over the beach to the ocean, Kevin leaned in, face resting on his hands eager to hear more. "So, tell me exactly what you'll be doing," he asked.

"I'm going to patrol the halls of Congress, seducing every important person I can find," Sally said, already feeling the wine a little.

"Seducing?" Kevin asked, a broad smile creasing his face.

"So to speak," She explained, forcing a fake sober look in her face. "Actually, I'll be rationally explaining the benefits of direct selling in the hope that those old fuddy-duddy Senators and Representatives will see the light and pass laws favorable to us."

"So, you'll be selling? I thought you said you were going to be an executive?" he asked.

"I prefer the word, 'persuading.' And everybody in the organization persuades, even big wigs like I'm supposed to be," Sally smiled coquettishly. "We'll see, though. It's far from a done deal."

"I know you, Sally. If you want it, you'll get it. And, if we can make it work, I'll be dating a lobbyist. How about that?"

"I like the ring of it, especially the dating part."

And just to underscore her point, she leaned across the small table and gave him a peck on the cheek. "That's just a small hint of future attractions," she said, her face flushed with joy, and passion. Kevin felt a fresh stirring in his heart too, as well as elsewhere.

******

As it turned out Sally didn't get the job in Washington and, over time, their relationship developed to the point where Kevin had almost forgotten all about Greta.

Kevin found Sally to be exciting and fun, in that he never knew exactly what she might say or do. But, on the other hand, he found their relationship comfortable, in that Sally was such an open book. Her love for him was unquestioned, and, when she asked him a question about something, he knew she was just curious, with no ulterior motive.

That was a refreshing change.

Kevin also was able to build a successful and comfortable career with Naval Intelligence in San Diego.

Over time, he had two supply officers reporting to him because much of the actual nitty-gritty investigative work in the office lent itself to the kind of training and experience supply officers routinely receive. So, net, net, Kevin was instrumental in building a capability that the investigative arm of Naval Intelligence had never had before.

Eventually, after a few years of dating, Kevin asked Sally to marry him and, soon after, they were wed in a Congregational Church near Del Mar. Over one-hundred people were invited to the wedding, and many more could have been.

Kevin wanted to invite all his new co-workers as well as his old shipmates, which numbered in the dozens. (Fortunately, he had nobody from El Centro he really wanted there, so that helped.) Cutting his list down to a manageable number wasn't easy.

But Sally's list was the real problem.

Everybody she knew from Avon corporate, and everybody she worked with in San Diego, loved Sally and considered her to be "their very best friend." In fact, if she just invited all of her "very best friends," they would have filled the chapel, leaving little room for any other guests.

Somehow, in the end, she worked it all out, and nobody was offended, something only Sally could pull off.

The ceremony went off without a hitch as well and the only slight hiccup for Kevin was, when he and Sally left the church, he thought he saw Greta across the street, watching the festivities from afar. The woman was too far away to clearly see her face, but her confident posture, with arms crossed and frozen posture, seemed like something Greta might do, just to let Kevin know it was her.

He and Sally settled into marriage comfortably, like they had been preparing for it all their lives. She continued to excel at Avon, once passing up a promotion because she didn't want to leave San Diego. As for Kevin, when it became time to leave the Navy, he re-upped for another four-year term. He kept saying to Sally that advertising would have to wait but, in his heart, he knew he wasn't cut out for that type of work anyway. Working for Naval Intelligence had an excitement that advertising could never match.

About a year after Kevin's wedding, Tom called Kevin into his office, shut the door, and told him, "I must admit I had an ulterior motive when I asked you to join me a few years ago."

"What in the world was that?"

"From the time our mutual buddy, Brad, defected I wanted, in the worst way, to bring him to justice. He played me for a fool. You must have felt the same way."

I did, Kevin acknowledged to himself, *But I understood the role Greta played in that. Was it really all Brad's doing? I don't know.*

Tom continued, "And I felt, having you on my staff would greatly increase the chance that, at some point, the Brad Smith case would be assigned to my unit, to us."

"There's a Brad Smith case?" Kevin asked.

"Of course there is. Did you think the Navy would just let him waltz off into the sunset with Greta and have a good life."

"I guess not but, honestly, what can we do at this point?"

"You'd be surprised," Tom said as he lifted a box full of file folders and other correspondence onto the desk. He had a big grin on his face.

"Here's everything the agency has on Brad and Greta at this point," a smiling Lt. Cdr. Brown said, "And you are going to be my point person on this. You need to go through everything and see if anything triggers an alarm."

"Aye, aye, sir."

"In addition, I put out what the police call All-Points-Bulletins, APB's, on both of them, with bio's, pictures, likes/dislikes, etc., and we've been getting quite a few possible sightings. You need to sort through those as well."

"Got it."

"But, also, you need to wrack your brain for anything Greta or Kevin might have said that could tip off their whereabouts. Ironically, not only are you our lead investigator but also our best source for information right now. You knew both of them better than any of us."

"You know, it's funny you say that, because I do remember something that could be important. I don't know why I never mentioned it. Wasn't asked I guess," Kevin confessed, "But Brad told me to contact a friend of his if I ever wanted to get together with him. It never entered my mind it might be relevant all these years later, but who knows? He gave me the guy's name and number. He lived in D.C., as I recall."

"I can't believe you never mentioned it before."

"And I can't believe you never mentioned there was a Brad Smith case before?"

"Touché," Tom replied, "So, anyway, Brad's your next assignment. Look over the files. Follow up on that contact he gave you. Then, together, we'll plot a strategy for dealing with whatever you discover."

Kevin went back to his office and hesitated briefly before picking up the phone. He knew he should look over the files first, and work on a strategy. But he had a telephone number, and might as well find out whether it was relevant right away. So, he made the call.

Kevin was very surprised to hear a woman answer "Russian Embassy" in somewhat tortured English. Taken aback, he said nothing at first, then blurted out that he was trying to reach Alexander, the name of Brad's so-called friend.

There was a long silence.

"What is Alexander's last name?" the operator finally asked, "We have several here."

"I don't know," Kevin answered. "He's a friend of a friend of mine named Brad Smith."

After another pause, she queried, "Can you give me your number, and I'll have somebody call you back?"

Kevin didn't have to wait long. Within minutes a Russian man called and identified himself as Alexander. He kept the conversation short and sweet, saying just that he would rather not talk on the phone but that he would be able to meet Kevin two days later at a diner in Washington, D.C.

"Come alone, please. And we talk about Brad."

Given the short time frame before the meeting, Kevin really had to scramble. Luckily, he was able to book a flight into Chicago the next day, and after a layover of several hours, catch a 'red eye' from there into Washington D.C. He arrived only a couple of hours before the scheduled meeting, which gave him just enough time to meet with his contact at Naval Intelligence headquarters, get wired up for the meeting, and find his way to the diner.

Once there, Kevin scooted into an upholstered booth near the back and scanned the other customers in the diner briefly, to see if Alexander happened to be there, but also wondering if he had back-up.

The closest possibility was a casually dressed, middle-aged couple at a Formica-topped table about ten feet away. They were picking at their food, and looking around the room, seemingly bored with both the place and each other.

A little further away were two bulky men, with athletic builds, who seemed like good prospects to be agents. They were engaged in a spirited conversation about the *Senators* baseball team. He overheard one snippet of their conversation, "…whether we're at war or peace, you can always count on the Senators finishing last in the American League." They were ignoring Kevin entirely, which could mean they were great undercover agents, or just great baseball fans.

Suddenly, a young, pale-skinned man slid into the booth, and sat directly across from Kevin. He was big-eared and small-framed, with tousled brown hair and shiny dark black eyes. A broad smile creased his face, which made him look friendlier than he probably was.

"Hello. Good to see you. You must be Mr. Boyce." The man said, as he extended his hand awkwardly and limply, allowing Kevin to grip as firmly or as loosely as he would like.

"I'm Alexander Kharkov," the man said in a whisper, "We talked briefly on phone. You know Brad Smith, right?"

Kevin's mouth was surprisingly dry, and he had to muster up some saliva before huskily answering, "Yes. We worked together back in the day."

Kharkov dove right in, "Then, like him, you in Naval Intelligence?"

Kevin hesitated a little before answering, "Well, at the time I knew Brad I was just a supply officer. We met overseas and kept in touch over the years. He gave me your name."

"Are you still in touch with Mr. Smith?"

"No," Kevin answered. "That's why I'm here. When we last talked, he said you were friends, and to contact you if I wanted to reach him."

"I'm not sure why he say that" the Russian asserted. "Was there reason you wanted to talk to me… officially, perhaps?"

"I'm sorry, Mr. Kharkov," Kevin responded cautiously, feeling the blood drain from his face, "I'm not sure what you mean. All Brad said was you could put me in touch with him."

"Look, Mr. Kevin. As far as we know, your friend has disappeared, and we want to find him as much as you do. Maybe more. A long time ago, he contacted our Embassy with some false information, which sent us on, how you say it, a mad goose hunt?"

"Wild goose chase. It's called a wild goose chase," Kevin clarified.

"Well, whatever. We don't like wild chases," the Russian waved his hand dramatically. "We don't know where Mr. Brad is but if we did, of course, we wouldn't tell you, unless you gave us reason to."

"I suspected that."

"Do you have any information for us, like maybe where you last saw him?"

"No, but if I did, I wouldn't tell you either, unless you gave me reason to." Kevin mimicked the guy a little, hoping to lighten the mood.

It didn't work. Alex Kharkov glared at Kevin for a second, in a way which would have been comical under different circumstances. Then, the Russian abruptly got up and stomped out of the diner without saying another word.

No sense of humor I guess, Kevin thought to himself.

A moment later, the two stocky men came over and slid into the seat across from Kevin, the one just vacated by Mr. Kharkov. They both had scowls on their faces.

One said sarcastically, "Well, that went very well, don't you think?" as a kind of icebreaker. "Have you ever done this sort of thing before, Mr. Boyce?"

"Not really. Did he know what was going on here?" Kevin asked.

"You think?" The man replied facetiously.

"Actually, this is what we expected," the other clarified, hoping to ease the tension a bit. "I don't know if he spotted us or not. But no matter. There was no way he was just going to meet up with you and start talking about one of their prize recruits."

"He was probably just sizing you up," the first man continued. "And your little wise-ass comment told him everything he needed to know."

"Maybe I shouldn't have tried to be funny," Kevin ventured.

Again, the first man responded, "You think?"

But the more conciliatory one tried to cut the tension again. "I wouldn't worry too much about it, Mr. Boyce. My guess is you weren't going to get anything out of Mr. Kharkov anyway. And now he seems to be really done with you."

It turned out to be a solid guess. Kevin never heard from Alexander or the Russians again. Which, although it didn't help their investigation, was probably a good thing.

After returning to San Diego and debriefing Tom, Kevin found a big manila envelope on his desk, with pictures in it. They were blurred and grainy but, to Kevin's eye, they were unmistakably photos of Brad. He had a beard, looked a little more stoop-shouldered, and his hair was graying a little. But the likeness was there.

The accompanying memo was from a guy named Gus Mortimer, a CIA agent posted in Berlin. It was brief. "This could be be the Naval Intelligence traitor you are looking for. But, best to get confirmation. Can you send somebody over to make a positive identification and follow up?"

Kevin knew immediately who that would be and, although the idea of taking a very long flight was unappealing to him, going to Berlin, or anywhere else in Europe, was exciting. As was catching up with Brad again.

CHAPTER 20

Unfortunately, Kevin's first trip ever to Europe started off badly.

Kevin was wedged in a center seat, between an overweight German man and a talkative, middle-aged lady from Georgia who welcomed the captive audience of one. She told him about her large family, consisting of four kids, several aunts and uncles, as well as a dozen cousins, all of whom Kevin came to know much better than he wanted to. He learned how she met her husband, what he did for a living, and why they moved to their small town twenty-five years ago this week. Among other things.

Thankfully, the German guy said nothing, but he did snore his way across the Atlantic Ocean, ensuring that Kevin got no sleep even when the woman from Georgia came up for air. So, early the next morning, when Kevin arrived in Berlin, he was beyond exhausted, and, after hiking from the plane to passport control to baggage claim, where his luggage came out second to last, he was peeved as well. Then, to top it all off, after finally collecting his luggage, Kevin exited the airport into a heavy downpour.

Damn, could I be any more miserable? He lamented, then remembered, *I'm in Europe for the first time, as an agent on assignment, for God's sake. We don't let a little thing like rain bother us, do we? Buckle up, buckaroo.*

Kevin had packed a raincoat, which he was able to pull out of his bag and put on over his suit coat, but it offered scant protection from the buckets of cold water pelting him as he waited in the taxi queue. When he finally got into a cab, his clothes were soaked through, and he was chilled to the bone.

"Where to?" the cab driver asked in surprisingly perfect English.

"The Armano Hotel," Kevin answered, and the driver scrunched up his nose, as if he'd smelled something putrid. "Really? Are you sure, sir?" he asked, which was Kevin's first hint that his accommodations might not be exactly first-class.

But, how bad could it be?

Pretty bad, it turned out. Kevin's first impression was horrible, and everything went downhill from there. The hotel not only lacked a sense of entry, with no sign, no awning, no doorman but, once inside, it looked more like a hostel than a hotel. It had no lobby to speak of. Just a small counter, and behind that, a gnarled old man, who looked eager to growl at whoever wanted to book a room.

After a brief but thoroughly unpleasant conversation with the guy, Kevin got his key and climbed the dark stairs to his second-floor room which, unsurprisingly, was small, smelly, and dated. All in keeping with the ambience promised by the tawdry lobby.

There was a radiator in the corner of the room trying, with limited success, to clang out enough heat to fend off a pervasive chill in the room. The carpet was nondescript gray, perfect to cover up anything the vacuum missed, which, based on the odor, was quite a bit. The windows were large, dirty, and opaque, with heavy, flowered drapes framing them. One overstuffed light blue chair sat across from the radiator, and next to it, a portable closet just large enough to accommodate the few clothes Kevin had with him.

There was no dresser. No desk. And no charm.

The only welcoming feature of the room was a lumpy-looking bed in the middle, with a gaudy red and yellow quilt bedspread tossed over it. The bed looked soft. Very soft. Too soft. And yet, it was beckoning Kevin, convincing him to forego any more unpacking until he could get some sleep. *Just thirty minutes or so,* he told himself.

He undressed quickly, laid his wet clothes across the radiator, then, pulled back the sheets, and slipped his shivering body underneath them, snuggling deep into the warmth. And, even with the cacophony of honking horns, banging garbage can lids, and occasional wailing sirens as background noise, Kevin was fast asleep in minutes.

But, shortly thereafter, the large, black telephone on his nightstand began to ring, loudly, like a fire alarm, and to bounce around on the table as if it was alive. When Kevin answered it, he heard an unfamiliar husky voice ask, "Where the hell are you?"

"Who is this?"

There's a perceptible sigh. "It's Gus Mortimer. Remember? I thought we were meeting for lunch."

"Not until noon. Right?"

A very pregnant pause. "Yes. But that was thirty minutes ago, and I have another appointment soon. So, up and at 'em, hotshot. I'll order you a bratwurst. OK?"

Kevin dressed quickly and walked the two blocks to the cafe where Gus was waiting. When he entered, he didn't see the guy right away. But then, as his eyes adjusted, there he was, a shabbily dressed, pathetic figure in a back booth. Droopy faced. Middle-aged. Ordinary height. No distinguishing characteristics of any kind.

The perfect undercover agent, Kevin told himself, *Gus would be invisible almost anywhere. Well, maybe except at an elegant dinner, or play, or opera. But here, his clothes and demeanor say 'Ich bin ein Berliner" as effectively as President Kennedy did a few years back.*

After quickly wolfing down their bratwursts and beers, Gus and Kevin went to work doing what agents do. First, they wandered around the neighborhood where Brad, if it was him, had been spotted. They cased the apartment house he seemed to live in. Then, they sat at a coffee shop down the street where he would often get his morning coffee. Next, they visited a neatly trimmed park a block further down and, finally, a restaurant where, according to Gus, Brad would sometimes meet with an attractive young woman, probably Greta.

The next day, Gus stayed just long enough to work out a stakeout plan with Kevin. He would hang out at the park first, then, the coffee shop, and, finally, the restaurant. If Brad didn't show at any of those places, then, Kevin should position himself across the street from the apartment house around the time his target might be returning from dinner.

"How do I reach you when I find him?" Kevin asked a departing Gus.

"Look, Mr. Boyce," Gus responded, "Arresting this guy isn't my job. I happened to see the bulletin, then identified the target, followed him around as best I could until you got here, and now, I have to get back to my day job. He's all yours."

"What if I find him."

"The German authorities have been alerted. Here's a number to call if you want them to arrest the guy. Other than that, you're pretty much on your own."

Kevin hadn't really expected that, but, in a way, he welcomed it. Even in this short amount of time, Gus had become a complication he could do without. As he departed, Kevin whispered, mostly to himself, "Okay, Gus, I've got the conn. And you're relieved of your duties," as if he was assuming control of the ship, which in a way he was.

Gus turned back, a smirk on his face, as if he heard what Kevin said. Then, he asked, "So you're sure you'll recognize the guy when you see him?"

Kevin answered confidently, "I assure you that won't be a problem. We go way back."

"Sounds like a story for some other time," Gus said, "But, thankfully, there won't be another time. So, good luck with your traitor friend, and I'll be watching the newspapers to see how everything turns out."

******

Patience never was one of Kevin's strengths. So, he was probably ill-suited to do stakeouts on his own, but there was only one way to find out.

The next morning, he positioned himself at the end of a bench in the small city park where Gus had seen the target a few days before. He was obscuring his face as best he could by pretending to read a newspaper.

Hopefully nobody tries to talk to me, he thought. *The fact I'm reading a German newspaper, but can't speak a word of it, might be a problem.*

But it was early in the day and the park was busy, with people hurrying to work. Nobody was pausing to enjoy the bucolic park, which was good and bad for Kevin. It reduced his chance of being outed, yes, but it also made his task of finding Brad, and identifying him, almost impossible. People were flying by at too fast a pace.

So, Kevin decided to move his surveillance to a nearby coffee shop where he could be less conspicuous and more observant. As he sat down, he was startled to see a woman who looked like Greta get up from a nearby table and disappear around the nearest building. Different color hair, yes. Oversized and dumpy clothes. Clunky shoes. But, that face. Who could forget that face, and those eyes?

Still, she mostly looks German, and I'm in Germany. So, probably a lot of women here look like that, Kevin finally admitted to himself, *I'm just a little jumpy. It's my first real surveillance assignment. And, in addition, lately, almost any attractive girl I see reminds me of Greta.*

Then, just thirty minutes later he heard, "Kevin Boyce. My God. is that you? What the hell are you doing here in Berlin?"

It was Brad himself, in the flesh. No doubt about it. But, in the year or so since Kevin last saw the guy, Brad had changed considerably. More flesh for one thing. Which, living in Germany, with their bratwurst and beer, was probably expected. And the beard, which made him look professorial. He was also slumped over a little, like an older man. With thinning, hair. And even given his ever-present grin, Brad looked sort of sad. Maybe it was the wrinkles, or the baggy eyes, or just his recent life experiences, which had to have been harrowing. But the ever-ebullient Brad was nowhere to be seen.

"I'm enjoying a little holiday, Brad. And you?" Kevin replied as innocently as he could.

Brad smiled broadly, and responded, "I live here now. Been here for about a year. You still in the Navy?"

"Lord, no," Kevin looked away as he lied, "I work for an ad agency in Washington D.C. now. Lots of government work. You'd be surprised how many tax dollars go into advertising."

Brad lifted an eyebrow but said nothing.

"Join me, please," Kevin said, gesturing toward the empty chair at his table, "let me buy you a coffee and a pastry. I'd love to catch up." He tried to sound casual, but getting a traitor to sit down and discuss his arrest was hardly that.

"Can't right now, buddy," Brad answered, "I'm late for a meeting, but how about dinner tonight, say the Frauhaus at eight? It's close by."

The Frauhaus was the same restaurant that he and Gus had scouted the day before, the one Brad visited with a woman who could be Greta. Hardly a neutral site, but Kevin wasn't in a position to suggest another one.

"Sounds good. I'll see you there."

"Look forward to it."

After Brad left, Kevin mulled over what just happened. He never expected the guy to just walk up and start a conversation, like everything was forgotten. In fact, he hadn't planned on meeting Brad at all. All he was supposed to do was confirm that it was him, from a distance, find out where he lived, and turn the information over to those who could arrest him.

Of course, he thought, *that could still be the plan. I could just notify the authorities where I'm supposed to meet Brad, show them his picture. And, if Brad shows up, which is unlikely, they could arrest him without me even being involved.*

But even as he considered that option, Kevin knew he wouldn't do it. He didn't fly all the way to Germany just to step aside at the last minute, especially not when he finally had the chance to have the candid conversation with Brad he'd been wanting for years. Who knows? He might even pick up some valuable tidbit that could lead them to Greta.

So, Kevin called the authorities to tell them that he wanted armed undercover policemen at the Frauhaus at eight ready to move on the fugitive at his command, but not before. He demanded, and got, complete control of the situation.

"The traitor I'm meeting is not just the target of this arrest," he explained. "But a source that could help us catch the Russian spy who recruited him. We need to handle this whole situation very delicately, and I know how to do that."

They went over the logistics several times, including the fact that nobody was to interrupt the dinner unless Kevin dropped his napkin. That was crucial. He wanted to keep open the option that Brad would agree to cooperate and surrender peacefully.

Kevin arrived at the restaurant around 7:45 p.m. and was surprised that fewer than half the tables were occupied. But, of course, by European standards, it was too early for supper.

The restaurant was very German in a rustic way. To Kevin, it seemed more suitable for a mountain village somewhere, than in a housing area of downtown Berlin populated with modest concrete high-rise apartment buildings. There was dark wood paneling on the walls, lots of shelves containing various knick-knacks, and rough-hewn wooden furniture that made up in discomfort what it lacked in taste.

Brad wasn't there yet, nor were the undercover police, at least as far as Kevin could tell. Kevin chose a table in the back of the room and began what he assumed would be a long wait, probably followed by the disappointment of a no-show.

But, a few minutes after the agreed-upon time, big as life, in walked Brad, a characteristically friendly smile on his face and a swagger to his step that was noticeably missing earlier in the day.

When he saw Kevin, he smiled even more broadly, as though he were meeting an old friend. *Not a bad actor,* Kevin acknowledged. *Unless he still believes I'm his friend.*

"I knew you would be early," Brad said. "Some things never change."

Kevin smiled and offered his hand. "And I figured you would be late for the same reason."

Brad frowned dramatically as he returned the handshake. "Touché. It's still me. A little fatter, maybe, a little balder, but still with the same bad habits."

Once Brad settled into a chair, and the pleasantries were over, the parrying began.

"So, Kevin," Brad inquired, "Tell me about your job."

Kevin shook his head, "No way. It's too dull. Why don't you go first?"

"Not much to talk about there either," Brad answered, "But let's order first."

After a few minutes looking over the menus, Kevin ordered the Wiener schnitzel and Brad the steak special. And, of course, a bottle of red wine to share.

"So, let's toast to the good old days," Brad said with a wink. "You remember those, don't you?"

"Your memory is better than mine," Kevin countered.

"That's a little unfair, Kevin. In the beginning there were a lot of good old days. Don't you remember? We were going to be heroes, slaying the Russian dragons," Brad commented, a twinkle in his eye.

"Didn't quite get there, did we?"

"I guess not. But don't let the bad ending ruin a very good story. And a good friendship."

Kevin looked down at the table, silently acknowledging that, to him, the bad ending was the story. There was an uncomfortable silence before the waiter arrived with the wine. The tension was building and Kevin could hear his heart pounding spasmodically, hopefully not so loud that Brad sensed it.

"Where were we?" Brad asked after the waiter had left.

"You were going to tell me about your work," Kevin replied as casually as he could given the thumping in his chest. In contrast, Brad seemed remarkably at ease, as if he had nothing to lose, which was certainly not the case.

"Oh yes, of course," he replied, "Well, there's not much to tell. I work at an insurance company figuring out actuarial rates. You probably didn't know it, but I was an accounting major in college."

Kevin was shocked, not by Brad being an accounting major, but by how normal he was acting, as if he really was an accountant talking about ledgers, and not a despised traitor to his country who might actually face the death penalty. There was something about the normalcy of their conversation that cranked up the suspense considerably.

Kevin nervously moved his napkin from his lap to the table and responded, "No, I didn't know that, Brad, but well-educated or not, I'm surprised you could just waltz into an insurance company in Berlin, and get hired."

"Well, I couldn't do that, of course," Brad answered, then paused, finishing off his first glass of wine and pouring another before continuing.

"As I'm sure you know, Kevin, I now have a whole new identity, courtesy of the Russian government. You're looking at Ivan Petrov, proud graduate of Lomonosov University in Moscow. According to my resume, I've been an accountant in Russia for years, and I'm working here under a visa issued by the Kremlin. I supposedly speak Russian fluently, although I doubt a Muscovite would agree with that. I speak some German as well, and English, which, since most in my department are non-Germans, is the language of choice."

"That's convenient," Kevin commented.

Brad smiled. "Yes. Everybody compliments me on how good my English is. Hardly any accent at all."

Kevin fingered his napkin anxiously. "Were you in Russia for a while?"

"Yes," Brad replied, "Several months, but it didn't work for me. It's not a very happy place, Moscow. So, after getting as much out of me as they could, we all agreed it was best if I moved on."

Kevin was straining to keep his face expressionless. "Why Berlin?"

Brad shrugged and answered, "Actually, it was Greta's choice. We intended to live together, and she felt it would be a good base for her. But, after a few months, that didn't work out for either of us, professionally or personally. So, we drifted apart."

"Where is she now?" Kevin asked casually.

"I have no idea. Unlike me, she's still an operative," Brad answered. "She could be anywhere, even in America, a country she particularly enjoyed. Of course, if you run into her there, you probably wouldn't recognize her. She can be a chameleon, hiding her bountiful assets or using them, depending on what the situation called for. She's one of Russia's best undercover agents, as I'm sure you know now."

"So, I've heard."

"But enough about Greta and me. What have you been up to?"

"Not much," Kevin began, bringing the napkin up to his face to wipe off one bothersome bead of perspiration, "Just the normal advertising things. I'm an Account Executive and I work with a number of government agencies, putting together boring, mundane ads. You know, Navy recruiting, and that sort of thing."

Brad didn't seem to be buying it. "Is Naval Intelligence one of your clients?" he asked.

"I doubt they're much into advertising. So, no. Why do you ask?"

Brad smiled, looked his old friend in the eye, and quipped, "Well, Kevin, I hear you're spending a lot of time with my old friend Tom, in San Diego. Great guy, by the way."

"Yes. I met Tom through a shipmate of mine actually. We have lunch every so often."

"And I know you contacted Alexander, my Soviet handler."

"Alexander who?"

"Oh, Kevin, you're still an awful liar. Personally, I thought you were too honest to work in Naval Intelligence back in the day," Brad confessed, a sardonic smile on his face, "But I guess Tom felt differently."

Kevin's heart skipped a beat, and he picked up his napkin again.

"I'm going to lay my cards on the table, Kevin. I know exactly what you do, and why you're here," Brad uttered, the smile now gone, "And, because I still consider you a friend, I'm going to make it easy on you. I'm ready to turn myself in peacefully. So, let's you and I just enjoy our dinner, shall we? It could be the last good one I have for a long, long while."

Kevin glanced around the now-full dining room. *There are any number of people here who could be undercover cops, so I'm not really at great risk. It seems like Brad considers me a friend, maybe even the last one he has. So, I might as well satisfy my hunger and my curiosity before going to the unsavory part of our get-together.*

"Okay, Brad, let's finish our dinner," Kevin tentatively agreed, "but I have a few more questions while we eat. I hope you're OK with that."

Brad opened his palms wide and answered, "Shoot."

Kevin stared at his old friend without blinking. "Why did you decide to face the music now?"

"As soon as I saw you sitting at that coffee shop, Kevin," a now subdued Brad answered, "I knew what I had to do. You're appearing out of nowhere was a sign. So, I decided, why not just do it today, with the help of my good friend Kevin. Get all the bullshit finally over."

"What bullshit?"

"I'm not cut out to be a traitor and a fugitive, living a lie. It's not who I am. I need to find my way back to the truth."

"It's a great place to be, or so I've heard."

"You're one of the good guys, Kevin. As honest as they come," Brad said in a hushed voice. "And I mean that sincerely. I wouldn't be turning myself over to anybody else."

The dinners arrived, with the smell of Brad's steak sizzling in butter on a hot plate taking center stage. After savoring his first bite and taking a sip of the wine, Brad looked up and gazed unblinkingly into Kevin's eyes. The sadness was gone from his face and, in its place was an unmistakable aura of serenity.

"Kinda like the last supper, huh, Kevin?" he said, "I suspect I won't get many prime cuts like this where I'm going."

"I still don't get why you're doing it?" Kevin asked again, "It's an incredibly high price, giving up your freedom for a jail cell?"

"Because, honestly, I'm not really free," Brad explained, after looking at the ceiling for a few seconds. "Despite all that I've done, in my heart I'm still an American, and I don't want to live out my days away from home, looking over my shoulder, and hating myself every day for what I did. Besides, I have information now that I can hopefully trade for a little leniency."

Kevin shook his head, still not fully comprehending. "It was so hard for me to believe back then, that you, a self-described patriot, would betray your country? Can you explain that?"

Brad sighed. "Simple question. Complicated answer."

"Was it because of Greta?" a curious Kevin asked.

"I suppose she was the catalyst," Brad explained after a pause to finish his bite, "You know how seductive she can be. But no. It wasn't just her. The more I learned about Vietnam, and our reasons for going in there, and the devastating impact it was having on the people there. Well, I began to side with the dissenters. The long-haired hippies were making sense to me, if you can believe that."

"I can believe it but siding with the enemy?" a confused Kevin asked, "How would that help anything. You could have gone to Canada."

Brad visibly flinched. "I guess that's where Greta really played a role. She was offering me a new, exciting life. Travel the world, make tons of money, and have a lot of sex with a beautiful woman. Greta was hard to resist."

She sure was, Kevin agreed silently, *I certainly fell for her, and I still wonder what my answer might have been had I been asked to go away with her.*

"Why didn't she try to turn me?" Kevin finally queried. The moment of truth.

"I've wondered that myself," Brad admitted, "In the beginning I just thought she preferred me over you. But, over time, I concluded that it was just the opposite. She might have actually been in love with you and didn't want to put you through the wringer she knew was in store for me."

A skeptical Kevin disagreed, "But she chose to be with you. And not with me."

"I was just an asset for her, nothing more," Brad said, "totally disposable, as I found out in Moscow."

"I guess I would have been disposable as well," Kevin mused. "

"I'm not so sure," Brad countered, "For some reason, after her charms didn't seem to be working on you, she turned them my way. Which, I'm proud to say I resisted for about a minute and a half."

"I didn't resist much longer, as I recall. She just never tried to close the deal," Kevin admitted, and then, they both laughed. Fortunately, the tension had eased considerably, although Kevin still had the napkin in his hand.

"I've often wondered how I would have responded had she asked me to switch sides," Kevin continued, "But thank God she didn't. Or we might be on opposite sides of the table today."

"I doubt that, Kevin," a suddenly disconsolate Brad admitted. "You were always stronger than me."

And Kevin decided it was time to drop the napkin.

Within seconds, their table was surrounded by several stony-faced armed men. But Brad didn't seem intimidated or scared. More resigned to his fate…and relieved.

Once Brad was handcuffed, the German police walked him outside the restaurant to a patrol car that was waiting to escort him to a downtown holding cell. A small crowd had gathered around the car to see what all the commotion was about, and they weren't disappointed by the drama seemingly taking place in front of them.

Brad came out, head down, hands covered by a coat, with Kevin in front of him. Suddenly, there was a screeching of tires on the road in front of the patrol car, and the onlookers scattered as a female motorcyclist sped by brandishing a military-style pistol that she was pointing at the two men.

Brad saw her first and shoved Kevin to the ground before a number of bullets ricocheted off the pavement and door, with one or two of them hitting Brad in the chest. He went down immediately beside an uninjured Kevin, who looked up in time to see the attacker was a woman in a green-and-black skin-tight leather suit. She wore a helmet with a dark shield that obscured her face, but Kevin knew immediately it was Greta.

Within seconds, she was around the corner and gone, leaving a few injured passers-by and a dying Brad in her wake.

Kevin bent over his old boss, who was now coughing up blood and trying to speak.

"I know who it was," Brad gurgled.

"So do I," Kevin said to Brad's fluttering eyes, "and she won't get away with it, I promise you that, old buddy. I'm going to get her for this."

Acknowledgements

I wish to acknowledge all who served with me on the *U.S.S. Buck*, but especially Rear Admiral Joseph Strasser and Bob Calvert, two members of that wardroom who kept in touch with me through the many decades since we served together.

And, of course, my daughter A.J. Czerwinski, her kids Will, Kacy, and Hannah, and my son Scott Morrow Johnson, his wife Erin, and their kids Drew and Molly.

And a special "shout out" to my soulmate and wife of over 60 years, Fran O'Brien Johnson, who shared so many memories with me, some of which inspired this book.

www.ingramcontent.com/pod-product-compliance
Lightning Source LLC
Chambersburg PA
CBHW060708190726
48289CB00002B/588